MODEL FOR MURDER

Also by Jeanne Wilson

Uncertain Heart
No Medicine for Murder
Take Time for Murder

MODEL FOR MURDER

Jeanne Wilson

LMH PUBLISHING LIMITED

The original version of this novel was published by Ward Lock and Company Limited
(London and Melbourne). 1968

2942

First Edition 1993
Reprint 2022
10 9 8 7 6 5 4 3

Cover design: Roshane Mullings
Typesetting: Lazertec Limited

Published by LMH Publishing Limited
Suite 10-11, Sagicor Industrial Complex
7 Norman Road, Kingston C.S.O., Jamaica
Tel.: (876) 938-0005; 938-0712 • Fax: (876) 759-8752
Email: lmhbookpublishing@cwjamaica.com
Website: www.lmhpublishing.com

Printed in the USA

ISBN:978-976-657-082-8

PROLOGUE

It was that somnolent hour between two and three in the afternoon, when the sun beats down relentlessly from a hot blue sky. A haze hangs over the lower slopes of the Blue Mountains, tantalising with a half promise of rain, and the white-collar workers wish that the siesta had been adopted in Jamaica from the nearby Latin American countries, and not the eight to four regime from a colonial past.

Inside an old wooden building, the Minister for Internal Affairs flicked his finger impatiently at a file marked 'Most Secret – Highest Priority'.

"What's been done about this? Why wasn't I informed earlier?" he demanded.

Major John Terrance sighed inwardly: here we go again. Aloud he said smoothly, his voice soft, taking out the implied sting before the smart was felt: "I tried to contact you, sir, on Saturday morning. I was told that it was impossible to speak to you, much less see you."

"Why didn't you say that it was an HP?"

"I did, sir."

There was a short silence: the Minister's eyes narrowed slightly.

"Somebody seems to have goofed – I'll check on it. In future, Major, don't take no for an answer in a matter of this importance."

"I won't, sir."

The Minister gave him a sharp glance, but the young major's face bore no expression but that of respectful deference.

"Well, what are we going to do about this?"

"If I may point out, sir, the delay has not been of any consequence as the possible date of arrival is not until tomorrow – or even the day after. According to my latest information – not in this file – the plans for departure are still rather fluid." Terrance paused. "Our agent over there has been most reliable so far but too many shipments have been getting through."

The Minister nodded, his dark grizzled hair curled tight against a dome-like skull, his eyes noncommittal.

"And what about this end?"

"Tricky, sir. I'd like some help."

"From whom?"

"May I suggest a member of the CID?"

The Minister nodded again. "Anyone in mind?" He showed approval at Terrance's reply. "If we can get him." He picked up the receiver from one of a number of telephones before him. "Get me the Deputy Commissioner of Police – and scramble it."

There was a short delay, during which time the two men eyed each other covertly. The Minister, in his early fifties, a man of the people and for the people. He had overcome his early lack of education by acknowledging the lack, and then had made a concentrated drive to remedy that lack. He then devoted himself to politics, rising doggedly from obscurity to head one of the most important ministries. He was shrewd, cynical, but with his country's well-being his one aim – if he benefited at the same time, what complaint should he make?

In sharp contrast was Major Terrance, tall, darkly good looking, with that svelte charm and assurance that came with a combination of a socially secure background, an education that included travel and the opportunity and ability to mix with a cross-section of European and North American cultures, topped by military training at one of the renowned officer training schools. He was the complete antithesis of the man behind the desk, yet there was no resentment on the one hand, or false condescension on the other: each respected the other for what he was, not for the social ground in which he had his roots.

The telephone gave a bleep; immediately the receiver was cradled against the Minister's ear. "Peter? – Ivan." He spoke quickly for a few moments. From the other end of the line came a series of staccato enquiries that reached Terrance clearly. Finally the Minister said, "Right – I'd be very grateful. Working together we may be able to wrap it up quickly." He looked triumphantly at Terrance as he replaced the receiver. "It's all yours, Major Terrance. Call upon me at any time if I can be of assistance." He stood up, shoulders hunched over his stocky frame, and shook hands in dismissal.

John Terrance left the shabby old wooden building that still housed the Ministry of Internal Affairs – apparently it didn't rate one of the newer ministry buildings that had mushroomed in the last three decades in a welter of steel and plate glass – and his steps rang with a hollow sound on the wooden floor, eaten in places by wood ants or chi-chi, as the vernacular had it. The full force of the afternoon sun hit him as he crossed the rutted driveway to the staff car parked under a poinciana tree. Despite the age and shabbiness of the building he had just left, it had been cool with its wide sheltering verandahs and high tray ceilings. He squinted his eyes against the glare and reflected ruefully on the way of all ministers who, when delegating a job, somehow expected its completion to be effected with great alacrity. He set his cap at its usual jaunty angle and jumped into the staff car.

Private Johns at the wheel sketched a salute as he asked, "Where to, sir?"

"Back to HQ, Johns, at the double."

He opened the file in the privacy of the car and settled back to study the contents. The Minister thinks that we can wrap it up quickly, does he? he mused. The fact that the police forces of France and Britain, with the assistance of Interpol, have had no joy, bears little weight with the old boy. Well, let's hope that he's right and be grateful for his confidence. That the confidence might be misplaced and should have been termed ignorance of the problem, John Terrance refused to acknowledge.

ONE

London's Heathrow Airport at eleven-thirty in the morning: the giant jet aircraft shuddered at the pre-take-off warm-up. The November sun, so weak that the eye could gaze at it without danger, barely penetrated the thin swirling mist that eddied against the insulated windows of the plane. A few wisps seeped into the brightly lit cabin, bringing the peculiar acridity of hot petrol and wet tarmac. It looked as if it would thicken by nightfall, thought the operators at the radar control tower, and there'd be a pileup of traffic for sure.

Inside the aircraft the passengers divested themselves of overcoats, leather jackets, the odd quilted car coat and an occasional full-length mink. The flight attendants moved easily down the aisles, making a last-minute check on each passenger.

In the club-class compartment, a high babble of French topped all other conversation, bringing a gaiety to the interior, after the wet, clinging drabness of the world outside.

Anna Morgan settled herself by the window and reached for her seat belt. She looked across at the rest of the party a little impatiently. This Gallic impetuosity was being carried too far, she thought, then felt annoyed at her impatience. She glanced at her watch: three minutes to take-off, then home to the sun, to Jamaica, for six glorious weeks. It would be good to get home again and revel in the sun and sea. She had been away for nearly four years. She had gone to Paris on a prize trip when she had placed second in a Miss Jamaica beauty contest. She leant back in her seat, recalling those first weeks in the city she had so often dreamed about, and the crowning magic when she was offered a job modelling for the House of Girot. The magic had dimmed a little over the succeeding months, but it had been a good time – she paused and amended, a good time most of the time. She shut her mind to some memories.

Now here she was, returning home with Girot himself on one of his overseas showings. The whole entourage of fitters, models, cameramen, seamstresses made up the troupe – the Circus, as the irreverent called it – and of course Roger Girot himself. Anna glanced across at him, his tubby figure impeccably clad in, ironically, a London-made suit that quietly stated its quality. His round face blended into his high balding head. His lips had a hard line in repose, belying the unctuous charm he kept for his clients. His eyes, light blue, and at this moment holding a wary coldness, met Anna's large dark brown ones. For a few seconds he held her gaze, his expression unchanging, then suddenly he smiled, the studied charm reasserting itself. Anna smiled back, but her mind held a question: how much of this charm was spurious? What manner of man was hidden under the artistic facade of the world-famous couturier? She sighed. It didn't really matter, she told herself lazily, nothing really mattered for the next few hours. While the outside world went on remotely, those inside the plane were in a world of their own. All too soon for many, they would have to return to the greater world and resume the problem of living. Anna reminded herself of the now of being in the plane – in one place, at one particular moment. Time would blur the memory...

She glanced around at the rest of the group, those whom she could see from her window seat. Across the aisle, Madame Yvette was settling fussily. Her admonishing voice was directing the flight attendant as to how her various boxes and endless pieces of hand luggage should be distributed – the House of Girot had booked the whole of the club-class compartment and had been allowed to dispense with the restrictions on hand luggage. This irritating insistence on the importance of trivialities belied her hardheaded shrewdness. She was the *Directrice Technique* of the House of Girot, the pivot on which the wheels of a smoothly running concern turned. Her greying hair was faultlessly styled, and her still trim small figure was impeccably gowned in a special Girot creation. Despite her age – which was never disclosed, but speculated by the staff to be on the wrong side of seventy – her skin was smooth and unlined, a tribute to the hours of care that she lavished on it. She caught Anna's gaze and smiled briefly. "It is always disturbing, this packing and unpacking, no," she stated rather than asked.

Anna nodded, "But exciting, eh, Madame?"

"Ah, excitement, always youth demands excitement." Madame dismissed the subject with her usual expressive Gallic shrug. Her voice was light and quick, bird-like, heavily accented. She glanced at the jewelled watch on her wrist. "We should be off soon, no?"

Anna nodded, "We should have been off five minutes ago – oh, what's happening?" A slight disturbance at the entrance to the compartment attracted her attention, as the cabin curtain was pulled sideways to admit a passenger.

Completely unruffled by her late arrival and exuding an aura of a striking personality, the woman made her way to her seat, clasping a large basket that was at variance with the rest of her immaculately groomed appearance.

"I'm sorry that I'm late," she was saying to the flight attendant in a light, rather breathless voice, as she passed Anna. "I had all the papers, but they were still fussing – it took ages to convince them. It was good of you to wait."

"Your ticket, madam." The flight attendant raised her eyebrows. "Both seats, madam?"

"Yes. I need the space."

The large basket was carefully put on the seat by the window and the late arrival seated herself on the aisle seat. Anna viewed her with curiosity: she was intrigued by the stranger's voice which, despite its lightness, had a caressing quality. She had close, cap-like, sleek black hair and widely spaced grey eyes, set in a pointed, heart-shaped face. She was slim but ripely curved. She looked vaguely familiar. Who could she be? Anna asked herself. From her coffee colouring – apart from the strange grey eyes – she was obviously West Indian; Jamaican probably, from her slight accent. She wasn't of the fashion world or Anna would know her. Television? Actress? She was obviously well off, as she had taken two club-class seats – and how had she managed to get seats in that compartment? Anna had understood that the whole had been reserved for the Girot group. Where had she seen her before?

Of course!

The answer came abruptly as old newspaper headlines flashed into memory.

Rachel Groome, wife of the doctor who had gone out of his mind and murdered the lawyer, Edgar Walton, and then the Vermont girl. Finally committed suicide. That must have been all of a year ago. Poor girl – woman, Anna amended – she must be at least thirty-five. One of those lucky woman who keep their youth and become more physically attractive as they get older. As if aware of the scrutiny from Anna's dark eyes, Rachel looked across the aisle: her gaze as her eyes met Anna's held a wary expression, then she relaxed and smiled.

A man's voice crackled over the intercom. "Good morning, ladies and gentlemen. This is your captain speaking. Captain Pangton. Welcome aboard. We regret the slight delay in take-off, due not to any technical fault, but to the boarding difficulties of a lady passenger – a feline lady passenger – which have now been resolved. Take-off will be in two minutes and forty seconds. Our ETA at Sangster International Airport, Jamaica, will be at four-forty EST. Thank you." There was a click as the connection was severed and the giant plane began to shudder as the revs increased.

So the basket held a cat, Anna thought.

There came a high bubbling voice from a few seats behind her. "A feline? A cat? Why do they allow animals in 'ere? Me, I do not like cats – they give me – 'ow do you say, the *shivairs*."

Oh God, Anna thought, I hope that Solange isn't going to have one of her temperaments: in this confined space it would be too awful. She was glad to see a flight attendant move quickly to Solange's side.

"It's quite all right, madam, she is just a kitten and will not be allowed out of her basket. Perhaps," the drama school type voice was professionally soothing, "I could take your order. The bar will be open as soon as we are airborne."

There were muted petulant murmurs as Solange Barnave, Girot's *première* model, settled down again.

The flight attendant made the rounds, taking orders for drinks. She paused by Rachel Groome's side. "Madam" – her voice was low – "the lady in seat six – she hates cats. You will keep her in her basket?"

Rachel smiled. "Of course. Do you want a peep? She's only a baby." She slid back part of the cover. A small bundle of fur, dark points beginning to show, blue eyes blazing at the indignity of being confined, was curled in one corner. The flight attendant laughed softly, "What a darling. What's her name?"

"Officially, Princess Ra San Dhu III – but I call her Bamboo. I expect that she'll be Bam before very long."

The attendant poked in a tentative finger then withdrew it with a cry as small needle-sharp teeth flashed.

"I'm sorry," Rachel apologised. "I should have warned you. She's got a temper like a prima donna – or –" she smiled wickedly, "like a top fashion model."

"That's all right, madam, it was more shock that hurt. What can I get you to drink?"

"Drink? Oh, a very light rum, please, on the rocks."

The attendant moved smoothly down the aisle and disappeared into the galley.

Rachel settled back, waiting for the lift of take-off. She wondered who the beautiful coloured girl was, across the aisle. One of the couture merry-go-round, I suppose, she thought. She looked familiar, she'd probably seen her in one of the fashion glossies. Oh yes, it was coming back now: Anna something – Anna Morgan. The girl who was the runner-up in the Miss Jamaica contest quite a few years back, went to Paris and made good as a model. The winner of the contest hadn't been heard of since. Rachel's thoughts raced on: why did she look at me like that? Did she recognise me? Oh God, I must get out of the way of believing that every time somebody looks at me they're thinking, It's Rachel Groome – do you remember the case? I didn't object to being looked at before.

The plane lifted sharply, the mist dropping away to reveal a pale grey sky, barely washed by the November sun. The signals "Fasten seatbelts" and "No smoking " flicked off. Rachel lit a cigarette with relief as the flight attendant brought her drink. She leant her head back against the pink linen-covered cushion and inhaled deeply, swirling the ice slowly in her glass. She was going home at last, after a year of running away from the past – a year of indecision.

She remembered again that day at the Manley Airport when she had said goodbye to Rowan Rodgers: it would have been so easy to respond to the plea in his black eyes, to say all right, I'll stay. I'll marry you if you want me to – or be your mistress – go on being your mistress, she amended, if you want me to be. But she hadn't said it. The shock and horror of the weeks before, culminating in the realisation that her husband's mind had gone – worse – that he was a murderer, had left her confused and unsure of her ability to make any decision – let alone the right one. She had said a little unsteadily, "I'm sorry, Rowan – I'm sure that it's best that I get away. If I stay and we're seen together – and if I stay we will be – it's only going to cause a lot of talk and speculation. You know how it is in the island?"

"How long will you be away?"

"I don't know. Six months – maybe a year – maybe..." The swift pressure of his hand on her arm and the sudden pain in his eyes stopped her from saying, "Maybe forever."

"You'll write to me?"

"I – won't promise. I – Rowan..." The tears were not far away. "Please don't make it harder for me. I don't want to leave you – but I must."

The final call for all passengers to board the plane had cut through his answer. He took her quickly in his arms and kissed her, the hard demanding kiss she had grown to know and exult in. She pulled herself free and almost ran through the barrier, becoming swallowed in a crowd of passengers. She hadn't looked back, she'd walked steadily across the hard tarmac, feeling the heat through the thin soles of her shoes. The plane shimmered in the rays of hot air that struck up from the ground, and the gleaming body glimmered through her unshed tears. She hadn't looked back as she climbed the gangway – and she hadn't written. She left no address for letters to be sent from Jamaica. Her only communication was through her bank, and there she had left orders that any letter from Jamaica was to be returned.

Why had she changed her mind, so that she was speeding at nearly six hundred miles an hour back to the warmth? She smiled at the recollection of the moment of decision and glanced down at the basket beside her. A red gleam from a partly hidden eye told her that the occupant was still awake, despite a sedative given before they had left for Heathrow.

She had been looking idly through the personal columns of the *Daily Telegraph* when an advertisement for a kitten show caught her eye. The pain that she had felt when she remembered Li Po was partly dimmed now, and she had stopped in front of a group of Seal Point Siamese kittens with only the slightest twist of pain. One was huddled apart from the others, shivering, its woebegone little face expressing utter misery. Its blue eyes were ready to slit with fury as Rachel bent over it.

"What's the matter with this little one? Is she sick?" Rachel asked the man in attendance.

"This gennelman can tell you, miss."

The owner, large, redfaced and hearty, with an out-of-date handlebar moustache, shook his head as Rachel asked about the kitten.

"Not sick, miss, cold. Can't get warm enough, that little tyke. Uster spend all her time under her mum, juster keep warm. Never known anything like it. Wish someone 'ud buy her and take her to India or some such place – then she'd be happy." Despite his rough exterior and speech he seemed genuinely worried and picked up the kitten in a stubby yet gentle hand. He tucked her into his coat front.

Rachel looked at the kitten with cautious enthusiasm. She was trying to restrain her sudden impulse, but asked, "Has she a pedigree?"

"Lord, yes, miss, long as yer arm. Princess Ra San Dhu III, that's wot she is. They don't come more royal."

He took the kitten from his coat and handed her to Rachel. The little body had that light, fragile softness peculiar to kittens, and her hands closed round the still-shivering creature. She opened the jacket of her fur-collared suit and tucked Ra San Dhu III inside.

"How much are you asking?" she asked crisply.

"Well, miss, she's class – no mistake about that, but this feeling cold like she has all the time, I..."

"That doesn't matter, I'm going to take her home to Jamaica – she'll be warm there."

"Jamaica, eh? Well, fancy that now. Well – ain't this your lucky day, Princess? I'll let her go fer five hundred quid."

Rachel didn't care whether she was being gypped or not. She took her copy of the pedigree without even reading it and paid the five hundred pounds.

On the way back to her flat, she booked her passage on the first available direct flight that would accept a cat.

"There is one tomorrow," the booking clerk said doubtfully. "There are only two vacant seats; the rest of the club class is taken up by a fashion group going to Sangster International Airport, Montego Bay."

"I'll take them."

"Both of them?'

She hesitated a moment, thinking, Oh dear, this is a lot of money I'm throwing away... then: Oh, why not?

"Yes, I'll take them both."

"What name, madam?"

"Rachel Groome."

"And the other passenger?"

"Princess Ra San Dhu III."

"Madam?"

"A Siamese kitten – but I need the extra room."

Rachel had hesitated about letting anyone know that she was returning. By anyone, she knew that she meant Rowan Rodgers. At last she shakily penned a cable: ARRIVING KINGSTON 6:30 PM ON THE 11TH. She thought a moment then added: LOVE RACHEL.

She came back to the present and peered out of the window. They were over the blurred coast of Ireland now and she looked down at the rivers and pockets of lakes. Then came a blinding white beach, curving by a sea of almost tropical colouring, with a scatter of bright green islands to the west. Then they were over the Atlantic, with Ireland receding to a smudged outline behind them; and suddenly Rachel felt alive and eager for what the future held – for whatever it held.

TWO

Superintendent Rowan Rodgers, of the CID, Jamaica Constabulary Force, tossed the last file into his Out tray. He reached for his pipe and leant back in the swivel chair, long legs stretched under the desk.

"Phillips," he called.

"Sir." The door into the outer office opened immediately and Detective-Sergeant Phillips, aide to Rodgers on many a case, came smartly to Rodgers' side.

"Relax, Phillips, sit down. We're on leave – as from," he consulted his watch, "five minutes' time. In precisely five minutes, you and I, Phillips, are on four weeks of glorious leave. Crime may flourish, but you and I will be blissfully unaware of the fact." He paused and grinned at Phillips. "Have you anything left to tidy up?"

"No, sir. I get everyt'ing finish off. An' that young Pearson, sir, 'im doin' all right, 'im a bright bwoy."

Rodgers gave an inward smile. Phillips could on occasion be alarmingly correct, if not pedantic in his speech, then he would consciously lapse into a broad local patois, heavily larded with idioms. He explained that he had to keep in practice for dealing with all members of the community.

"Good," Rodgers said. "What are you doing with your leave, Phillips?"

"Well, sir, I do a little gardening an' tidy roun' the yard. Take the kids to the beach. Maybe we go to the wife's mother for a little, she have a property in St Ann. And you, Mr Rodgers, sir, what you plan to do?"

Rodgers got up abruptly and tapped his pipe with unnecessary vigour against the ashtray on the desk, then walked to the window and gazed out unseeingly.

"I don't know, Phillips. A month of freedom and I don't know what to do with it."

Phillips surveyed the broad back of this chief with a worried frown. The wide muscular shoulders had an unaccustomed droop, there was an air of dejection about his whole stance that made Phillips realise that the chief was still moping like a schoolboy. He was well aware of the situation, not that he could really blame the chief. That Mrs Groome was one hell of a woman – but to go on like this after nearly a year, this was more than he could understand.

There was a knock at the door. A young police constable entered, stood rigidly to attention and said crisply, "Cable, sir. Received and delivered." He handed the blue and white envelope to Rodgers, still with an exaggerated concern for correct procedure that Rodgers inspired in young constables just out of the police academy.

Phillips watched tolerantly as Rodgers read the cable. He didn't have to be told from whom it came or the message that it contained. He noted the new gleam in Rodgers' black eyes, the sudden smoothing of trouble lines across his brow, and asked casually, "She coming back, sir?"

Rodgers laughed and slapped him on the back. "Nothing much escapes you, does it? And you've developed the impertinence of the devil. Yes, she's coming back, thank God, and now I don't have to wonder what I can do with a month's leave."

Phillips' reply was drowned by the loud shrill of the telephone on the desk. Rodgers picked up the receiver. "Rodgers speaking." There sounded a crackle of speech and Rodgers said, "Yes, sir."

Phillips knew from Rodgers' answering tone that the caller must be either the Commissioner or the Assistant Commissioner. He watched in consternation as his chief's carefree look changed to the cold, set expression he always assumed when confronted with a new problem.

"Yes, sir," Rodgers was saying. "I was, sir. Today – now, in fact. Yes, I realise that... Yes – yes, I could, sir." He looked across at Phillips and went on. "Yes, I think so, sir. I think that I can arrange that. Goodbye, sir."

Phillips could see, almost physically, his holiday receding from him. He knew that he was entitled to his leave. He'd earned it, he'd given it up many times in the past and if he stuck out for it now, no one would blame him. But he knew from the look on Rodgers' face that something big had come up and that the chief was relying on him to be at his side. He stoically accepted the fact that one more holiday had passed him by.

Rodgers replaced the receiver carefully. He looked down at the cablegram that he still held, his expression thoughtful. Then he looked up and grinned cheerfully at Phillips. "Contrary to your obviously gloomy thoughts, leave is not entirely cancelled – plans altered, yes, but maybe to some advantage."

"Sir?" Phillips sounded wary.

"Can't give you any details. Top secret, top priority. Pick up your wife and family and proceed to Rocklands. It's a little village between Runaway Bay and Rio Bueno. There's a cottage right by the sea, it'll have been taken in your name for a month. If we wrap up the case before then, you still have the rest of the month to spend how you like – at the government's expense. I shall be staying at the Santa Gloria Hotel – half a mile to the east of you."

"Yes, sir." Phillips' stolid acceptance was typical.

Rodgers went on, "I can give you no details – I know very little myself. I just want you there, in case of trouble. Tell your wife as little as possible. How are you going to explain the change of plans and the cottage?"

"I win a little bread at Caymanas, sir. I keepin' it as a surprise."

Rodgers laughed, "You'll do. Nice and anonymous – a story that can't be checked. Right – I'm leaving for MoBay in half an hour – got to meet a plane at Sangster. I'll see you on the beach between your cottage and the Santa Gloria at eleven-fifteen tomorrow morning. By then I should be able to put you more in the picture. Right?"

"Right, sir."

Five minutes later Rowan Rodgers, at the wheel of his veteran dark grey Mercedes SL, was weaving his way through the Half-Way-Tree traffic on his way home. He'd phoned his housekeeper, Maisie, from the station, asking her to pack some clothes for him as he was going out of town for a week or two. By the time he reached the small, luxurious bungalow where he lived, his bags were packed, steaming coffee and man-sized sandwiches waited on the shaded patio and Maisie, her dark face split by a wide smile, was awaiting orders.

"Nothing much, Maisie. Just look after everything as usual, but take it easy. If you need me urgently, I'll be at the Santa Gloria – here's the telephone number and the address."

He took a quick shower and changed into dark grey pants, matching short-sleeved shirt-jac, with a dark red cravat at the neck. The cravat was his one affectation, but his outward appearance and physique offset any adverse comments that might have been made by the men under his command. He brushed his short hair, which was greying slightly at the temples. The face reflected in the mirror was a strong one, long with a determined jaw, the nose aquilinely dominant over a full-lipped, sensual mouth. His eyes were unbelievably black; at this moment they were reserved and thoughtful, but they could on occasion hold a melting softness that had caused havoc to many a feminine heart and sensibility.

Exactly thirty minutes after leaving the station, he was on his way to the north coast. He turned thankfully onto the Washington Boulevard, out of the press of uptown traffic. At that time of day, the traffic along the highway was fairly light, apart from a laden country bus and the maniac minibuses. The early afternoon sun beat strongly down and made the road ahead glimmer and glisten, as if there were innumerable pools of water on the surface which disappeared on closer acquaintance. The hills on his right were stark against the pale sky. Wide, barren clefts threw into highlight patches of deep green and stressed the purple pockets shadowed by rocky outjuts. The hills fell away as he approached Spanish Town, giving way to high fields of cane, green and lush, giant grasses waving in the stiff breeze that came in from the unseen sea on his left. It was crop time; some cane had already been cut and there were large areas of brown stalks and trash drying in the heat.

The miles sped by. The long, smooth, curving, undulating

Ewarton Highway was passed and the climb up the famed Mount Diablo began. Rodgers smiled as he remembered the bogey to drivers it had been when he'd been a schoolboy. The road then was unpaved with a surface of crushed white marl, rolled smooth. But the heavy seasonal rains would quickly reveal pockets in the surface, which did untold damage to tyres, shock absorbers and axles – not to mention the wear and tear on the nerves of drivers and passengers. In those days, he reminisced, it would take a good four or five hours from Kingston to the north coast, but now he could do the journey easily in one and a half hours, as the towns of Spanish Town, Bog Walk, Linstead and Moneague were bypassed by the now not-so-new highway. Then along the coast road to Montego Bay in another hour and a quarter: Apart from the surface, though, he thought, swinging the car up a one-in-five gradient and round a hairpin bend at the same time, the road was also much wider, even if it did give tourists heart flips on first acquaintance. He was nearly at the top now, and the view beneath him on the right was magnificent: a deep green valley, the tops of palms far below him, their leaves feathering in the sunlight. Here and there was the spreading grandeur of a silk cotton tree, a familiar sight to islanders since the days of the Arawaks. A graceful stand of bamboo bent its fronds by a still, algae-covered pool. A few small houses, the walls roughly daubed, the roofs of sheet zinc, were perched at intervals at seemingly impossible angles down the mountainside. Away across the valley the mountains rose again. Then the road dropped swiftly as he neared the north coast, passing little settlements, isolated separate communities in the mountain serenity. Now he was going down Fern Gully, dark and mysterious, its steep sides thickly covered with vegetation. Lianas swung from branch to branch and orchids grew in wild profusion, ferns of every size and description flourished in the dark humidity, as only the faintest wash of sunlight penetrated the depths and overhanging branches. Then he was out into the sunlight again and so to the coast and the magnificence of the sparkling sea.

Rowan Rodgers drove mechanically through villages and

settlements, almost without being aware of them. As he drove, he went over in his mind his conversation with the Assistant Commissioner – not that much had been said – just enough to point out the importance and urgency of the case. He would be contacted at the Santa Gloria by Major John Terrance of the JDF, Military Intelligence. So it was something big, if MI had been brought in. Oh well, speculation would get him nowhere. Time enough to worry when contact had been made.

He switched his thoughts to Rachel. After her long absence she was coming back: she was coming back to the island but was she coming back to him? The fact that she had cabled him made him hopeful, but not completely confident. In a way he could understand her running away and not writing. Their relationship, so short and passionate, had been under such adverse circumstances, that he could well see that she feared it was an outcome of the circumstances and might easily die after the situation was resolved and normal life resumed. What now? he asked himself. If Rachel could be persuaded to stay at the Santa Gloria, it would make good cover. He grinned to himself; Rachel would indeed be flattered at his thoughts, though probably she would be the first to suggest such a course if she knew the set-up. She mustn't be told, though, top secret etcetera. He gave an inward groan. Keeping anything from Rachel was not easy. Her quick mind and sensitivity would immediately grasp that he was not on the north coast strictly for pleasure.

He was driving fast along the Queen's Highway, the miles flowing by smoothly under the Mercedes. The Caribbean Sea was on his right, patches of aquamarine side by side with deep emerald, shading to silver grey or pale yellow, as the depth of the water changed. The sands were blindingly white, reflecting the heat from a sun which had beaten down on them all day. There were patches of shade from a few palms, bent grotesquely by the prevailing winds into attitudes that had charm in their very extravagance. The sea had an unnatural calm, a stillness of surface that appeared oily. At that hour of the afternoon there was no one in sight, he might have been alone on the island. He glanced at his watch; he should be in

MoBay by four o'clock – the plane was due at four-forty. That would give him time for a sandwich and Red Stripe at the airport coffee shop. He tried to stifle the feeling of anticipation he was experiencing at the thought of seeing Rachel in less than an hour.

His thoughts were interrupted by the sound of a car coming up fast behind him. It hung at his rear bumper for a few minutes, then cut out sharply and overtook him at such an angle as to force him onto the soft shoulder. It stayed in front of him as he righted the Mercedes and regained the road, then accelerated with a burst of engine power and shot away.

Rodgers swore briefly. What did the fool think he was up to? He glanced at his speedometer: eighty-five. The idiot must have been doing close on a hundred – on this particular stretch of the road it was suicidal. He wondered what was behind the incident. There had been plenty of room to overtake – it looked deliberate, the careful hanging back, then the crowding to the side. Why then did he stay in front for as long as he did after the incident? Rodgers hadn't seen much of the driver, probably European, heavy dark glasses, but the car he could never fail to recognise if he saw it again. It was an Audi 100 Turbo Quattro, surely the only one of its type in the island. Its coach was a pale lemon yellow, the upholstery black. Very snazzy – must have cost close to a million. Not many had that sort of money – shouldn't be too hard to find out to whom it belonged. Probably some expatriate villa-owner with more money than sense.

He was well off the Queen's Highway now, bend following bend. The surface was good, but even then with the power of the Mercedes he had no hope of catching the Quattro; with its turbo charge it could outdistance anything on the road.

He dismissed the irritating incident and concentrated on getting to the airport and the warming thought that he would soon hold Rachel in his arms. Or was he being too optimistic? Perhaps Rachel wouldn't want to be in his arms. Perhaps her passionate love for him had burnt itself out by its very intensity. He sighed and clamped his teeth firmly on the stem of his unlit pipe.

He was nearing the airport now and the very character of the island had changed. He was on the outskirts of Montego Bay and gay modern houses became more frequent. Lush gardens gave way to private beaches. Great masses of bougainvillea were a dramatic foil to crisp white walls. Roof gardens abounded with brightly painted outdoor furniture on which were bikini-clad figures soaking up the sun. There was a pervasion of wealth and good living that was nearly tangible. Montego Bay – the resort of millionaires, the famous and the infamous. The place to be seen in. To be photographed for the glossies. Not to have been there at some time or other, was something to which one didn't admit.

Rodgers mentally contrasted all the opulence with the hovels in the ghettoes where the inhabitants hardly ever knew where their next meal was coming from. All men are born equal, but some are fed with a bitter bread.

The hotel area had a bustling sophistication not to be found elsewhere in the island, with the possible exception of Ocho Rios. To the travelled visitor, an unremarkable quality; to the ordinary Jamaican, confusing on first acquaintance, alien, a looking-glass world. Once in the town itself, a degree of normality returned, but the business of tourism was still dominant. Rodgers always felt like a stranger or a tourist himself. He was from St Ann and a friendly rivalry persisted between the two 'Bays'.

Rodgers was glad that he didn't have to pass through the town to reach the airport and he swung off the highway into the entrance to Sangster International with relief. He slid into a parking space. The yellow Quattro was two bays away. He walked over to it. It had an air of careless affluence in its perfection. He looked through the side window; there was a woman's briefcase on the seat and an airline identification tag hung down. He could just make out the name: Diana Barrington. Well, well, well. Diana Barrington. The car had been driven today, though, by a man. The manner of driving had been masculine – although from what he had heard of Diana Barrington, she was mad enough for anything. He'd have a chance during his stay at the Santa Gloria to satisfy his curiosity about the car – and its owner.

THREE

The giant plane was bathed in a golden glow from a westering sun as she skimmed in to land. The roar of the jets heightened as they went into reverse thrust, then she taxied smoothly to the disembarkation bay. There was a moment of intense sound, which sank to a whisper as she came to a lumbering halt. The ground staff were ready with the gangways, and to Rowan Rodgers, watching from the VIP lounge, the moment between the opening of the hatch and Rachel's appearance stretched into eternity. He had radioed a message for her to disembark at Sangster, instead of going on to Kingston as she had planned.

A colourful collection of people spilled out of the plane; a high-pitched babble in some foreign language drifted across to him on the light breeze that was coming in from the sea. He watched them idly, whilst raking the group for a glimpse of Rachel's sleek dark head. She was the last off, supervising a steward carrying a large wicker basket. Good God, he thought, what on earth is she bringing back? She was scanning the visitors' waving gallery, not looking in his direction. There was disappointment on her face which dispelled his fears of a cool reception. He tapped on the window as she passed into Immigration. She stopped, her eyes wide and questioning, the glass between them. Then she smiled, that smile that he'd missed even more than he had admitted. It's all right, he told himself exultantly, she's come back, she's come back to me. He filled and lit his pipe, content now to wait. Although she had been last off the plane she was first through Immigration and was suddenly by his side.

"Hullo, Rowan." That same slightly breathless voice, which when heard over the phone always made the caller feel that she had just come from, or was about to make, a romantic assignation.

The large basket was held in front of her, making an effective barrier. Anyway, Rodgers doubted if it was politic at this stage to take her in his arms.

"What on earth have you got in that basket?" he demanded.

She laughed, realising the reason for his gruffness. "Well, *really!* I go away for a year and you greet me with, 'What's in the basket'."

He laughed back at her. He'd forgotten her sense of humour. "Well, what is it?"

"It's a cat, a Seal Point Siamese kitten. Princess Ra San Dhu III – Bamboo to you."

"I see." His eyes softened. If she's recovered enough to get another cat, he thought, then there's hope for me.

She sensed his thoughts. "I'll tell you about it later."

There was a renewed babble of French and English from the members of the House of Girot, as Customs officers tried to sort out the pile of luggage.

Rachel's two pieces had been passed without comment or inspection, but the Girot group were asked to open every piece until a member of the Tourist Board made his way through the crush. He spoke in a low voice to the Customs officer, who nodded in relief, then marked the numerous cases and boxes without further comment.

Rodgers loaded Rachel's luggage into the boot of the Mercedes, and carefully placed Bamboo's basket on the floor in the rear compartment. As he slid behind the steering wheel, the yellow Quattro roared by. The driver was the same, now obviously a Latin type, sleek dark hair, light open-necked sports shirt. There was a girl with him, blonde, svelte, exquisitely dressed.

"Who's that, do you know, Rachel?" Rodgers asked.

"The man, no. The girl, yes. She was on the plane. One of Girot's group, a model by the name of Solange Barnave. Why?"

"Not important." He switched on the engine. "I'll find out later."

"Why did you ask me to get off here, rather than in Kingston?"

"Because I'm staying over here; got a few days' leave. I've booked you into the Santa Gloria. Thought it would be more your speed than one of the all inclusives. All right?"

"Wonderful, nothing to do but laze in the sun and look at marvellous clothes."

"Marvellous clothes? Where do you think that you're going to see them? It's generally lack of clothes in this part of the world."

She laughed and moved closer to him. He took his left hand off the steering wheel, reached across the gear lever and held her hand.

"I can see that I'll have to change my car – these bucket seats are most inconvenient."

"I thought that the police deplored one-handed driving?"

"We do... but there are the acknowledged experts."

"Expertise of this sort.comes from extensive practice, surely... I mean it's not the sort of thing you're born with?"

" 'What a question, should any lewd interpreter be by,' " he quoted, then said gravely, "We take a special course in one-handed driving....didn't you know? Very thorough, our training, prepares us for any... emergency."

"Oh, Rowan, you fool," Rachel laughed, relaxed now for the first time since her arrival. "That's the first time I've really laughed... for a very long time."

He squeezed her hand before he released it to change down for a deep corner.

"What was all that about marvellous clothes?"

"Oh, yes. Well, you noticed that rather airy group that got off the plane, and the blonde girl who drove away with your mystery man?"

He nodded.

"Well, they are all from the House of Girot... Girot is the rather fat little man with the balding head... and he is going to present a selection from his latest collection on the north coast. The blonde, Solange Barnave, is his top model."

"Hold on a minute... would you kindly translate that into English? And *who* is Girot?"

Rachel gave an exasperated little snort. "You *must* have heard of him. He is one of the top dress designers – *couturiers* – of Paris. His clothes are fabulous, he always sets the trend about two years ahead of his rivals. Part of his collection goes on tour every year with his own models, cameramen – the lot. This year it's Jamaica and, to make it even more exciting, one of his models is a Jamaican. Don't you remember Anna Morgan? She was runner-up in the Miss Jamaica competition – oh, three or four years ago?"

"Vaguely – slant eyes? Long black hair?"

'H'm, you do remember, don't you? I recall at the time that you and – and," she paused, then went on slowly, "you and Bill said that if you both had been on the panel of judges, she would have won hands down."

Rodgers ignored the hesitant reference to Bill. She's got to get used to mentioning him, he thought.

Aloud he said, "This becomes much more interesting. Where is this – er – collection to be shown?"

"At the Santa Gloria! We'll have a ringside seat as well as seeing them all off duty."

"At the Santa Gloria? Is it now? H'mm." Rodgers was looking thoughtful. His large, well-shaped hands gripped the wheel lightly as he negotiated the numerous curves.

As Rachel glanced at him sideways, her heart gave a little skip. No, he hadn't lost any of that wild attraction that he had held for her, that attraction that had sprung up so suddenly between them. She knew that she would have to make up her mind before very long.

Not now, though. She pushed the future out of her mind.

"Well?" Rodgers asked.

"Well what?"

"You've been gazing at my profile for the past five miles. Forgotten what I look like?"

Rachel felt suddenly breathless. "No, I hadn't forgotten. Rowan," she went on quickly, "when did you come over to the north coast?"

The change of subject took him by surprise and he answered before he realised the interpretation she would inevitably place on his reply. "This morning – or rather this afternoon. Why?"

"So it's not a holiday? You're on a case?"

"Why do you think that?"

"Oh, Rowan, I'm not a fool. If you were planning a holiday, you would have met me in Kingston and asked where I would like to go. You wouldn't have whisked me off without a word. If you were on leave, you would have been here longer."

He pulled into a lay-by and switched off the engine. He lit two cigarettes and handed her one. "Sorry, do you still smoke?"

"I'm trying to give it up. All the hype about cancer is getting to me. Oh, well, one more won't make any difference."

The swift nightfall of the tropics had turned the sky to a welter of red-gold clouds, paling to a silver-green where it met the blue pocketed mountains. The sun was dropping like a fiery ball into the sea: suddenly it was gone and within seconds the reds and golds had turned to a deep green. Finally the sky became a dark blue whilst the few remaining clouds retained for a little their outlines of green, tipped with silvery pink.

Rachel took a deep pull on her cigarette and surveyed the surrounding beauty.

"I'd forgotten how lovely it all is," she said, then asked, "Rowan, what do you have to tell me?"

"That's the trouble – I can't tell you. It's top secret and highest priority. Military Intelligence is involved, so it must be something really big. I'm over here ostensibly on holiday. I only knew of this after I got your cable. You can help me in this. Together we can really give out the carefree holiday approach."

She sighed. "Yes, but you know how people talk. Everyone will know that on my return, one, I was met by you at the airport, and two, we immediately spent a holiday together. My reputation will be in shreds."

He took a deep breath before he said, "There is one sure way to stop all gossip."

"I know." Her voice was low, the moment she had expected had arrived too soon. "But Rowan..." She was saved commitment by a wail from the basket in the back. "Heavens, Rowan, we must get on. Poor little Bamboo must be starved; she wasn't allowed to eat before the flight. I hope that they won't object to her at the Santa Gloria."

"Better hadn't," he murmured inelegantly as he slid the Mercedes into gear and moved smoothly out of the lay-by, privately cursing 'poor little Bamboo' for her inopportune intervention.

"I'll meet you in the Patio Bar at – seven-thirty?" Rodgers asked some thirty minutes later. They were in Rachel's room.

Rachel nodded. She smiled up at him; she'd forgotten how very tall he was.

"Would you like to meet the princess before you go?"

"The princess? Oh, yes."

She carefully undid the fastening on the basket and lifted out an irate Siamese kitten. Her points were just becoming definite but her body was still creamy-white. Blazing blue eyes glared up at Rodgers. He took her gently from Rachel and lightly stroked the soft fur. Immediately her eyes changed to a limpid blue as a surprisingly powerful purr came pulsing out.

"The little minx," Rachel said, "she's a man's cat. Look at her, exercising her charms on you. I'll get her something to eat." She took a tin of cat food out of the basket and opened it.

Bamboo ate with concentration, her recent instant adoration for Rodgers subjugated for the moment to assuaging her hunger.

Rachel curled up in the corner of a cane settee upholstered in wild flaring yellows. She nodded at the little cat. "It's because of Bamboo that I'm here. I'll tell you some time."

He bent down and pulled her to her feet. "I don't care on whose account you're here, as long you are," he said. "But I would rather that it had been on mine."

His arms tightened round her as he kissed her. Her slight resistance crumpled, and she was clinging to him, all the remembered desires flooding back. "I've missed you so much," she whispered when at last she could speak. "I ran away – I couldn't be sure. It was so difficult..."

"I know," he said gently. "But you're here now – and I love you. Nothing has to be decided – yet."

While he showered and changed for dinner, Rowan Rodgers felt a lightness of heart and spirit that he hadn't known since Bill Groome died and Rachel went away. He recognised the fact, though, that Rachel's presence was both an asset and a complication whilst he was on this new case. He wished that he knew more of the set-up but he assumed that his contact, Major John Terrance, would get in touch with him soon. He knew Terrance slightly, in the way that everyone knew everyone else in the same social circle in the island. There was a constant meeting and re-meeting at government functions and receptions, so that it almost seemed that certain people existed solely for, and had no apparent existence apart from, such activities. Terrance was one of them, an acceptable young man, said to have a liking for and a way with the ladies. Like Rodgers, he was unmarried. He certainly gave no impression of ever working at anything serious, yet, thought Rodgers, that was presumably the impression that he wished to create. If he was deemed worthy for Military Intelligence he could not be entirely the fun-loving type that he showed to the world.

Rodgers was a few minutes early in the Patio Bar, which opened out of the larger Pirate's Lair and had a secluded intimacy under the stars, with the sound of the surf breaking gently on the distant reef. He slowly filled his pipe while he waited for Rachel and watched the occupants of the Pirate's Lair. The central bar was circular, the ceiling above draped with fish netting, giant conch shells on the counter substituting for ashtrays, with two cheerful barmen in pirate dress, their white teeth flashing in gleaming dark faces. The bar was quite crowded despite it being the dinner hour. The tourist season, though not starting officially until the middle of December, seemed to be in full swing a month early. Many of the guests drinking, smoking, chatting volubly were, as far as Rodgers remembered, from the House of Girot. The blonde French girl, Solange Barnave, was perched on a stool, talking with expressive Gallic gestures to a tall, fair, almost effeminately good-looking young man in a ruffled silk shirt, plum-coloured silk jacket and grey and plum striped trousers. They were joined by a slim dark girl. That must be Anna Morgan, thought Rodgers, noting the slant eyes and the long, smoothly coiled black hair. She seemed to sense that she was being watched and turned her head. Despite the distance and the darkness, her eyes met Rodgers'. She looked at him for a long moment, her eyes wide. Rodgers had the impression that she believed that they had met before, but he had no recollection of the occasion.

"Sorry to be late," Rachel's voice broke into his thoughts. She surveyed him with an amusement tinged with annoyance and her voice held a slight tartness as she said, "I see that you haven't wasted the time, though. What is the phrase that novelists use? 'Their gaze was locked across the crowded room.' "

She slipped into the seat beside him.

He laughed. "I note that you still give your admirable jealousy act – so flattering to the male ego. But I defy any man not to admire those two damsels – though 'damsel' may not be quite the right description. But to admire from a distance is as much as I want to do. What will you have to drink?"

"Oh – rum, please – very light – on the rocks."

"Since when have you been drinking rum? Thought you didn't like it."

"I didn't, but I came to the conclusion that it was the mixers I didn't like, so now I take it on the rocks."

He handed her a cigarette. "You're looking gorgeous," he said. "That dress is quite – something."

She glanced down doubtfully. "You really like it? I had it before I went away. My dressmaker in Kingston made it. I never wore it, always felt that it was a bit too much. But I saw something vaguely along this line in Paris, so I thought I'd wear it – but I still have doubts."

"Don't – I like it. Though at the moment I would like whatever you wore or ..." He paused and smiled; she grinned impishly back at the uncompleted sentence.

Their drinks arrived and at the same time a waiter appeared at the net-hung doorway. He glanced round the patio then wove his way to their table.

"Superintendent Rodgers? Sorry to disturb you, but the manager is asking you to see him in his office."

"What's it all about?"

The waiter shrugged, "I don't know, sir, but Mr Deleon said it was important that I fetch you *right away*."

FOUR

Oh God, thought Rodgers, who'd be a policeman? He left Rachel at her door and made his way to the manager's office. It was a pleasant room with deep wicker armchairs, gaily upholstered. A large, flat-topped desk adorned with a straight-line phone, a more complex-looking machine with a variety of buttons and a computer whose screen gave off a flickering green light, faced a large plate-glass window, through which was a vista of gardens that led down to the beach and the ever moving waters of the Caribbean.

The manager, olive-skinned and with a somewhat Semitic mien, greeted Rodgers with a worried frown. "Superintendent Rodgers? Amos Deleon." He extended a small, well-tended hand. "How good of you to come. I hesitated to disturb you as you are on holiday, but Mr West assured me..." He petered off and raised his elbows in a resigned, expressive gesture.

It was only then that Rodgers became aware of a third person in the room. The long body of Superintendent Richard West was stretched out in a long chair by the window. He raised a limp hand in greeting as Deleon mentioned his name.

"What's the problem?" Rodgers asked.

"One of our guests has been found – dead." Deleon spoke in a low voice.

"Dead? Where?"

"On the beach." The manager was becoming more anxious as the enormity of the situation penetrated his mind. "What this is going to do to the bookings – just at the start of the season..." He sighed heavily.

"Well, it was the end of the season for our friend," Rodgers said shortly. "What happened, West?"

Richard West rose slowly to his feet, his thin body almost anguine. He had a long melancholy face, a light coffee-coloured complexion with sad brown eyes to match. Behind this facade of louring apathy was a quick analytical mind and an often caustic wit.

"A guest from here has been killed."

"Name?"

"Simon Soulis."

Rodgers glanced at Deleon who was becoming increasingly upset; sweat gleamed on his oily forehead. "Simon Soulis? French?"

"I – believe so. He spoke, though, with hardly any accent. He arrived a few days ago; we didn't see much of him. He was very friendly with ..." Deleon stopped in mid-sentence.

"Yes? Friendly with whom?" Rodgers prompted.

"No. I was about to repeat – just gossip."

"Sometimes gossip is very useful and informative; it often helps to unearth facts. Maybe we could hear it sometime?" Rodgers turned to Richard West. "Who found the body? And when?"

"One of the bellhops. He'd been sent down by a guest to retrieve a forgotten beach bag." He looked at his watch. "Just about an hour ago. They phoned me, but couldn't contact me right away."

"Right, let's go see." Rodgers turned to Deleon. "Mr West will want to question the bellhop. OK, West?"

"OK. I waited until you got here. Touched nothing. Let's go."

He nodded briefly to Deleon and led the way through a door beside the picture frame window. A flight of stone-flagged steps led down through the terraced gardens. The night sounds were all about them as they made their way through a studied tangle of tropic vegetation. Bougainvillea spilled cascades over a pergola, their daytime brightness washed with grey in the brilliance of the moonlight. They passed through a cactus garden, whose spiky shapes set in a bed of stones gave a touch of fantasy. Giant feathery ferns brushed them gently as they descended. The crickets and tree frogs were in full chorus, making a musical background, with the occasional harsh stridency of a lone croaking lizard to mark a contrast.

The garden ended in a smooth patch of close-cut lawn, dotted with chairs and umbrella-topped tables. Then another flight of steps led down to the beach, gleaming whitely in the moonlight.

Along the beach were outjuts of sharp honeycomb rock; broad-leaved, flat-topped, wild almond trees cast well defined shadows on the silver shore; and the surge of the sea grew louder each moment as they drew near to it. West led the way across the soft still-warm sand, to an overhanging outjut of rock. From the base of this, a churned-up track led towards the sea, the whiteness stained with a dark fluid that glistened stickily in the rays of the moon. On the edge of the softly lapping sea lay a crumpled darker shadow, more solid than the others. A uniformed constable standing by came to attention as the two officers approached.

"All right, Goodbody," West said crisply. "This is Superintendent Rodgers, CID, Kingston."

"Sir." The young police constable's stance grew even more rigid. This would be something to tell the boys. To think that him, country bwoy police, just six weeks out of Police Academy, to work wit' big-time CID Super from city. That Mr Rodgers, he'd read about his exploits in the press... Rodgers' voice cut into his rosy thoughts.

"You will say nothing to anyone of my being here, Constable. I am here on holiday and no connection must be made between my presence here and this case. That's an order. Right?"

Goodbody's dreams of being the star performer and recounting his activities to admiring cronies faded and died. There was something about Rodgers' quietly snapped 'Right' that precluded even the contemplation of disobeying the order.

"We haven't moved him. We'll wait until the doctor has seen him. I phoned Dr Montgomery – unlike you city folk, we don't boast a police surgeon. The flash boys should be here soon," West said.

"I'd appreciate it if you'd give as little publicity to this as possible, for the time being," Rodgers said in a low voice. "It may be important, maybe not. Maybe just another senseless mugging. If there are any enquiries from guests or staff, say it was an accident – a fall from the rocks – anything plausible. Just keep it quiet for a day or so."

"Right, if you say so, " West agreed with his usual gloom.

Rodgers bent over the body, then straightened. "Here's a couple of lines of enquiry you may care to follow up," he said. "He was driving a pale yellow Audi Quattro earlier this evening, went out to the airport and drove one of the visiting French models back here – a Mademoiselle Solange Barnave. The car belongs to Diana Barrington – lives at Ripple – half a mile along the coast."

An admiring gleam crept into Richard West's melancholy eyes. "You're really cool, man. D'you generally have such seemingly useful lines at the start of a case?"

Rodgers grinned. "Luck, man. He nearly drove me off the road, that's why I noticed him. If you could make those interviews soon and let me know the outcome?"

"Right, will do"

There goes the rest of the evening, West thought dolefully.

The cameramen and Dr Montgomery arrived within minutes of each other. The doctor was a tall, spare man, spare of figure and words. He was dressed for dinner in a black tie and carried a long case. "Sorry to keep you – I was dining at the Beach Club. They took some time to find me." He waited while the camera crew photographed the body from all angles. "Right, Doc," one of the crew said as he took the final shot. "He's all yours."

Dr Montgomery handed a flashlight to Constable Goodbody. "Just direct that as I tell you."

"Yes, sir."

The doctor knelt down and examined the dead man in silence. Then he grunted as he straightened up and said shortly, "Messy – very messy. Stabbed through the sub-clavicle with some sharp jagged instrument. The area is torn outwards, which is not consistent with a normal knife wound, and rather rules out the mugging theory. Death instantaneous. Occurred between half an hour and one and a half hours ago."

"Any idea what could have caused such a wound?" Rodgers asked.

"Not with such a brief examination and under these circumstances, I'll be able to tell you more after the PM."

Rodgers left Superintendent West and his men to carry out the routine enquiries. At least they weren't hampered by curious sightseers. Most of the hotel guests were still at dinner and the area where the body lay was well away from the main beach used by the guests.

With the preliminary examination completed, Constable Goodbody was left to superintend the transfer of the body to the ambulance, and Richard West returned to the hotel lobby and sent for the bellhop who had discovered the body. He was young, about fourteen, short and slim, with a neatly cared-for head of curling black hair. His dark eyes shone from his mahogany-coloured face with a youthful intelligence which led West to hope that he could expect reasonably intelligent answers.

"What's your name, son?"

"Carlisle," the boy answered, stressing the second syllable.

"Carlisle what?"

"Sir?"

"Is Carlisle your first or last name?"

"Is firs', sir. Carlisle Linton." Again the second syllable in each name stressed.

West nodded. "Right. How long you work here?"

"Six week, sir. I leave school in July, an' work a little at garden, clear up de lady yard dem, den me cossin get me here, sir."

The ubiquitous cousin, thought West. In every walk throughout the island a cousin seems to be involved.

"What your cousin do?"

"Him de barman in de Pirate Lair."

"I see. His name?

"Sir?"

"What you call your cousin?" That outward intelligence went no deeper. West clung to patience.

"Is Delroy, sir." Carlisle caught West's eye and added hastily, "Delroy Simit, sir."

"Smith?"

"Yes, sir, Simit."

"Tell me, Carlisle, what happen this evening? How you on the beach after dark?"

"One o' de lady dem." The boy slipped deeper into the vernacular as he gained confidence and lost his awe of West. "She say she leave she glasses, she shade, she not sure where, sir. She say me mus' look 'pon de beach, nuh mus' go back till fin' me fin' dem." He paused and swallowed. "Me look fe dem good."

"How, in the dark?" West asked sharply.

"Me tek a flashlight, sir." Carlisle looked at West in reproach.

"So?"

"Me look all over, an' me jus' give up, when me 'ear a sinting."

"What sort of something?"

"Is a – cry. A kin' a – cry, sir," he struggled with his limited vocabulary to describe the sound.

"All right, you heard a sound. Like someone in pain?"

"No, sir, like frighten 'im frighten, then it cut off, sir."

West nodded, remembering the wound. "It figures," he murmured.

"Sir?"

"Nothing – go on. You heard a sound, did you hear anything else – or see anything?"

"Me hear a sinting fall, sir, an' me hear de boat..."

West grasped the boy's arm. "You heard a boat? Did you see it?"

"No, sir, it don't have no light."

"So you went to look?"

"Me study up me brain an' t'ink it funny-like. Me climb down de rock dem, an'..." his dark skin took on a greyish tinge at the recollection of that moment – "me a'mos' fall over 'im, sir. Me shine de flashlight an'..." The boy shuddered at the memory.

"You turned the flashlight on. Could you still hear the motor of the boat?"

"Yes, sir, it come up close. Me did t'ink it comin' in, den it go off fas' fas'. Me did wonder wh'appen."

"It came a bit more inshore? You still have the flashlight on?"

"Yes, sir. Me shine it out but me don' see not'ing."

"You're quite sure about that?" West asked. "Could you make

out the size of the boat or who was in it?"

"No, sir, me try but me frighten, sir, an'..."

"Yes, son, I expect that you were." West glanced at the boy's strained face. His colour had improved; he didn't seem to realise the implication of what he had said. "Look, son." West's normally curt tone had softened a little. "Do something for me?"

"Yes, sir?"

"I don't want you to talk to anyone about this, y'hear, boy? Not anyone. Not about what you saw or heard, or what you didn't see and didn't hear. Not until I say that you may. Right?"

The boy nodded solemnly.

"A' right, sir, me won' say a t'ing."

West slapped him on the shoulder, gave him a two-dollar bill and dismissed him with a, "Right, son, see you tomorrow." He watched the boy go and wondered if he should have warned him more strongly against talking of what he had seen and heard. He didn't want to worry the boy unduly. He dismissed the matter with a shrug as he got into his car and drove along the coast road towards Ripple. He glanced at the clock on the dashboard: nearly nine-thirty. Too late to call on the lady? He thought not – and anyway with a murder on his hands a little thing like unconventional hours was unimportant. From what he had heard of Diana Barrington, she didn't know the meaning of the word convention. She had been married and divorced three times, widowed once – that's where all the money came from – and it was rumoured that she had a long, ceaselessly changing line of lovers – despite the threat of AIDS.

He was driving west along the coast road, the sea slapping incessantly on his right, high craggy rocks coming down to the edge of the road on his left. The turning into Ripple was sharp; he came upon it unexpectedly, so that he had to reverse before he could make the turn. The drive was narrow and unpaved, rising, it seemed, almost vertically through continuous hairpin bends – double hairpin bends for the most part. Certainly discourages the chance visitor, he thought, then grinned at the implication. With all her money, Diana Barrington could have afforded a better surface on her driveway; its only virtue was that it was well cambered. He swung round the last bend into a wide, flat car park. There were three cars in a line: a Jaguar 4.2, a Metro Mini and the pale yellow Audi Quattro.

He must have climbed a few hundred feet in a matter of minutes, he thought, looking at the coastline spread out below him. East he could see as far as Flat Point, west almost to Falmouth. The sea appeared dark blue in the brilliant moonlight from that distance, in sharp contrast to the silver-white sands that curved away in either direction.

He turned towards the house. It was, to his surprise, a perfect reproduction of an old great house, not the angular modern steel and concrete type he had expected. He took in its beauty for a long moment: it must be a reproduction, he thought, one would never find a great house so near the road, and this wasn't near the site of an old sugar plantation, as far as he knew. He felt reluctant to face the coming interview and lit a cigarette, watching the play of light on the sea far below, then turned back to the house and noted the soft gleam through the jalousied window. A welter of assorted dogs suddenly came tumbling through the wide-open mahogany doors. A houseman, trim in black trousers and pale monkey jacket, white shirt and black bow tie, followed the dogs. West came to a decision and threw away the cigarette in a wide curving arc of sparks as he mounted the elegant outer double stairway. The houseman raised his voice over the babel from the soft growls of a couple of miniature Chihuahuas, the deeper tones of a Great Dane and the high yap of a poodle.

"Sorry, sir. They won't do you nothing."

West flapped a hand. "Shoo, boys." The dogs circled him once then scampered back into the house. West stepped into the hallway. "Good evening. May I see Mrs Barrington? I know that it's late but my business is most important. Superintendent West."

"This way, please, sir."

The man motioned West to a chair and went softly away into the shadows. West looked around the hall. It was large and square; in the centre was an elegant mahogany staircase leading down to the ground floor. There were deep-piled white rugs scattered over the darkly gleaming floor, a few perfect period chairs – Georgian, he thought - and a couple of Spanish chairs, with supple black leather backs and seats which smoothly flowed one into the other, and high fan-shaped headrests which were intricately carved, as were the armrests. He rose as the man returned.

"This way, please, sir."

He led the way through an archway to the left of the staircase and onto a wide, cool verandah overlooking the terraced garden. The sea shone distantly in the bright light of the moon. Deep bamboo-cane chairs and long settees were in keeping with the setting. The cushions struck a vibrant neoteric note, thick foam covered with a rough, tweedy material, shaded from light yellow through burnt umber to dark brown. This scheme against the deep ivory of the bamboo had a restful vitality.

As West stepped through the archway, a woman rose from a chaise longue.

"Superintendent West? I'm Diana Barrington."

He took the hand she held out to him. Her handshake had a quality that he could not define. He remembered suddenly a doctor whom he had once met who said that all that he needed to know about a women was told to him by seeing her lower lip in profile and by shaking her hand.

This woman was, he decided, all woman.

She was tall, five feet eight or more, he guessed. She looked athletic, without being in the least muscular, rather she had a trim litheness. Her hair was short, a deep red-gold – naturally so, he would swear. This colour made a striking combination with eyes of golden brown against a skin of warm coffee cream, darkened still further by a patina of suntan.

She was dressed in a white lace jumpsuit, lined in a shade of coffee to achieve the nude look. She exuded an aura of sex, but without effort and seemingly without care.

"Well, Superintendent?"

There was a trace of irony in the emphasis that she placed on his rank. It was the voice of a woman accustomed to male adulation. A woman, he thought once more, to be reckoned with. He was quite unperturbed by her mocking tone or by the fact that her hand had been in his for so long.

"My apologies for disturbing you, Mrs Barrington, but a matter of some importance has occurred and I would like to ask you a few questions."

"Dear me," she murmured as she lit a cigarette and sat down, this time on a wide, swinging settee. She patted the seat beside her. "Do sit down. You make me feel nervous – standing there like vengeance. Tell me, do you have a little opening speech like that ready to meet all occasions?"

He ignored her flippancy and sat down opposite her. Her lips twitched slightly as she asked, "Would you like a drink? I think that you will find most anything." She indicated a large liquor cabinet behind her.

He shook his head. "Thank you, but you forget, madam, I'm here on duty."

"For God's sake, don't go all Scotland Yard on me – and don't call me 'madam'."

He didn't move.

The brown eyes snapped. "Well, at least get me one – Scotch – on the rocks."

He went in silence to the cabinet and poured a drink. On second thoughts, and having established his point, he poured himself one. He went back to the settee and sat down beside her. She accepted her drink without a word, but the warmth in her eyes acknowledged his capitulation.

"Yes, Mr West?" she asked after a pause.

"Mrs Barrington, you lent your car – the pale yellow Audi Quattro – to a friend of yours? Simon Soulis?"

"Yes." Her voice was even, almost bored. "What's he done? Smashed it up?"

"No. You don't know, then, that it has been returned?"

"No, has it? I told him that he could keep it overnight. He was picking up some French doll."

"How good a friend – have you found him?"

"What an odd choice of words." Her eyes narrowed. "It was a deliberate choice, though. What's happened?" There was a note in her voice that demanded the truth.

"He's dead."

"Dead? How?"

"He was – murdered – rather nastily."

She paled under her tan, then drank deeply from her glass.

"How? Who..." she began.

"Perhaps you will now answer my question. How good a friend was he?"

"He..." She was regaining her calm now. "Not so much a friend as an acquaintance. I met him in Paris – two – three years ago. He's been out here, off and on..."

"Are you in the habit of lending acquaintances valuable cars? Just like that?"

She looked at him levelly. "Why not? I do a lot of things – just like that. A car is only valuable because it costs money. That I have plenty of."

West waited, his eyes on hers.

She held his gaze, then burst out, "Don't be such a prude. For God's sake, in this day and age. So – he was a lover. Note, I say 'a' – intimating one of many. He wasn't important – in that way. An amusing diversion." She stopped and lowered her eyes as she stubbed out her cigarette with a hand that was completely steady.

"So," said West at last. "It didn't matter to you that he borrowed your car to meet a charming model?"

She laughed suddenly. "Mind? God – no. Do you think that some little chit in her twenties is any threat to me?" She faced him, challengingly, arrogantly.

West got up – in self-defence? he wasn't quite sure – and walked to the rail of the verandah. He stood gazing out towards the darkling sea. He caught a glimpse of white in the shadowed garden. He peered through the night and discovered that it was a flight of rough cut-stone steps leading downwards.

"Where do those steps go to?" he asked over his shoulder.

She was by his side, her perfume heavy and intrusive.

"Down to the beach – rather to the road – then down to the beach."

"I see."

He took out two cigarettes unthinkingly, and held one out to her; she accepted it with a twitch of amusement. He flushed and said with more harshness than he intended, "Where were you between six-thirty and eight-thirty this evening?"

"Right here, Mr West, right here."

"Were you alone?"

"You mean, do I have an alibi?"

"Just that, Mrs Barrington."

"No, I was alone. Except for Peters, my handyman, who can confirm that. The other two cars were not used today – and the third you say was returned – when?"

The last word had a hesitancy that the others, mockingly assured, did not.

"How would I know? Perhaps Peters could help. May I ask him a few questions?"

"Don't be so damned polite. You know that you'll ask him, whether I say yes or no." She rang a handbell with unnecessary energy. The elderly Peters came silently through the archway. He gave an old-fashioned bow.

"You rang, Miss Diana, ma'am?"

"Yes. Mr West would like to ask you a few questions."

Peters' rather rheumy eyes turned slowly to West. "Peters, when was the Quattro returned?"

The man hesitated. "Quattro, sir?"

"Who bring back the yellow car, man?" West rephrased the question and added a strong local inflection.

"I don't know, sir. I go into town to do a little shopping, at aroun' five o'clock, an' when I reach back, I see the car."

"What time you reach?"

" 'Bout seven."

West was well aware that 'about seven' could mean anything between six-thirty and seven-thirty, and that 'town' was the little group of shops half a mile away. He turned to Diana, his eyebrows raised.

"All right," she snapped. "So I was alone then. I'd forgotten that I'd told Peters that he could have some time off. I was in my room – over there." She nodded to a door opening off the far end of the verandah.

"And you don't know when the Quattro was returned? Are you sure that Simon Soulis didn't bring it back?"

"I've told you, I don't know. If he did, I didn't see him. And if he did, why didn't I see him – and how did he get back to the hotel?"

"Those are a couple of questions that I would like answers to. Are you generally so casual about lending cars?"

"I've told you," she flared, regardless of the still present Peters. "Cars are only worldly goods – of which I have plenty."

"You're fortunate," West commented dryly. He turned back to Peters. "What time did you serve dinner?"

Peters hesitated, cast a sidelong look at Diana, then said, "I tek a tray to Miss Diana 'bout half pas' seven."

"You stayed to serve?"

"No, sir. I put it on the verandah, here," he indicated a round table. "Miss Diana was in the shower."

"So you didn't see her?"

"No, sir. I jus' hear the water running."

"Did you speak to – Miss Diana?"

"No," Diana cut in. "It's just routine. I always have a tray if I'm alone. I called out, 'Thank you Peters, I'll be right out.' " She was looking straight at West as she spoke.

"Will that be all, sir?" Peters asked hesitantly.

"Yes." West regarded him thoughtfully. "That will be all – for the moment."

Peters gave his little bow. "Goodnight, sir." He went, his face inscrutable.

West swung back to Diana. "Thank you, Mrs Barrington. May I congratulate you on your fortitude?"

"Don't be so pedantic. What in hell are you talking about?"

"Your stoic acceptance of bad news..."

"Oh," she interrupted him with studied rudeness. "You mean Simon's death? I don't feel anything, Mr West, not anything." She looked at him defiantly for a moment, then turned and went to the verandah rail.

"You didn't tell me – how – how he was killed," she said after a pause, in a completely different voice.

"He was stabbed through the sub-clavicle," he indicated the position at his neckline. "With an as yet unidentified instrument."

She drew in her breath. "Where – did it happen?"

"On the beach – the Santa Gloria beach. I wonder how – and why?"

She didn't answer. He left her there, still standing at the verandah rail, gazing across the little bay to where the lights of the Santa Gloria blazed in the warm night air.

As West passed the Quattro, he paused and peered inside. The rich smell of leather assailed his nostrils from the black upholstery, mingled with a mixture of perfume and cigarette smoke. The keys hung from the ignition switch: he looked at them thoughtfully for a moment, then walked slowly to his own car. The keys wouldn't tell him anything, any prints would be superimpositions. He negotiated the drive with respectful caution and it was with relief that he swung once more onto the main coastal road. A gleam of white attracted his attention; the cut-stone steps from Ripple and, across the road on his left, the corresponding flight leading down to the beach. He pulled off the road onto the grassy verge. The sound of the sea was insistent now, mingling with the constant chorus of tree frogs and crickets, the whole an off-beat symphony. The peeniewallies blinked on and off among the trees, tiny moving spots of light.

He walked slowly along by the low retaining wall until he came to the white steps leading down to the beach. At the head of the steps were two concrete posts which supported a wrought-iron gate. A notice painted on wood warned: RIPPLE. PRIVATE PROPERTY. TRESPASSERS WILL BE PROSECUTED. The gate swung open at his touch; a padlock, open, hung by its staple. Carelessness or haste? Or was someone down there now? He opened the gate fully and went down the steps on silent feet. The steps were steep, each tread causing discomfort; care was needed in ascent or descent. He reached the bottom and scanned the surrounding area. To his left was a beach house, the sides of bamboo, the roof thatched with coconut palm leaves. To his right, moored to a heavy stanchion and rocking lightly in the shallows, was a powerful looking, but compact, motor launch.

He removed his shoes and socks, rolled up his pants to the knee and waded through the gently lapping water to the boat. He peered over the side, then vaulted lightly aboard. Blue flippers and skin diving equipment were jumbled carelessly on the deck. He searched the craft thoroughly: the small galley was well stocked with tinned food, and the cabin had swimsuits and beach towels in a tiny closet; apart from that – nothing. West looked thoughtfully at the flippers and the rest of the equipment. "I wonder," he said aloud.

Then he sniffed: there was a lingering smell of warm engine oil in the air.

With a final look around, he left the boat and went back up the steps to his car.

He left the padlock on the gate as he had found it. When he was approaching the Santa Gloria, he glanced at the clock on the dashboard. Nearly ten-thirty – he hoped that the little French number was still up and about.

FIVE

When Rowan Rodgers left Richard West to take care of the routine enquiries on the beach, he returned to the hotel and went immediately to Rachel's room.

"Shall we finish that drink after dinner?" he asked. "I'm afraid it's not the end of my work for this evening, otherwise I'd suggest that we had it here."

Rachel nodded as she picked up her handbag, then paused to stroke Bamboo, who was curled in a tight cream ball on her bed. "Downstairs will be fine," she said primly as she went through the door. They went to the Columbus Room; but both discovered that their appetites had fled.

"I'll settle for a small shrimp salad and coffee," Rachel said. "All these steaks and so forth turn me off."

"Me too. Shrimp salad and coffee it is – and a bottle of champagne to welcome you home."

"You know that I can't say no to champagne."

After their light dinner, they settled themselves in the Pirate's Lair. When their drinks were before them, Rachel asked, "What happened? Can you tell me?"

Rowan told her about the body on the beach. "The dead man was the driver of the overtaking Quattro. His name was Simon Soulis. He arrived a few days ago and spent much of his time at Ripple – Diana Barrington's home. I'm keeping out of it, for the moment. I don't want to get too involved unless it's certain that the murder has any bearing on why I'm here. And I won't know that until my contact gets in touch. There's a good man over here in charge, Richard West. He's making all enquiries and will report back to me later."

"Do you think it's likely that this man's death does have some bearing on your case?"

"I don't know, it may have. I rather hope that it does, then the whole thing won't be so tenuous." He glanced round the bar which was quite full now.

"Who's the fat little balding man at the bar?"

Without even checking, Rachel said, "That is the great Girot himself. Why?"

"You seem to have made a conquest. He's been gazing steadily at you ever since we sat down."

"I doubt the conquest bit. I'm not exactly – the type – shall I say? He's probably thinking 'what a frightful dress'. I told you that I had doubts about it."

Rodgers laughed. "You're probably right, on second thoughts. It's not an admiring gaze, rather puzzled and faintly annoyed."

"Really, Rowan, I don't look that awful."

He took her hand across the table. "Sweetheart, I don't care what that arty little man thinks – I adore you, so let's forget him."

She sipped her drink as she looked down at his large, dark, well-shaped hand which enveloped her own slim one. "I'm glad that I came back," she said. Before he could take advantage of this encouraging opening, a piratically dressed waiter stopped at their table.

"Excuse me, sir, madam. The gentleman at the bar – him say if you an' the lady would join him for a drink?"

"Which gentleman?"

The waiter indicated the rotund figure of Girot, who acknowledged Rodgers' look of enquiry with a half – but wholly Gallic – bow. Rodgers turned back to Rachel and raised an eyebrow. "Do we accept?"

"I suppose so," she said doubtfully. "After all, he is a world figure. But I wonder why us?"

"My compliments to M'sieur Girot – the lady and I will be delighted."

They followed the waiter through the crowded bar. Girot had moved from his former position and was now installed at a table at the edge of the Patio Bar, facing the sea. The soothing, silky slither of the surf on the reef reached them with an oddly mesmeric sound.

Girot rose as they approached. He was dressed in wine silk suit, white ruffled shirt, wine bow-tie and cummerbund, ruby studs and cuff links – rubies that held the deep glow of authenticity. His round face and the high, bald dome of his forehead gleamed with moisture. His eyes belied his smile of welcome: coldly blue, they surveyed Rachel almost inimically.

"Roger Girot. *Enchanté*, madame." He bowed over Rachel's hand as he kissed it. She felt a shiver of revulsion. She knew that she should have been thrilled at meeting the great Girot – at his own request, too – but she was repelled by his manner, as well as his person.

"Rachel Groome, and this is..." She hesitated, then for some indefinable reason, decided not to give Rodgers' rank. "Mr Rowan Rodgers, a friend of mine."

"Delighted, m'sieur. Do sit down. What may I order?"

A hovering waiter took their orders.

There was a pause.

What's the matter with the man? Rodgers thought with annoyance, he asks us over then sits glowering like a clam – he gave an inward grin at the unlikely simile.

Rachel bridged the silence by saying, "M'sieur Girot, it is indeed an honour to meet you. I saw you on the plane today, of course."

"Madame, the honour and the pleasure are all mine – ah, *merci.*"

The waiter placed the drinks before them; Girot was silent during the procedure. He waited until they were alone, then lifted his glass with a fussy little flourish. "To your very good health, madam – m'sieur."

They acknowledged the salutation and waited. Girot placed his glass carefully on the round mat in front of him. He seemed reluctant to speak but said at last, "Madame, enchanted as I am to make your acquaintance, it is rather a matter of business that I wish to discuss with you."

Rachel glanced swiftly at Rodgers. His face was impassive.

"Business? I'm afraid I don't understand."

The smile had left Girot's thin lips. "No? Madame – forgive me – but where did you buy your gown?"

Rachel's grey eyes matched Girot's for coldness. "My gown? Really, Mr Girot..." she made to rise but he put out a restraining hand.

"Please, madame – do not take offence. I wish to know for a very good reason, please to tell me."

Rachel glanced at Rodgers again; his eyes had taken on a new watchfulness. He give an almost imperceptible nod.

"Well," Rachel sat down. "I wouldn't describe it as a 'gown'. It's just a little dress that my dressmaker ran up for me. I know that it's rather advanced – but..."

"In Kingston? Here in Jamaica?"

"Yes, about a year and a half ago. I..." Girot's look of amazement and disbelief deepened. "A year and a half ago? That is – very hard to believe."

Rachel's temper was rising. Girot or no Girot, she was not accepting this sort of treatment. She made to rise again, but this time it was Rodgers' hand that stopped her. "Mr Girot," he said smoothly, "you are causing Mrs Groome some embarrassment. I am sure that you do not intend that, so perhaps you will explain your interest in her dress."

Girot surveyed Rodgers, his light eyes speculative, then he gave a bobbing nod.

"But yes, m'sieur. I feel that I have been – how do you say? The bull in the china. Forgive me, madame, but that 'little dress' that your 'dressmaker ran up for you' – " he seemed to shudder inwardly at the irreverent phrasing in connection with the high altar of the world of couture – "that, madame, is a copy of one of my creations – a creation that has not left my workshop in Paris until yesterday. It has never been shown to either the press or the public. It was to have been one of the highlights of my showing here."

"But – this is impossible..." Rachel began, but Rodgers cut in.

"Mr Girot, what are you implying?"

"Simply, M'sieur Rodgers, that this gown, worn so elegantly by this lady, was made from one of my sketches. It could not have been copied from the original – not over a year ago. Only the sketches were in existence then – there was not even a *toile* – that was made later, then destroyed."

"What is a *toile*?"

"It is a – how do you say? A prototype, made of inexpensive white cloth. It would be foolhardy to experiment with exclusive dress material, you understand?"

Rodgers nodded and Rachel sat forward, all anger gone, an expression of intense interest on her pointed face. "I see," she said. "You say that a dress like this was made into a *toile* and later destroyed. Why?"

Girot took a sip from his glass. He seemed less antagonistic, bent now on displaying the well-known Girot charm.

"You ask why, madame. Because in the world of couture many, many sketches are made – some are never used. Some get as far as being translated into *toiles* – only a few are made into gowns. If, when a *toile* is made, it is decided that it is not – er – good enough for the final stage, then both the *toile* and the sketches are destroyed. But if it is considered perhaps too advanced – or out of keeping with the line or trend of the rest of the collection – as this one was – then the sketch will be retained, the *toile* destroyed. The sketch may be used again later when the new line is established and accepted."

"But why is the *toile* destroyed?"

"For the very reason that I am embarrassing you now, madame, because it may be pirated."

Rachel looked down at the dress with a new respect, tinged still with doubt. "You mean that this dress was made from one of your sketches which was – stolen?" She turned to Rodgers. "May I have a cigarette, please? I'm quite confused with all this."

Rodgers held out a packet of Dunhills then, as he struck a match, asked, "Mr Girot, how can you be so sure that this dress is one of your creations?"

Girot gave him a scornful look. "Mr Rodgers," he pronounced it in the French way, "to ask a couturier how he can recognise his own creation is like asking a mother how she knows her own child."

Rodgers bowed his head, mockingly meek.

"But, Mr Girot," Rachel leant forward, her eyes wide and puzzled. "How did the sketch get out here? As I told you, I had this made – oh, at least eighteen months ago. It was –" she stopped and drew back in her chair, and blew out a cloud of smoke to hide the sudden change in her expression. Rodgers looked at her sharply. He knew her too well not to realise that she had remembered something that she didn't want to reveal.

Girot didn't seem to have noticed and went on, "That, madame, is something I should like to know. It is one of the hazards of the couturier, this piracy – but it does not often happen before the first showing."

"How are these sketches pirated?" Rodgers asked, tamping down tobacco in his pipe.

"Oh, it is a ceaseless struggle, ceaseless. There are five classical methods. The most distasteful is by the treachery of a member of staff. If one chooses one's staff carefully that can be eliminated, for after all it is to the benefit of all the staff not to betray the House."

"And the other methods?" Rodgers sounded professionally interested now, and Rachel wondered again why she hadn't introduced him by his rank.

Girot passed a plump white hand across his glistening forehead and said, "Well, if at the press showing unscrupulous representatives abuse the privilege of the press, it can happen then. Quick sketches, even photographs by concealed cameras. I will not bore you with details of the other methods because in this instance it must be due to treachery amongst my staff – a conclusion I reach with distaste and sorrow." He turned to Rachel. "Madame, you have been most patient, but you must understand that it was a great shock to see you in one of my creations." He fingered the material and ran his eye over Rachel with dispassionate professionalism. "It is beautifully executed," he admitted grudgingly. *"Who is your – dressmaker?"* He hesitated over using the word, then went quite still and a wary look crept into his cold blue eyes."Who is she, madame?" His voice held a new intensity.

The old boy has remembered something, thought Rodgers.

Aloud he said, "Mr Girot, I am quite sure that Mrs Groome has no idea of how the sketch was pilfered."

"The name of my dressmaker can mean nothing to you," Rachel said. "I chose this dress from a sheaf of sketches, which I understood to be by a boy with a flair for clothes – a graduate of the School of Art. Surely, this may well be a coincidence, like – like two scientists discovering a new drug at the same time?"

"Madame, I wish that I could convince you that it is no coincidence. I *know* my own work, I cannot be mistaken. This piracy in my profession can be crippling."

Rachel rose to her feet. "I'm sorry, of course, Mr Girot. You have had a most distressing introduction to my country, but I can add nothing to what I have already told you. When are you showing your collection?" she changed the subject.

Girot rose, all unctuous charm now. "Tomorrow night, in the ballroom. You will be there, of course?"

"Of course, I'm looking forward to it so much. Goodnight, m'sieur. If you will excuse me, I have a headache – jet lag, you know."

Girot bowed over her hand, then stood watching as Rodgers followed Rachel from the table. Rodgers cupped her elbow with a firm hand. "Let's go down to the pool. The fresh air will do that 'headache' good."

She smiled up at him. "You know me too well," she murmured.

"Well enough to know that travelling doesn't tire you and that you very rarely get headaches."

They were standing by the pool, the sound of its pump throbbing in the quiet night. Rodgers said, "Damn this case coming up just now, and damn Girot for making us waste valuable time." He bent to kiss her but she drew away.

"No, Rowan. If you kiss me now we shall both go up in flames. Give me a cigarette, please."

He lit two and handed her one. "Now," he said, "what about that pirated sketch? What did you remember whilst talking to Girot?"

"So you noticed? Well, my dressmaker..."

"Name?" he asked automatically.

"Susan Taylor. She's very good – even better than I thought, after Girot's rather grudging praise." She paused, then went on slowly, "She was in Paris for a while, two or three years ago. She could possibly have obtained the sketch then. Also, when she showed me the sketch she said – I can't remember the exact words – but something to the effect that Paris would be wearing this line soon. I didn't think anything of it at the time. Sometimes – whatever Girot says to the contrary – a new line is duplicated by two or even more unrelated designers, quite unwittingly. It's like – like inventions..." she finished lamely.

Rodgers laughed. "I see your point, even though it's rather obscure. So you are being led to believe, despite your fierce defence, that your Susan Taylor might be implicated?"

"Anything's possible – people are always doing things that one would swear are completely out of character." She sighed, then said, "Rowan, would you mind if I went up to bed? I am tired, really. I know that you have to stay up to see this man – West, is it?"

He nodded. "You go up." He put his hands on her shoulders and drew her close to him. "If I'm through at a reasonable hour, may I see if you're awake?"

The touch of his hands made her limp and unresisting in mind and body. "Even if it's an unreasonable hour and I'm asleep, you may – wake me up." She twisted from his grasp and went quickly into the hotel.

Rodgers slowly lit his pipe and watched her go: he was wondering, among other things, just what it was that Girot had remembered during their conversation. Something relevant to the situation but not to be revealed.

He asked himself why – then dismissed the whole dress episode as something quite divorced from the case that he was on – and wondered for the umpteenth time, just what the case was all about.

SIX

Richard West scanned the Pirate's Lair: a haze of tobacco smoke hung in the dimly lit room – nobody here heeding the warning of the Surgeon General, he thought. The smell of tobacco mingled with the many perfumes and heavy aftershaves, with an overall pervasion of alcohol. West noted that many of the Girot group were present together with a few ordinary tourists and a group of local gays.

Solange Barnave, svelte in a black dress that left one shoulder bare, was sitting on a high bar stool, talking volubly to Roger Girot. Her pale silver-blonde hair gleamed in the half light. West threaded his way through the crowd until he was behind her.

"Excuse me, Miss Barnave?"

She stopped talking and slewed round on the stool so that her face was level with his. A pair of widespaced, hazel-green eyes stared at him.

"Yes, m'sieur? I am Solange Barnave. And you, m'sieur? I do not think that we 'ave met?" Her tone was light and mocking,heavily accented.

God, West thought, this is my night. Two women, but women, man! Aloud he said blandly, "No, we have not met before – unfortunately for me." He gave a little bow and she smiled in the way of a woman used to male admiration. "My name is Richard West, Superintendent of Police." The smile left her face, to be replaced by a wary look. He held up his hand. "Don't be alarmed, Miss Barnave. May I have a word with you in private? Excuse us, Mr Girot."

Girot asked testily, "What is this that has to be said in private? We arrive this afternoon – tonight we are questioned by the police – is this 'ow you treat your visitors, *hein?*"

West achieved an almost Gallic bow. "Indeed no, Mr Girot. There is nothing for you to be alarmed about. I merely wish to ask the young lady a few questions."

"What about, M'sieur West? Anything you wish to ask me, may be asked in front of M'sieur Girot." She smiled at him in a provocative way but West felt suddenly that the smile was for effect only, that the picture that she presented was calculated for the world to admire and appreciate, not for him as a person or as a man. He felt repelled after the initial attraction and said stiffly, "If you wish Mr Girot to be present, that is perfectly all right, but perhaps we could go where it is a little more private?"

"Oh, all right – such a bore." Solange slid effortlessly off the high stool. As she stood beside him, he realised that she was very tall, even for a model. She must be nearly six feet, he thought, but as she moved away from him, weaving a sinuous way through the crowded tables, he noted that she was wearing four-inch heels. She led the way to the entrance foyer of the hotel, which was deserted at that time of night, with the exception of a bored looking desk clerk.

They sat down. The circular rattan chairs were not as uncomfortable as they looked.

"This is quiet enough, no?" Solange settled herself fluidly, impatiently refusing the cigarette that West offered.

Girot refused. "Thank you, m'sieur, but I have my own brand." He lit a fat, oval, gold-tipped cigarette. The scent of the curling blue smoke was not easily identifiable: Turkish? No. Egyptian? No. Russian?

Girot was smiling at him. "You wonder, Superintendent, about my cigarette, no? It is a special mixture, made for me alone."

West nodded and turned to Solange. "Miss Barnave, you were met at the airport by a man called Simon Soulis. You know him well?"

Her eyes flashed. "M'sieur West, is it a crime in your country to..."

He held up his hand. "Miss Barnave, I am not criticising you, I am merely asking for information. Do you know this man well?" He framed the question purposely in the present tense.

Her lips tightened, giving her a shrewish look, in complete contrast to the limpid innocence she normally presented. "I do not see why you 'ave to ask questions about who I know or who I do not know," she began shrilly, then caught West's forbidding expression and stopped in mid-sentence.

You stubborn little bitch, he thought, I'd like to put you across my knee and whack your elegant little bottom. Aloud he said wearily, "All right, Miss Barnave, if you won't cooperate, you'll have to have it the hard way. Simon Soulis is dead. He died between one hour and one hour and a half after bringing you to the hotel. Now will you answer my question?"

Solange paled under her make-up. Her eyes went blank. She tried to speak but no words came. It was Girot who exclaimed. "Dead? but how – why?"

"You knew him too, Mr Girot?"

"But of course..."

"Why didn't you say so?"

"You did not ask me, m'sieur."

West's jaw tightened. Solange was still sitting in shocked silence. He kept his attention on Girot. Remember, he told himself, he's an important visitor, don't let him ride you. "Right, sir. Can you tell me about Soulis? He was a friend of yours?"

"Friend? No – business only. He was a newspaperman: a fashion photographer. He always covers my collection when we travel. We have our own in-house photographer, Peter Horton, but he does all the internal work: stills, studies, records, throughout the year. Soulis was for publicity in the press and the fashion magazines."

"I see. But he didn't travel with you – he arrived here at the hotel a few days ago, I understand."

"So. He was in the States, I believe. He is not of the House, you understand? I do not know what or where he is when he not working for me."

"I see." West turned back to Solange. "Sorry, Miss Barnave, but you did bring this on yourself."

She nodded; a little colour had crept back under her make-up. "What do you want to know, m'sieur?"

"How well did you know Simon Soulis?"

"You mean why did he meet me when I could have travelled with the rest of the group from the airport?" She was recovering her mocking tone. "Well, I will tell you, Mistaire West. There was not, as you are probably thinking, any romance between us. We were good friends – but only that. We 'ave worked together for many years. 'E always take my pictures. It was 'is pictures that made me – 'ow do you say? The *cover* girl!" Her voice broke a little. "Always 'e meet me at the airport, wherever we went. Then on the drive in, we talk – about the collection, the latest line, the new trends – and 'ow 'e will approach it..." She broke off, then asked, "Please, m'sieur, may I 'ave a drink? I am..." She shut her eyes. She was more affected by the news than her hard sophistication would admit.

"Of course." West signalled a passing waiter. When the drinks were before them, Solange took a deep pull at hers, then she put the glass down carefully. "I'm sorry, M'sieur West, I am not so – 'ard boiled? – as I believe." She achieved a small smile.

West smiled back: for the first time he felt that the real person, someone likeable, was showing through the well executed veneer.

"You did not say..." she hesitated, then went on slowly, "'ow Simon died."

West considered his answer: Rodgers had asked him to keep the cause of death quiet for a day or so. He had not done so in the case of Diana Barrington, mainly because he believed that she would not talk about it. But in this instance, with Girot and the girl living in the hotel? Better play it safe.

"We don't know exactly," he said slowly – which was true. "We feel that he may have fallen from some rocks" – which may have been true. "Perhaps he suffered a heart attack, then fell. The doctor will have his report for us, after the post mortem – autopsy," he added, not sure which term they used in France. "Miss Barnave, what time did you reach the hotel this evening?"

"Well," she wrinkled her forehead, "the plane get in at – er – about a quarter to five. We go t'rough custom quite quick, though at first they make the trouble and say open everything, 'What 'ave you got in this box?' – we would still 'ave been there, but a nice man from your tourist board said it was all nonsense and to let us t'rough. I am so sorry, I forget, what was I suppose to tell you?"

"What time," West's patient tone belied his feelings, "did you get here – the hotel?"

"Oh yes. It was just about 'alf past five, maybe a little later – no, no, no, I remember, it was near to six. Simon looked at 'is watch and said 'Just on six, just time for a drink before I take the car back...' I forget the name."

"Diana Barrington?"

"Yes, that was it. She must 'ave a lot of money, to 'ave a car like that."

West kept his voice carefully neutral as he asked,"And did he?"

"Did he what, m'sieur?"

"Did he take the car back?"

"I suppose so. We 'ad a drink, then I went up to my room – he said he would see me tomorrow..." She stopped and bit her lip.

"You're quite sure that you didn't see him again?"

"Quite sure, m'sieur."

"One last question. What time was it that Soulis left to take the car back?"

She tossed her head, her momentary sorrow at Soulis' death forgotten by the insistence for coherent factual answers to questions she considered irrelevant. "Always what time! I do not know – I do not watch the clock and remember what it is that I do every moment. We 'ad a drink – maybe two – I do not remember."

"Where did you have this drink – or two?"

She gestured impatiently towards the Patio Bar.

"I see." West stood up. "Thank you, Miss Barnave, Mr Girot. I'm sorry to be the bearer of such bad news. When I learn further details I will let you know." He left them and made his way to the Patio Bar, then sent a waiter to page Rowan Rodgers. While he waited he went over the little information that he had gleaned. So it seemed as if Soulis had taken the car back himself. If so, why did Diana lie about it? You've got a few more questions to answer, my lady, he thought. The necessity of questioning Diana further pleased him. She had impressed him in a way that no woman had impressed him for years. It was her sheer femininity, he told himself, pure undiluted sexual magnetism. From these pleasant thoughts he was roused by Rowan Rodgers who dropped into the chair opposite him.

"Hi, how goes it?" Rodgers signalled a waiter. Over their drinks, Rodgers' pipe smoke mingling with West's cigarette smoke, West recounted the events of the evening.

"So," said Rodgers thoughtfully, "Diana Barrington was lying when she said that she had told Soulis that he could keep the car overnight."

"Or perhaps Solange was lying when she said that he told her that he had to take it back. Or maybe he was lying to Solange."

"The fact is that the car was taken back. Now how did Soulis get back to the Santa Gloria beach? Walked, maybe, along the beach, it's only two to three miles. Oh well, speculation will get us nowhere. What do you think?"

Richard West wasn't listening. "That little bitch of a Solange, she'd lie to save her own skin, no matter who got hurt."

"Rather anybody than Diana, eh?"

"Good God." West looked startled. "Does it show that much?"

"Plastered all over you. Careful, man, that woman is dynamite. Anyway," Rodgers went on, "you're a big boy now and should be able to handle the lady. Back to Soulis: if he or Solange were lying, the fact remains that the car was returned. Diana says she knew nothing of its return – which I find difficult to swallow. She won't tell – and Soulis can't tell."

"Well," said West, "I'll question the staff here tomorrow – or rather, later today. Someone may have seen the car drive off."

"Right, do that." Rodgers glanced at his watch.

"Let's call it a day."

West agreed: tiredness had descended on him suddenly. The intricacies of the case were beginning to be assertive and the unexpected emotional impact of Diana was in itself an added burden. He gave Rodgers a terse goodnight and left.

Rowan Rodgers sat on for a moment after West had gone,

wondering if he should check as to whether his contact, Major John Terrance, had arrived. He decided not to; it was very late and these cloak and dagger boys, he thought wearily, always liked to plan their entrances. To pursue the analogy, they didn't like anyone stealing the spotlight, upstaging them or pre-empting their lines. The decision taken to postpone any active part in the affair that night, he rose abruptly and went along to his room. As he passed Rachel's door, he paused and looked at his watch: five past one. He wondered if she would consider that an unreasonable hour. He tapped softly on her door.

"Yes?" Her voice was sleepy.

"Rachel," he called in a low voice. "It's Rowan."

"Come in, the door's not locked."

He glanced along the corridor, carefully opened the door, then closed it with the faintest click.

Rachel was half asleep against the pillows, her bare shoulders dark against the white sheets. The little cat was curled in the curve of her waist. She shifted a little so as not to disturb Bamboo, and held out her arms. "I thought that you'd never get here," she said.

SEVEN

A ten o'clock sun was beginning to get unbearably hot as it beat down on the silver-white sands. The sea, brilliantly patched in shades of emerald and sapphire, was lapping lazily between the reef and the shore. Beyond the reef the morning breeze whipped frothy little whitecaps on the slow swell of the waves.

Rachel Groome lay in the shade of a palm-thatched beach shelter, her white swimsuit a delightful contrast against her coffee-cream skin and the burnt-orange beach towel beside her. She was remembering, with a sensual relaxed delight, the last few hours. She could feel again the taut muscles of Rowan's shoulders as he held her close. Now she was wondering why she had stayed away so long. She tried to push from her mind the inevitable gossip and speculation that their association would occasion – and thought wryly that even though such associations are a commonplace in the nineties, Jamaica was still a small island.

"Good morning." The voice above her was difficult to place, but familiar. She sat up and took off her sunglasses.

"John! John Terrance! What on earth are you doing here?"

"Much the same as you, I should imagine – soaking up the sun and forgetting the world."

He sat down beside her. She surveyed him thoughtfully; there had been a time, she remembered, when John had threatened to be quite a problem, which she had simply avoided by non-contact. His dark good looks had always attracted her, but there was a quality of ruthlessness behind that easy charm that had made her wary of any involvement. She gazed at him in appreciation; he was slimly built, but lithe and muscular. He was tall – though not anywhere near Rowan's height – perhaps a bit under six feet. He was clad in a pair of pale blue swim trunks, a beach towel draped over one shoulder. Behind his dark glasses he seemed to be laughing at her.

"You look," he said as he stretched out beside her then propped himself up on one elbow, a move which brought him disturbingly close, "you look like a woman who had just been made love to – effectively, I should hazard. Who's the lucky man?"

If it's that obvious to him, it must be equally so to the rest of the guests at the hotel, Rachel thought, then laughed. Not to take him seriously, that was part of the charm. She remembered the way in which he would make outrageous statements or suggestions lightly, daring one to take exception.

"Don't be ridiculous, John," she said, hoping that she wasn't blushing, a habit that she had never outgrown.

"Not ridiculous at all, my love. Perfectly natural and highly desirable." He bent his head suddenly and kissed the hollow by her shoulder. "M'mmm, heavenly perfume."

She drew away. "*Arpège*," she said shortly.

"Not *Arpège* – I know *Arpège*, and this is quite different."

"I ought to know what perfume I'm wearing," She was annoyed at her feeling of irritation over such a trifling argument. John rolled over onto his stomach, which brought him far too close for Rachel's comfort.

"Not *Arpège*," he repeated. "Woman – essence of Woman. Rachel, why don't you take me seriously? You know that I adore you."

Rachel got up impatiently. "For heaven's sake, John, don't make extravagant statements. There's only one person whom you adore; John Terrance." She ran lightly down the hot sands into the warm water that closed around her like liquid silk. She swam furiously towards the reef and the floating raft nearby. My God, she thought, I've been back less than twenty-four hours and my life is becoming entangled already. She stopped swimming and trod water, then felt two hands grasp her shoulders from behind and turn her round. The next moment she was being thoroughly kissed. She pulled herself free and, despite the hindrance of the water, brought her hand up and slapped hard. "I told you..." she began furiously, then saw with dismay that it was Rowan. There was a shout of laughter from the raft. She looked up to see John Terrance looking down at them.

"I gather that was meant for you," Rodgers said as he pulled himself onto the raft. He smiled down at Rachel, who was still treading water, a set expression on her face.

"Well – you shouldn't have taken me by surprise," she said lamely. Rodgers opened his mouth to reply then closed it with a snap. Terrance looked from Rachel to Rodgers, a thoughtful expression in his eyes. Then he turned to Rodgers and said lazily, "Glad you dropped by. Could we have a chat?"

Rodgers smiled at him. "Nicely done, John," he said in a low voice, then called to Rachel, "I've left my pipe and pouch in the hotel. Be an angel and get them for me. I'll soon be out – I just want to have a word with John."

Her eyes snapped as she realised how she had been manipulated into their plan. She nodded, turned and streaked back in a fast racing freestyle – which she could never have achieved if not spurred by anger. On the raft, Terrance's surface gaiety left him.

"Sorry, man, hope that I haven't caused a rift?"

"Nothing," Rodgers said shortly, "that can't be mended – with ease," he added.

"I see – like that. I wondered."

Rodgers dismissed the subject by asking, "Well, what's on? Why all the elaborate casualness?"

Terrance rolled over onto his stomach. To the random observer from the shore the two men would seem to be enjoying a rest from swimming. Terrance's face was towards the horizon; even so, his lips hardly moved as he spoke quietly.

"In short – drugs. It's long been felt that Jamaica plays a major role in the drug trade in this part of the world. Well, we have evidence that there is a nice little traffic going on in this specific area of the north coast. This seems to be the clearing house for traffic to the other islands and certain parts of South America. It's a two-way traffic – one drug coming in, another going out. Not the usual cocaine either. The incoming drug is mainly pethidine, a synthetic allied to the morphine group. The medical authorities here have become acutely alarmed at the increase in addiction in the island.

It's spreading rapidly in the schools, with the age group becoming lower. It's rife among university students; most of the addicts started on the weed and 'graduated.' I tell you, Rowan, man, it's one big headache."

Terrance paused and Rodgers asked, "Any idea how it's getting into the country or where it's coming from?"

Terrance raised his head. "Don't be a fool, man, that's the burning question – or rather, questions. If we knew how we could track it from there, which hopefully would lead us to where."

"So?"

"So – that's the incoming drug. It's possible, of course, that it's made here, but the number of plants capable of such production have been carefully vetted and unless somebody is being very clever and with big resources behind him – which doesn't seem probable – though of course, always possible..."

"Surely, though, anyone in this racket on an international scale, would be very clever, with big resources behind him?"

Terrance snorted in disgust. "God, Rodgers, man, come up with something worthwhile."

"Sorry, it's newer to me than to you, I'm just sorting ideas." He paused, then asked, "And the outgoing drug? What's that – ganja, I suppose?"

"The inevitable ganja. They're getting it out somehow. We've had word from Britain that supplies appearing recently on their market point to this part of the world as the source, but we can't track it down."

Rodgers got up and walked to the edge of the raft and flexed his shoulders as if preparatory to diving. "We've been confiscating and burning shiploads of the stuff for years."

"Yes, we nabbed a whole container at Newport recently. Worth millions. The vast majority of the stuff that gets through that we know of goes to the States. It's the traffic to the UK that beats us."

"So what's the programme?"

Rodgers dived into the clear water, swam round the raft a couple of times then clambered out and flopped on his stomach. John

Terrance lay still, apparently asleep.

"We have an agent in Paris who has sent word that a shipment of pethidine was due for delivery this week. This agent is a good man; he's come up with some first-class info in the past – that's why he was put on this. He's certain of this fact, and further, that contact would be made with an agent at this end – and through him to me. So far, sweet nothing. We play the waiting game. We have a constant watch at both airports, just looking out for anything unusual, anything offbeat. Anything with you? Anything unusual?"

Rodgers kept quite still. The only connecting link was – Paris.

"Paris?" he murmured. "You know that we have this invasion of the House of Girot?"

"Yes, and they've been thoroughly vetted – both here and there."

"And then," said Rodgers. "There is – or rather was – Simon Soulis."

"Simon Soulis?"

"A French fashion photographer." Rodgers told Terrance of the recent death in detail. "Could he be your missing contact? That's why – no contact?"

"Could be – we'll check on Soulis. We'll just have to play it off the cuff and hope for the best – and a good strong lead."

"Right." Rodgers stood up. "I'll go in now. You could still make your play for Rachel – it'll be a point of normal contact."

"I wish it could be, man, I wish it could be," Terrance called cheerfully as Rodgers dived cleanly off the raft.

Rachel was not on the beach when Rodgers waded through the shallows, but Anna Morgan was. She lay on her back, eyes closed, a bright green towel spread under her. Rodgers paused beside her. She opened her eyes and looked up at him in a questioning manner.

"Good morning," he said. "Don't take too much of the sun at this time of the day. Not till you get used to it – again."

She sat up. "I know that I'm being stupid. It was just being *able* to – you know?"

"I know," he agreed gravely. "Come over to the beach hut and I'll order you something cool to drink. What's the matter?"

She had begun to laugh as she gathered up her beach towel and the usual trivia that a woman takes to sunbathe. She coloured slightly at his question.

"Silly of me, but your invitation sounded like a quote."

"A quote?" He thought a moment then laughed. "Of course – Lady C. No there were no improper intentions behind my invitation, Miss Morgan."

"How do you know my name?"

"Well, you're not exactly unknown – or unforgettable. My name is Rowan Rodgers."

She looked up at him, her large brown eyes puzzled. "Your name is familiar. When I saw you in the bar last night, I felt that I knew you from somewhere, yet I'm sure that we've never met."

"You probably know of me. I'm a policeman." He supplied the information shortly.

"Of course – I remember..." She paused in confusion, then added lamely, "I must have seen your picture in the paper." The intimacy that she had noticed between Rachel Groome and this disturbingly handsome policeman precluded comment about the publicity a year ago.

He offered her a cigarette, which she refused. "If you hesitate over the recollection because of possible embarrassment to me or to Mrs Groome, it makes it much worse. She will get used to it eventually. Painful at first, but you can learn to live with most things."

They were sitting under the beach shelter now. Rodgers signalled a waiter. "Tell me about yourself," he invited, while they waited for the drinks. "How do you like working for the great Girot?"

"I love it. It's an honour to work for him; it's the plum of all modelling jobs. But don't you believe all you hear about a fashion model's life – it's one percent glamour and ninety-nine percent hard work."

"Like many of the much vaunted glamour professions. Do you want to make it your life's work?"

She didn't hesitate. "No, it's too much an artificial world. All the temper tantrums, jealousy etcetera – very like the stage, I should imagine. It's fun for a while – and lucrative. But no girl should think of modelling as a life's work – you're old and *passé* at about twenty-four or -five." She gazed down at the white sand.

Rodgers studied her thoughtfully. "Do you make many trips like this? With the – er – collection?"

She was suddenly very still, then she looked straight up into his eyes: they were carefully impersonal: she relaxed.

"This is my third trip. We – the House – go every six months, after the Autumn and Spring showings are over in Paris. Girot always makes some special clothes to suit the climate where we show. Those aren't shown in Paris."

"Must be fun," he said lazily. "Where were the other two trips?"

"The Spring collection was in Trinidad – we stayed at the upside-down Hilton. We just missed Carnival, but all the costumes were on display in the foyer. They were unbelievable – have you ever been to Carnival?"

He nodded. "A couple of times – I'm getting too old for such activities now."

She made no polite protest and he realised that he must seem quite elderly to her. The thought was somewhat deflating.

"The Autumn collection was in Caracas. Such wealth – and such poverty. It was lots of fun, one meets all sorts...Oh, I mentioned tantrums a while ago – here' s Solange."

"Solange? Oh yes, of course."

"Solange Barnave. Now she is very much the world's idea of all that a model ought to be – and Girot's pet." There was no envy or bitchiness in her voice, just a plain statement.

They watched as the tall French girl came slowly along the beach, her slim figure hugged by a black swimsuit that seemed to be mostly net. Her blonde hair was covered by a black scarf and huge sunglasses hid her eyes. She was accompanied by the fair, long-haired young man that Rodgers had noticed the night before.

"That's Peter Horton with her. He's the resident photographer to the group, not like Simon, who does the glossies."

So, Rodgers thought, she doesn't know yet about Soulis.

Solange's high voice carried clearly to them, as she swung round and façed her companion. She waved her hands to emphasise her words. "I will do what I want. Why should I do or not do, what you say? Always, wherever we go, it is the same..." She broke off as Peter Horton put his hand on her arm and spoke quietly but with a forcefulness that belied his appearance. Solange listened sullenly then shook his hand away. "I don't care what you say, I do what I want – always."

She flounced away from him and down to Anna and Rodgers.

"You see what I mean?" Anna asked softly.

Aloud she said to Solange, "Hullo there, getting some sun? Have you met Superintendent Rodgers?"

Solange flashed him her much photographed smile, all signs of temper gone.

"We 'ave not met, but I see you last night in the bar, no? I am so much liking your island – it is all and more that I've 'eard. Ah, Peter – "she turned as Peter Horton joined them – "There you are, *cheri*." The scene that they had just witnessed might never have taken place.

Rodgers studied Solange with interest. She had made no mention of the death of Simon Soulis, neither did she show any sign of grief. It was unnatural for one of her type not to dramatise the event. So why was she behaving out of character?

Anna had risen at Peter Horton's approach and was pinning up her long black hair. Horton, elegant in a yellow and brown patterned cabana set, raised his brows in languid surprise. "My dear Anna, you're not going to swim? What energy! In this climate surely one can only relax? Oh, but of course, you're used to it, aren't you, darling?" His voice held a barbed note that was not lost on Rodgers and clearly resented by Anna.

"Yes," her voice was flat, "I am. Peter, have you met Superintendent Rodgers? Mr Rodgers, this is Peter Horton, our official photographer."

She barely waited for them to acknowledge the introduction, but said to Rodgers, "What about that swim? Race you to the reef?"

She was running lightly down the beach before he could reply, and was sitting on the raft when he pulled himself out of the soft warm water and flopped down beside her.

"You were in a hurry to get away from those two," he remarked, glad that Terrance had gone.

"I know, I'm sorry." She unpinned her hair and it came tumbling down. "Peter always upsets me – it's stupid. I shouldn't let it affect me, but of all the people I've worked with over the years, he is the only one who is colour conscious. He always manages to impart or imply a barb. As for Solange, she's just purely decorative."

Rodgers laughed. "I'm not sure that I would apply the word 'pure' to that young lady. Tell me about her."

"There's nothing much to tell. She won a beauty contest..."

"Like you."

"Not like me. She won, I was only placed second. She got into the fashion world – like me..." she forestalled him. "But unlike me she went straight to the top and looks like staying there."

Rodgers rolled over onto his back and gave a quick glance at his watch. Nearly ten-forty-five. He'd arranged to meet Phillips at eleven-fifteen.

"And why won't you get to the top? I should have thought that there would be no difficulty at all."

She hesitated a moment, then said flatly, "I'm afraid that I don't sleep with the right people."

"I see. So what? You sleep with the wrong people – or no people at all?"

She got up abruptly, a spark of anger flashing. "I know that I brought that on myself, but no gentleman would be so mean as to – to..." she finished lamely.

He laughed. "My dear girl, I'm not going to apologise. For a girl in the world of fashion, rat race that I understand it to be, you seem singularly naive and delightfully old-fashioned. It's something that I thought had died many years ago – prudery in the young – but if you make remarks to others as you did to me, then expect them to be capped."

She smiled and sat down again. "I'm sorry. I quite often say things like that, wanting to be thought free-thinking and sophisticated – then I find that I haven't the courage to follow through and find myself with another embarrassing moment."

He nodded. "But what you said about sleeping with the right people – that was true, wasn't it? Not just a flip remark?"

"Yes, that was true."

"And Solange? She sleeps, I gather, with the right people?"

She nodded.

"But," Rodgers continued, "who are the 'right' people? From the little that I've seen of the circus up at the hotel, the men don't seem quite the ladies'-man type."

She looked at him, an expression of distaste about her eyes and mouth. "Mr Rodgers, are you asking me these questions because of perverted curiosity or from a professional standpoint?"

He rose lazily to his feet and smiled down at her. "Let us say from a mixture of motives. You don't have to answer." He flexed on the edge of the raft.

"Coming?"

She shook her head. "I think I'll stay here for a bit."

He dived deeply into the blue-green water and swam in a powerful breaststroke to the beach. Rachel was nowhere to be seen. He hoped that she hadn't seen him spending so much time with Anna and was paying him back in his own coin by spending time with John Terrance. Solange was posing against the curved trunk of a palm tree, being photographed by Peter Horton in an unhurried, efficient manner. His effeminacy seemed less obvious while he was working and Rodgers wondered if it was an assumed pose. He passed them with a wave of his hand, packed up his towel, his pipe and tobacco pouch. There was no time to find out if Rachel was annoyed.

He untied the mooring rope of one of the small boats, commonly termed runabouts, that the Santa Gloria provided for the convenience of guests and slid her smoothly into the warm sea, leaving a sharp indentation in the silver-white sand.

As he skilfully piloted the small craft through the emerald and sapphire patched water, he thought over his conversation with Anna. Her rather prudish reactions belied her appearance and manner. Was she sincere or was she trying to make him believe that she was other than she was? Why should she? He was seeing ulterior meanings in normal, everyday conversations. It was this blasted case; with so little to go on and not knowing what to look for, he was apt to look at everything and everyone with suspicion.

He scanned the shore. He must be quite close to the beach cottage by now. The sun beat down on his bare shoulders from a hot blue sky and the glinting reflections from the sea struck back at his eyes. Should have worn glasses, he thought, squinting against the glare.

Just then a runabout like his own shot out from the beach and bore swiftly down on him. He cut the motor and let her drift in the practically still water as he recognised the powerful stockiness of Sergeant Phillips, unaccustomedly clad only in swimming trunks. The two boats floated together, their sides bumping gently.

"Morning, Mr Rodgers, sir."

"Morning, Phillips. Why the cloak and dagger meeting?"

Phillips grinned, white teeth gleaming in his dark face. "Adassa bit curious-like, sir. I think she swallow the story 'bout my winning little money at Caymanas, for she go on at me 'bout gambling for two hour straight. So me did think maybe it not a good thing if she see us meet – she might jus' think again."

Rodgers laughed. "Right, man." He recounted briefly the events of the previous evening: the death of Soulis, and Richard West's preliminary investigations.

"Whether all this has any bearing on our job, remains to be proven."

"Did you find out anything 'bout our case, Mr Rodgers?"

Rodgers briefed Phillips on what Terrance had told him earlier, then asked, "Yesterday evening, did you notice anything or hear anything?"

Phillips nodded, "Could be, sir. Didn't think anything of it at the time. Well, it was a bit odd-like. We get here at about five last evening – I bring young Pearson, sir, we may need him. Hope that's all right, sir?"

Rodgers nodded. "Fine. What was odd-like?"

"Well, sir, after we settle, an' while the missis getting a little supper, I come out on the beach with a Red Stripe. It peaceful, like," His dark eyes swept the emptiness of the Caribbean Sea. Lord, thought Rodgers, I hope this isn't going to be one of Phillips' poetical mornings. "Yes, sir, it peaceful – not like Kingston, all noise and bustle. Well, me drink a little Red Stripe when me hear an inboard motor boat, moving fast. I look out but can't see nothing. From the sound I'd say it was about fifty horse-power, doing a good twelve to fifteen knots. I look good but can't see nothing – it carry no light at all."

"No lights?" Rodgers asked sharply.

"No, sir. Contravention of international shipping law. It was about a quarter-mile offshore. And," Phillips concluded with the presence of an actor delivering the curtain line, "it return in exactly fifteen minutes."

He paused, waiting for Rodgers' question, which he obligingly asked: "And at what time did this world-shaking event take place?"

"It pass going east at six minutes past seven an' return going west at twenty-one minutes past seven."

Rodgers' eyes narrowed. "And Soulis was killed around that time. M'mmm. I wonder. Phillips, let us take a little cruise to the west. No sense in checking the time factor from here to where your mystery boat went – we couldn't approach that speed. But – you say it was doing about twelve to fifteen knots?"

"Could have been more, sir, twenty maybe. Difficult to judge under the circumstances."

"Agreed. Right, let's say it was doing sixteen knots: this baby can't do more than about four or five at the outside. Four into sixteen is four, that means a quarter of the speed, which means four times slower. So where your boat took fifteen minutes – that is seven and a half there and seven and a half back..."

"But, sir," Phillips broke in, "we don't know if him turn or if him stay."

"You're right. I was called a fool earlier this morning, I'm inclined to agree with the description. Let's just go and see."

Phillips gave a nod of agreement. The two outboard motors roared into life, and the runabouts cut through the water, leaving a frothy wash, white against the jewel-coloured sea. The coastline was jagged, with jutting honeycomb rocks a dark grey contrast to the white sands. Almond trees crept almost down to the water's edge in places and palm trees softly rustled their feathered fronds in the wind now coming in from the north-east.

They rounded a promontory and cruised into a small bay. A curving beach of pure white sand made a perfect picture. A palm-thatched beach hut was halfway between the shoreline and a flight of white cut-stone steps, which wound up the rocky hillside. Outside the hut was a heap of brightly coloured beach towels, and beside them the prone body of a woman. A large sign attached to a rock at the water's edge stated: PRIVATE BEACH. TRESPASSERS WILL BE PROSECUTED. A white-painted launch, about eighteen feet long, was moored to a stanchion. This then, thought Rodgers, is the Ripple beach and that could be the boat Phillips heard last night.

"Phillips," he called softly, bringing his craft alongside his sergeant's, "in view of that notice we'll have to play it off the cuff. Take your cue from me."

"Right, sir."

Rodgers over-throttled the engine, then shut it off. He started it again and over-choked it. The engine sputtered and died. He was glad that the strong smell of gas was exhausted under water and would not be wafted to the woman on the beach. He called loudly to Phillips, "Hey, Phillips, give me a hand. The damned engine's died on me."

Phillips drifted alongside and examined the outboard motor. "Look like you out of gas, sir," he announced.

"Well, look, I'll drift in here and you nip back to your place for some. Right?" He lowered his voice, "This could be the place where your boat came from, but go further along the coast and see if there's another possibility. Take your time – at *least* half an hour," he added softly.

"Right, sir." Phillips went off in a froth of spray.

Rodgers dived over the side and towed the runabout by the mooring rope into the shallows then beached the small craft. He padded silently towards the woman. The sands were hot and softly yielding to his bare feet.

The woman had not moved. She lay stretched out on her stomach, her hands crossed under her cheek. Her hair was a coppery golden-red, glinting in the sunlight. She was quite naked, and her body, naturally coffee-coloured, was evenly tanned to a deep bronze. Rodgers gazed down in admiration at what seemed a perfect figure. He bent and picked up a towel from the heap and lightly placed it over her. Without opening her eyes she said, "Who the hell are you? Can't you read?"

"I'm sorry," Rodgers said, "but my boat ran out of fuel. A friend of mine has gone to get some – I hoped that you wouldn't mind."

She twisted round and sat up at the sound of his voice, the towel only a token cover. Her eyes, dark golden brown, heavily sensual, regarded him levelly. She examined him leisurely. His six feet three inches towered over her as she half reclined at his feet. His black hair shone in the morning sunlight which struck highlights from his gleaming dark shoulders.

"No," she said at last. "I don't mind – I don't mind at all." She got up in a lithe fluid movement and he caught the towel and wrapped it round her. "Why so prudish? Haven't you seen a woman naked before?" she asked, then added, "I can't believe that."

He grinned down at her. "Not prudish – just susceptible – and I'd hate to have you take in in for indecent exposure."

She laughed, "Take me in? Don't tell me that you're a policeman?"

"Yes, but off duty."

"Good. My name is Diana Barrington."

"Rowan Rodgers."

"Oh, yes – I've heard of you. You say that your friend's gone for some fuel? Let's hope that he'll be a long time." She moved towards the beach hut. "I'll put on some clothes – as you're *so* worried about this," she gave the towel a provocative flip, "then perhaps you'd like a drink."

She disappeared inside the hut. Rodgers walked down to the moored launch and examined it. From its size and its lines it could easily be the one that Phillips had heard the night before. It had all the regulation lights: white amidship directed forward: green to starboard and red to port. He tried them, they worked. Tossed on the deck was scuba diving gear. A spear fishing gun without the spearhead caught his attention; he bent and peered at it. The nylon connection line was severed. whether by accident or design it was impossible to ascertain. He straightened as Diana came out of the hut, carrying two tall lager glasses.

"I took a chance and brought beer. OK?"

"Very much OK."

He looked down at her. She was in pale green shorts and a loose, dark green shirt. Against the rich patina of her skin and her red-gold hair the effect was disturbing.

She smiled at him. "Well?"

"Very well," he raised his glass. "To you."

She drank deeply then sat down under a wild almond tree, the broad leaves casting uneven patterns on the white beach. Rodgers remained standing. He found, as had Richard West so recently, this woman more than disconcerting. He had heard so many rumours about her but he was unprepared for the reality. She got up and went towards him. "So you're a policeman – on holiday?" He nodded. "People on holiday should learn to relax. Why don't you?" She was close to him and put her arms round his neck, still holding the half-filled glass of lager. "I'm a very good teacher," she murmured, her mouth against his.

Rodgers thought of Rachel and his hands went up to disengage hers. Then he remembered that this woman might know something, she might be important to the case. He reached behind, took the glass from her and dropped it on the soft sand then loosened her hands and secured them behind her back as he pulled her body against his.

"Now," he said lazily, "you can't do a thing."

He bent his head and thought, what I do in the cause of duty. He found too soon that all thought of duty vanished. She responded to his kiss in a way that was completely uninhibited, completely satisfying. He released her hands and she slid down onto the warm yielding sand, pulling him with her.

"Why don't you make love to me?" she said.

In answer he kissed her again.

The sharp sound of an outboard motor interrupted them as the return of Phillips round the promontory brought an end to something which had hardly begun. It was Rodgers who said, "Hell – what a time to return."

She looked up at him. "But you'll come back?"

He nodded, committed now.

"I quite often swim at night," she said.

He hesitated. "That might be difficult."

"Do you have a demanding wife or anything?"

He hesitated again, then laughed. "A very demanding wife – and six assorted offspring." He took her hands and drew her closer for a moment. "I'll see you soon, somehow."

She smiled.

He swam out to the waiting Phillips, towing the runabout behind him. Phillips made some pretence of re-fuelling; the engine sputtered back to life.

"Thanks." Rodgers looked at Phillips' carefully expressionless face. "You arrived just at the right moment."

"Yes, sir?" There was a trace of disapproval in Phillips' dark eyes. "All in the cause of duty, sir?"

"Indeed, yes. In the cause and in the course."

EIGHT

Richard West had spent the morning making careful enquiries regarding the death of Simon Soulis. He had telephoned to headquarters requesting information from Paris. This request was passed back, ironically, to John Terrance, who sent the query in code to his counterpart in Paris.

West had checked at the morgue, but Dr Montgomery had been out all night on an emergency call and had telephoned to say that he would perform the post mortem at eleven that morning. It was now nine-thirty. West lit a cigarette, and told the sergeant in charge at the station that if needed, he could be contacted at the Santa Gloria, then he got into his car and drove thoughtfully along the winding coastal road. Sunlight filtered through the deep green of the giant ferns that grew wild on the precipitous rock face, rising sheer and craggy from the roadside. Strangely shaped trees, festooned with wild orchids, bent at odd angles, mingling their foliage to form a kaleidoscopic leaf arrangement. To his left, the rocks seemed to cascade down to the white beach below: an intense, blinding white in the sunlight. The road curved in a deep U-turn, descending in a gradient of one in four. The rocks fell away and the sea came nearer as he approached the hotel.

The Santa Gloria car park was nearly full. West eased his Rover 220 Turbo Coupé between an ancient VM and a seven-passenger tourer with the name of a well-known travel agency emblazoned on its side. A group of chauffeurs lounged against their vehicles, talking in pseudo-American accents copied partly from the tourists but mostly from second-rate television programmes and old movies.

There were not many guests in the lobby when West entered the hotel. It was markedly cooler than outside where even at this early hour the sun beat down with a fierce intensity. "Good morning," he greeted the desk clerk. "I would like to see the manager."

The clerk flicked an indifferent eye over West's beige twill pants and brown patterned sports shirt. "Mr Deleon busy. In conference – all morning," he added, hoping to prevent any argument.

"Then," West's voice was deceptively mild, "you go into that conference room and tell Mr Deleon that Superintendent West is waiting to see him."

The clerk gave a nervous cough and reached for the house phone. "Yes, Mr West, sir. Right away, sir." He spoke rapidly into the mouthpiece. "Yes, sir. Now, sir." He replaced the receiver. "Mr Deleon say to go right in, sir. You want me to show you his office?"

"No, thank you, I know where it is. You on duty all morning?"

"Yes, sir, till noon."

"Good, I may want to ask you a few questions." West walked away, not bothering to answer as the clerk said weakly, "Me, sir?"

The hotel was a pleasant place to stay, West thought, as he made his way towards the manager's office. A wide verandah ran the whole length of the seaward side, and beyond were terraced gardens planted with exotic flowering shrubs, giving way to the cactus garden he remembered from the night before.

Deleon rose from behind his desk, nervously fussy. "Mr West, good morning. What can you tell me?" He waved West to a chair. "But first, may I offer you some refreshment? Coffee? Red Stripe or something stronger?"

West hesitated – he was tired, but as much as he would appreciate a cold beer at that moment he said, "Coffee, please. I'll take a rain check on that Red Stripe."

Deleon gave an order over the house phone, then asked again, "What have you to tell me, Mr West?"

"Soulis was murdered – he didn't acquire that wound by accident. But by whom and why – well, that's a mystery at the moment. Perhaps you can help me find out?"

"Me?" The pudgy face paled. "What should I know about him?"

"Well, he was a guest in your hotel. Just answer my questions carefully. How long was Soulis here?"

"He arrived last week, about four or five days ago. The room clerk will give you the exact date."

"Right. Had he been here before?"

"No, not that I can recall. And we generally remember our guests, as we don't have a very large capacity."

"Where did the request for a reservation come from?"

"From Paris. From Mr Soulis himself."

"How long ago was the booking made."

"Just a moment." Deleon opened a drawer in the large mahogany desk and took out a file. He ran a well-manicured fleshy finger down a page. "Ah, here we are. He made a reservation in October – the twenty-eighth of October."

"And when," West's voice was almost bored, "when did the House of Girot make reservations?" Deleon consulted the file. "A little before that – on the twenty-second, to be precise."

West reached for a cigarette as a waiter entered with a tray of coffee and Danish.

"Mr Deleon – you realise that we cannot conceal this man's death for much longer? I know that you have this big fashion show here tonight, which will naturally attract a great number of visitors."

Deleon nodded, becoming more apprehensive as West continued.

"We don't have the post mortem report yet. I hope to have it by noon. I shall spend the day making discreet enquiries, but after tomorrow morning the news must be released."

Deleon nodded again, unhappily. "This will ruin the season – ruin it. And we're booked out from now until March."

"Never mind," West said as cheerfully as he was capable of sounding. "It may pack them in. People love a good murder. And, who knows, we may find that he wasn't killed by a local person at all."

"Yes, indeed." Deleon became less morose at this ambiguously comforting remark.

West poured a second cup of coffee, decided to pass up the Danish and asked, "Tell me, what sort of a person was Soulis?"

"What sort?"

"I mean, was he friendly, outgoing? Reserved, withdrawn?"

Deleon pursed his lips as he considered the question. "He didn't strike me as a person on holiday, somehow. It seemed that he was here for a purpose and although he went around with his camera all the time, I somehow got the impression that *that* was not his purpose." He paused and looked at West a little helplessly. "I'm afraid that I'm not explaining my impressions very clearly."

"On the contrary." West eyed the pudgy little man with more respect. "On the contrary, sir, you were very astute and helpful. Did you know that he was a fashion magazine photographer and that he was going to cover the Girot fashion show here?"

"No, I didn't know that. Perhaps that's why he seemed restless – he was just waiting."

"Perhaps. Did he mix with the other guests?"

"No, he always seemed to be alone, until..." he faltered.

"Yes?"

"I – er – you understand that this is only hearsay, one hears all kinds of gossip, most of it exaggerated, about local people from the staff, but I understand that he met Mrs Barrington – you've heard of her? Yes, well, she lives at Ripple, a mile or so along the coast. She often drops in for lunch or a drink, dinner very occasionally, and apparently she met Soulis in the bar. After that he was hardly ever in the hotel, and when he was seen he was driving Mrs Barrington's Quattro."

"Met in the bar? Had they known each other before?"

"The barman said not from their conversation. Barmen can usually be relied upon to make accurate judgements in matters of this sort."

So Diana had lied as to the length of time that she had known Soulis, thought West. Last night she had told him that she had met Soulis in Paris, three or four years ago. And now it seemed that it had been a casual pick-up in a bar. Which was the truth and why conceal it anyway? And who had done the picking up? Diana or Soulis? Perhaps the barman could enlighten him.

West thanked the by now heavily sweating manager for both coffee and information, and made his way to the bar via the desk clerk who now greeted him with a healthy respect. He flashed white teeth in an ingratiating smile.

"You get through, sir? Get everything you want?"

"Not quite, perhaps you can help me on one or two points. When did Mr Soulis arrive at the hotel?"

"Mr Soulis? The French gentleman in room – er – Room Ten." He consulted the registration book. "November the twelfth, sir. He was booked in on the eleventh but his flight was delayed. He's not in trouble, is he sir? He seems like a nice man!"

So, thought West, the grapevine had missed out on this. One up for security.

"No" he assured the man, "he's not in trouble." He felt like saying that all his troubles were over now, but feared that the intelligence of the desk clerk might just raise to the level of appreciating the significance of the cliché.

He thanked the man again and went into the main bar, the Pirate's Lair. Even with the sun outside rapidly reaching its zenith, the shaded lights were on and the curtains drawn, so that the tawdry appearance most bars assume in the light of day was avoided. It was practically deserted, except for a couple of European visitors who seemed to believe in the theory of the biting dog, and a cheerful round-faced barman, polishing glasses and softly whistling the latest reggae hit. "Yes, sir?" He gave a deft wipe to the spotless hardwood counter top. "What's your pleasure?"

West considered a moment then concluded that he'd get more co-operation as a customer. "Red Stripe, please, and join me."

"Thank you, sir. Staying here? Thought I saw you last night."

"No, I'm not staying here. You don't know me?"

"No, sir. Sorry, sir."

"I'm Superintendent West. In charge of this area. What's your name? You new here?"

"Yes, sir." The revelation of his customer's status left the man unmoved. "Came over from Kingston two weeks gone. My name is Casbert Blackwell."

"Well, I'm glad to hear that some people are coming *out* of Kingston."

"Sir?"

"No matter. Tell me, you see a guest, one Mr Soulis, in here often? He arrived on the twelfth – that's four days ago."

"Mr Soulis? I may have seen him, sir, but I don't rightly recall the name."

West took a deep draught of the ice cold beer. "You know Mrs Barrington?"

"Yes, sir!" Blackwell beamed in appreciative recollection. "She's a very well known lady, sir."

"So I gather," West said dryly, then went on, "I hear that one evening she met Mr Soulis in here. A French gentleman." He could see that something had registered in the barman's mind. "Did you happen to be on duty that night?"

The barman shook his head. "Smith was on that night, sir. He told me about it."

"Smith? Young Carlisle Linton's cousin?"

If he felt any surprise at West's precise knowledge of the relationship of two members of the staff, Blackwell concealed it admirably. "Yes, sir. Carlisle is his cousin."

"And what did Smith tell you about the meeting?"

"He said, sir, that the French gentleman asked two-three times when Mrs Barrington was likely to come here, and to let him know if she came when he was not here."

"Did he, indeed?"

"Yes, sir. If you'd like to wait a little, Smith is due on duty soon."

Knowing that in the local acceptance of time 'soon' might mean anything from two minutes to two hours, West thanked the man and left. So, he thought, the meeting with Diana was not by chance and not by her connivance. He returned to the manager's office. "Mr Deleon, sorry to bother you again, but could you let me in to Soulis' room without anyone knowing?"

"'But of course, Mr West." He opened a drawer and took out a bunch of keys. "This one will open his door; it's the master key for that corridor. Take the second corridor on the right when you leave here."

"Thanks."

West made his way to Room Ten. Inside, it was just as Simon Soulis had left it. West had left orders the night before to leave it untouched. The bed was slightly rumpled, a damp bath towel lay in a heap on the floor. A half-filled glass of some golden liquid was on the bedside table.

West sniffed.

Rum – and ginger probably. It had the vapid, sickly smell of stale alcohol.

He noted an expensive camera on the dresser top. So he hadn't taken it on that last trip. He opened the sliding door of a closet. A black dinner jacket hung beside a heavy tweed suit and some lighter wear more appropriate for the tropics. West searched quickly through the pockets. In the heavy suit he discovered a small sac within the breast pocket which contained a notebook, the size of a personal diary.

He opened it. It was half filled with jottings, from the tabulation presumably dates and names but, West noted with a quickened interest, in some form of code. He slipped the notebook into his hip pocket and decided that he would pay a second visit to Diana Barrington.

NINE

Rachel Groome stretched out on a long chair by the pool, a tall glass on the table beside her. She glanced again at her watch: it was nearly lunch time. Rowan had been gone the whole morning. After she had left him on the raft and had swum back to the shore, her anger and embarrassment had abated and she was ready to laugh at the whole incident, but being made to wait like this was bringing back her annoyance.

John Terrance stopped by her chair. "Am I forgiven enough to dare to hope that you will have lunch with me?"

She was hesitant for a moment, then smiled. "You are indeed. I was just hoping that I wouldn't have to eat alone."

He took her elbow as she rose from the low chair. "You don't have to do anything alone – not while I'm around." She wasn't listening. "What is it?" he asked. "My proposals aren't usually treated with such indifference."

She frowned. "My dressmaker has just gone into the dining room – with Anna Morgan."

"And why is that a cause for such a worried look?"

"I don't know. I'll tell you about it over lunch." Over devilled black crabs and salad, Rachel recounted the story of the pirated sketch and Girot's reaction to her when she wore the finished dress. "And just now," she concluded dramatically, "I see Susan Taylor, my dressmaker, walk in with Anna Morgan – one of Girot's models."

Terrance looked across to the wide verandah, where Anna's sleek, dark head could be seen bent towards a small, middle-aged, nondescript woman.

He turned back to Rachel. "Let's not speculate. Let's take the simplest way. Let's ask – when we've finished our lunch."

She smiled at him. "For such an apparently feather-brained young man, you sometimes come up with some good ideas."

"Rachel." His voice was serious. "I know that it's none of my business, but how involved are you with Rowan?"

"I don't know, John. I thought that I did – up to just a little while ago – but now, I don't really know. After the episode at the raft and no word since then."

"I asked because you've always attracted me, but you were out of reach. Now you seem to be much closer. You realise that given the slightest chance I'm going to make love to you?"

She didn't answer.

"Did you hear me?"

"Yes, but as well as chance – there must be something else. Don't rush me, John, I like you so much as a person. Don't let us complicate matters. Let's keep it as it is for now."

She finished her coffee and they got up.

"Are you going to find out?" He inclined his head towards the verandah.

"Oh, yes. Thanks for reminding me."

She passed through the archway onto the verandah and stopped by Anna's table.

"Why, Susan Taylor, what a surprise!"

The woman jerked her head up, her dark eyes startled for a moment. "Why, Mrs Groome, I didn't know that you were back. How well you're looking. Have you met my niece Anna Morgan?"

"Your niece?" Rachel tried to keep the surprise from her voice.

Anna smiled in recognition. "We saw each other on the plane," she said. "How do you do, Mrs Groome."

"How nice." Susan Taylor was relaxed now. "Mrs Groome, I'm so thrilled. Anna has asked me over to see the Girot collection. It's the chance of a lifetime."

Rachel frowned slightly; Susan seemed sincere, and yet... "But surely when you were in Paris two or three years ago, you went to one of his showings?"

"No – no, I didn't." The denial came a little too quickly and Rachel noted that Anna was taken aback by her aunt's reply.

"Well, my mistake," Rachel said easily. "It's nice to see you again. We'll all be there tonight for the showing." She left them and rejoined John Terrance. "Did you hear?"

He nodded. "Unless she's a good actress, she's quite innocent – although she was lying when she said that she hadn't seen the collection in Paris. The niece was surprised at her answer too."

"That's what I thought, which seems to make *her* innocent also. But if Susan had nothing to do with the pirated sketch, why conceal the fact that she saw the Girot collection? It doesn't make sense."

Rachel left Terrance with some relief. She couldn't endure any more complexities in her life at the moment and John was threatening to become quite a problem. She went up to her room. The afternoon sunlight slanted through the Venetian blinds onto the bed where Bamboo was asleep. The kitten woke with a delighted whicker and stretched voluptuously, her darkening tail curled above her arched back. Rachel picked her up. "Poor darling, I've left you too long. Hotel life is not for you."

She held the little cat against her shoulder and wondered again where Rowan was. She knew that he was on an important case, but a feeling of resentment was beginning to rise at being neglected. Deep down she knew that she was being selfish and irrational, but dammit, she'd been back less that twenty-four hours... A light tap sounded on her door. "Come in," she called.

A waiter, trim in black trousers, short-sleeved white shirt and a black bow tie, entered carrying a box. "Mistress Groome? For you, ma'am."

"For me?" she asked in surprise. She reached for her bag and gave the man a tip. Now she knew she was home. That deliciously old-time form of address, 'Mistress'; she hadn't heard it for a long time. The box was about ten inches long, elaborately wrapped. She opened it with care. It was a bottle of perfume. *ILLICITE, Girot, Paris.* A note was attached:

My dear Madame Groome,

Please accept, with my esteem, this little token. It will suit your personality. I am sure that you are quite ready to discard the dress that led to our meeting, saying you wish never to see it again. Please don't! Wear it tonight at my showing, where you will be my most honoured guest, as will your handsome escort, M. Rodgers. Remember kindly, and possibly with some affection,

Girot

Rachel laughed, her good humour restored. Girot was quite right, she thought. She had said that she would never wear that wretched dress again. Yet why the gift? After his antagonism of the night before? Was he trying to make her view the episode as a mistake on his part – or to stop her asking questions that he didn't want to answer?

She opened the bottle. The perfume had a heady pungent scent, the type she loved. She didn't hear the door open and jumped when Rowan said behind her, "What's all this? I leave you for a few hours, then discover you opening presents." He sniffed. "H'mmm. Very nice."

She gave him the note to read and told him of her doubts as to Girot's motive.

He took her in his arms. "Let's forget Girot. I've missed you."

"Have you? I was beginning to wonder. Just what have you been up to all day?"

He led her onto the balcony and gave her a brief resumé of his activities but not in elaborate detail.

"Diana Barrington, eh? I used to know her quite well – two or three husbands ago," Rachel said when he'd finished. She looked at him thoughtfully. "Just be careful. She collects men as other women might collect china dogs. And," she held tightly to his shoulders, her nails digging into the hard muscles, "I'd hate to compete with her."

"Sweetheart! You don't compete with anyone. You must know that. I don't want you to be upset if I do see her again. I feel that she's important – somewhere – in this case."

"Would you like me to see her? Oh, not instead of you," she said lightly. "But I did know her fairly well at one time and I might be able to find out something. What am I supposed to be looking for?"

"That's the hell of it. We're groping in the dark."

"To slightly paraphrase your quote to me yesterday, 'What a sentence if any lewd one be by'." He laughed, and she went on, "She'll probably be at the showing tonight, anyway."

"Yes. If she does turn up, renew the acquaintanceship."

The phone by the bed rang. Rachel went in and answered it. "Yes, he's here." She called, "Rowan, it's for you." She handed him the receiver. "My reputation is in shreds. They phoned here for you from the desk. It's urgent," she added. "Kingston."

"Rodgers here."

There was a series of clicks and then the Assistant Commissioner's voice rasped in his ear. "Rodgers? You can talk freely, it's scrambled. Are you alone?"

Rowan's eyes met Rachel's "Quite alone, sir. Safe to talk."

"Good. Any developments?"

"Nothing yet that seems to have any bearing on the case in point – although this may." He recounted the death of Soulis. "By a long shot there may be a connection. I hope so. It'll make it easier; something to hang on to, perhaps. I'm still waiting for the PM report."

"Right, keep me posted." The AC sounded worried. "For Christ's sake break this, Rodgers. We've had a hell of a telling-off from London that a large consignment must have got through. There's ganja for sale on every street corner. Another lot was confiscated at Heathrow, bound for France. All indications are that it came from this part of the world."

"We'll do our best, sir."

"I know you will. Goodbye."

"Goodbye, sir."

He replaced the receiver and drew Rachel down beside him as he sat on the edge of the bed. "Sweetheart, we're not going to have much time together. I'm sorry, it's not the homecoming I would have chosen for you. Would you like to go back to Kingston?"

"Are you trying to get rid of me?"

He kissed her. "I'll show you how much I want to get rid of you." He got up and went to the door and locked it, then on second thoughts, put on the chain as well.

It seemed only minutes before the phone rang again. Without thinking, Rowan picked up the receiver. "Rodgers here."

"Hold on, sir," the desk clerk said.

Rowan laughed softly at Rachel's expression and covered the receiver. "Whatever they're thinking – they're right."

The phone crackled. "Montgomery here."

"Ah, doctor. Got something for me?" He listened intently. "You'd like me to come down?... Right... right away. See you in about ten minutes."

He looked at her after he'd hung up. "I've got to go – I want to stay."

Rachel gave a little laugh. "This is almost as bad as a doctor's house..." she broke off. "Oh God, how could I say that so – lightly?" She covered her mouth, her hand shaking.

"Rachel," Rowan said gently, "you've got to get over that. It's past – understand? Over. Think of the now, now and us."

"I'm sorry." She was abruptly withdrawn. "You must go. It's important and I'm holding you back."

"I'll make it as brief as I can. Have a rest, then perhaps we could have a swim before dinner?"

"Yes." She was still unsmiling. "Do go, Rowan, you'll be late." He gave her a quick hard kiss and went.

The post mortem room at the local hospital was cold and clinically uninviting. The body of Simon Soulis lay stretched under a white sheet. Dr Montgomery, looking more relaxed in his hospital garb, greeted Rodgers briefly.

"An unusual wound," he murmured. "The flesh had been torn and lacerated outwards. The cause of death was due to the carotid artery being severed as a result of a deep, wide, laniary wound."

"What do you think would have caused this type of wound?"

Rodgers asked.

"Some form of hook, I should think."

"Hook – or perhaps – a spear gun head?"

"Could be. That would account for such extensive damage."

"H'mm." Rodgers sighed. "A new type of weapon to worry us and probably at the bottom of the sea by now."

He left the hospital and drove thoughtfully through the little country town. The streets were narrow and crowded with country buses, cars, bicycles, heavily laden donkeys, their panniers overflowing with produce from the outlying districts: yams, the white flesh showing through the red earth that clung to them: green bananas, firmly curved in hands: yellow and black ackees: ripe pawpaws and yellow grapefruit. The whole was a melee of machines, goods and assorted humanity. A babble of voices assailed him, as higglers shouted their wares and barefoot children chased each other, screaming at the tops of their voices. Chickens pecked in the refuse heaped at the side of the road, or fled squawking at the approach of a vehicle. The shops, open-fronted, spilled out a cacophony of sounds and an assortment of smells: the pungent scent of pimento and coffee: the sharp acridity of saltfish, mixed with the odour of kerosene and wood smoke from a nearby cooking yard.

Rodgers swung the Mercedes round a tethered mule and narrowly missed a big dray that pulled unheralded out of a side street. The driver's vision was obscured by a pile of coconuts that filled the back of the dray.

Rodgers swore in a mixture of standard English and Western Kingston patois. The man replied with a choice of expletives that left Rodgers chuckling in admiration.

"Right, man," he called as he drove by, almost brushing the nose of the leading mule.

"Right, sah," the man replied without a sign of rancour, his black face wrinkled and wizened.

The encounter had cheered Rodgers' spirits and cleared his mind. He thought back to the morning: there had been a spearhead missing from Diana Barrington's boat. That much was certain, but did the two facts of the type of wound and the missing spearhead correlate?

TEN

Madame Yvette was superintending the sequence in which the models would show later that night. She inspected the ballroom that had been reserved for the event. She nodded; it would do. At this moment, she felt that anything would be acceptable. Oh, she was getting tired, so very tired of these trips – and the heat. She was certain that her face was showing through the careful make-up. She hoped that the girls weren't staying in the sun too much; red blistered shoulders were not an added advantage. *Mon Dieu*, but she was tired; this must surely be her last tour with the house. She hadn't yet inspected the *cabine* – dressing room they called it. She walked quickly across the highly polished floor towards the shell-shaped stage, high heels tapping a staccato beat. One side of the room was composed of folding doors, jalousied to let the air in when closed. They were folded back now and beyond the wide verandah a terraced garden led down to the sea. She paused for a moment looking out at the scene. It was incredibly beautiful – but, *mon Dieu*, how could one live with elegance in this heat? She continued on her way to the dressing room behind the stage. The sound of Solange's voice, shrill with anger, reached her. "...Always looking and listening. Curious – like a cat. I will teach you that I do not like curious people – or cats."

There was the sound of a sharp slap. As Madame Yvette entered the room, Solange was confronting Anna Morgan, whose hand was pressed against her cheek.

"Girls, what is this? Solange, control yourself."

Solange dropped her still upraised hand. She was trembling. "I will not 'ave anyone prying. Look at that." She indicated an open fitted leather beauty-case. Powder was spilled inside and scattered over the dressing table top. She swung back to Anna. "What were you looking for? Tell me that."

"Solange!" The note of authority in Madame's voice at last

quietened Solange.

"Now tell me, what has happened?"

Anna took a deep breath as she felt her cheek tenderly. It was still burning from the ringing slap. "Madame, Solange gave me no chance to explain. My beauty-case is exactly like Solange's. I brought mine down and put it in here earlier; I don't know where it is now. I came down a few minutes ago to check my make-up for tonight and opened this. I thought that it was mine. It was only when I opened the powder box that I realised that it was not my case; I use a much darker shade. Then Solange came in like a raging virago and startled me. I dropped the box and spilt the powder." She turned to Solange. "I don't see why you wouldn't let me scoop it up – it's such a waste."

Solange scowled, all her spurious surface charm gone. She held the square powder box firmly in her hand. "I do not want you to touch my things." She turned her back.

Madame Yvette put a hand on Anna's arm. "I am sorry, *ma petite*. We will leave it for now, eh? I will speak to this one tomorrow – after the showing."

"All right Madame, but I must find my beauty-case, I need it."

Anna left the dressing room with its battery of mirrors and bright lights and hurried to the desk in the lobby. She reported the loss of her case.

"Why, hullo there." Rodgers' deep voice by her side made her swing round. "What's the matter?" he asked, noting her flushed face.

She told him briefly.

"That young lady needs a good spanking." He looked down at her. "Is there anything more to tell me?"

She hesitated. She remembered the look, almost of fear on Solange's face as she snatched up the half emptied box of powder. And she remembered – though she couldn't be sure – that the box, which had seemed full before she dropped it, was not. She could have sworn that she had seen what must have been a false bottom to the box. Not enough powder had been spilt for her to have seen the true bottom. And yet, she couldn't be sure without checking. It was such a little thing and would sound so foolish in the telling. She shook her head. "There's nothing more to tell."

Rodgers was sure that she was withholding something but decided to let it pass.

"Miss Morgan." Carlisle Linton, the bellhop, was at her elbow. "This your case, ma'am?" He held out a white leather case.

"Well, it looks like mine." She opened it and rummaged inside. "Yes, it's mine – but there is face powder spilt all over – and the box itself has gone. Odd." She looked at Rodgers in bewilderment.

"Very odd. Two lots of spilt face powder. Where did you find it?" he asked the boy.

"A gues' fin' it, sir, on the beach."

"Oh the beach? But I put it in the *cabine*. How could it have got there?"

"Just a moment," Rodgers cut in. "Let me handle this. Could you possibly do without the case for an hour or two?"

"Yes, but..."

"I'll explain later. Don't worry, you'll get it back as soon as possible." He took out his handkerchief and gingerly picked up the case by its body. "Do you know the name of the guest who found the case?" he asked the bellhop.

"Me don' rightly know, sir. Me jus' 'ear that it 'anded in to los' property, an' then me did 'ear Miss Morgan say 'er own case did lose..."

"All right, son." Rodgers dismissed the boy with a ten-dollar bill.

"Mr Rodgers, why do you want to take my case?"

"I don't know yet. It may be important, maybe not. But somebody took your case and then abandoned it. Why? It's probably only some petty thief who mistakenly thought it contained something valuable. But I'm a policeman, Miss Morgan. I like to know why these things happen. So we'll dust it for prints, just as a precaution. You say that the powder box was missing? Powder boxes seem to be in the forefront this afternoon," he said lightly.

"Yes." Her tone didn't match his. He waited but she didn't elaborated. "Well, I'll get this back to you as soon as I can," he said.

She watched him go, her dark eyes worried. Why hadn't she told him the full story? But what possible connection could the theft of her powder have with the incident with Solange? One of those strange coincidences. I must examine the box of Solange's, she told herself. But when? Everyone would be in and out of the *cabine* from now until the showing. During the showing it would be impossible – but afterwards? Surely then she would have an opportunity.

Rodgers stopped at a phone booth on his way to his car. He put through a long-distance call to Kingston. "Petrie? Rowan Rodgers here. Listen, I want you to get me some information." He spoke rapidly for a few minutes.

"But honest to God, Rowan, man, I'm a lawyer, not a private investigator," Petrie protested. "I can't divulge my client's private affairs..."

"Don't give me any of that ethical guff. This is top secret. Just get the information. I give you my word that if your client is innocent the information will be destroyed and forgotten. Right?"

Petrie made a few further feeble objections but finally agreed to Rodgers' request.

"Right, man, I'll let you have it as soon as possible – probably early next week."

"By tomorrow at the latest."

"Don't pressure me, man, I don't even..."

"Petrie," Rodgers' voice was more serious than the easy-going Petrie had yet heard, "I'm trying to get it across to you – it's vitally important."

There was a pause, then Petrie capitulated with a resigned, "Right, Rowan, man, tomorrow."

Rodgers swung the dark grey Mercedes into a parking place outside the police station. He strode into the bleak station room. "Superintendent West in?" he asked a constable seated at the desk, who was engaged in filling up a form with a bored slowness.

"Me not sure." The constable didn't even glance up.

"Then find out at once, man. Tell him that Superintendent Rodgers, CID Kingston, is here to see him."

"Yes, sir!" The constable's lethargy evaporated and the vigour with which he sprang to his feet knocked over the chair. He went out with an excess of smartness in an endeavour to undo any adverse impression that he might have created. He returned in seconds. "This way, sir!"

Rodgers was ushered into a big square room, with an old-fashioned high tray ceiling. West sat behind a large mahogany desk, littered with papers. For a moment Rodgers had the impression that he was surprised and not too pleased to see him, but this was immediately dispelled by West saying, "Glad that you dropped by. I was just about to ring you. Forbes, bring us some coffee, there's a good chap."

"Sir." Forbes practically clicked his heels.

Rodgers placed the white case carefully on the desk. "Could you have this dusted for prints? Be careful of the contents, though. And at the double. The lady's almost lost without it."

West grinned as he picked up a phone and gave the necessary orders. "Thought you looked a bit odd, toting a beauty box. What gives?"

Rodgers told him briefly.

West pursed his lips. "Won't do any harm to have it printed. Probably it's of no significance, but we can't afford to take chances."

Rodgers said slowly, "You know why I'm here, then?"

"No." West got up from behind his desk and crossed to the window. "I was just told to give you any assistance that you might require – and not to ask questions."

"I see. Have you got anywhere on Soulis' death?"

"Nowhere." West spoke more sharply than he had intended. He rather resented Rodgers' interest in the crime committed in his territory whilst he was excluded from something that must be big in the same territory. Why bring in someone from Kingston and tell him not to ask questions?

He had gone back to Ripple earlier in the day. Diana was down on the beach, he was told. West thought back to that moment: he'd asked Peters about the night before.

"When you took in Mrs Barrington's tray at dinner time, did you see her?"

"No, sir. Miss Diana, she in the shower."

"So?" West prompted.

"Well, sir..." Peters hesitated; the rheumy eyes in the dark wrinkled face were wary. "I put the tray on the table on the verandah, same as always. I call out to Miss Diana that I bring the supper."

"And did she answer you?"

"I not sure, sir. The water in the shower, it run fas'."

Peters had given virtually the same answer as he had done the night before. West thanked the man and left, once more negotiating the steep driveway with respect. So Peters had not seen or heard Diana Barrington. Was she in fact there? He stopped his car at the steps leading down to the beach. He stood at the top and looked down. Rowan Rodgers' dark head was bent over Diana's red-gold one. Their kiss was long and, even when seen from a distance, passionate. In the bay, a runabout cut through the shallows with a burst of noise. It was piloted by the stocky figure of Sergeant Phillips. Another runabout was beached by the moored launch. West watched as the two broke away, then Rodgers ran down to the beached runabout and towed it out to the waiting Phillips.

What in hell gives? West asked himself. He'd been under the impression that Rowan and Rachel were lovers. Not that he blamed Rodgers. He himself had succumbed quickly enough to the strong emanation of pure sex that Diana exuded from every pore. He went slowly down the steps as Diana looked up and saw him. Her face was hard and set, not the expression that he had expected. When he reached the bottom step, she looked at him levelly for a moment then her expression changed as she said, "Good morning, Mr West. This place is swarming with policemen this morning. Is this a friendly or a professional visit?"

"Perhaps not as friendly as your last visitor."

She laughed, not at all embarrassed. "Your thoughts are obvious. I lost one lover yesterday, so set about finding – another one?" She ended on a questioning note. Then said, "Don't look so unbending. Come and sit down, have a drink and tell me what's happened."

He lowered his long body into a reclining beach chair. "I came to ask questions, not to gossip."

He accepted the drink that she offered and looked at her critically. She seemed somehow different from last night. Then she had been angry and abusively honest. Today she had shed some of her hardness and appeared to be amused at the situation: because she imagined that she had made another conquest in Rodgers? Or was this her normal self? Last night something had happened that had angered her – or frightened her? Some people respond to fear with a show of anger.

"Well?" Pushing his legs aside, she sat on the end of the long chair. "You've been gazing at me for ages. What did you want to ask me?"

He took a sip from his glass. "When Peters took your tray into your room last night, what did he say?"

"Say? God, I don't know."

"Try and remember."

"Something like 'I bring the supper, Miss Diana.' That's his usual formula."

"Did you hear him say that?"

"I suppose so. What does it matter?"

"You *suppose* so. Were you in fact having a shower or were you out there in that boat?" He flung his hand in a gesture towards the sea and the white boat rocking in the shallows.

Diana was very still.

"Why should I say that I was in the shower if I was out in *Katinka*?"

"Why? Because at just about that time, Simon Soulis was killed on a rocky outjut just a few miles along the coast – killed from a boat like that."

She got up abruptly, spilling her drink. The anger was back and her brown eyes blazed down at him. "You get the hell out of here! I don't care who you are, you understand? You have no proof – either that I was where I say I was, or any damn place else. I'm just a convenient peg to hang a murder rap on. And with my reputation you could probably make it stick. But you've no proof – and no motive."

He finished his drink, stood up and looked down at her. He felt again her disturbing attraction and wanted to take her in his arms and say, 'Forget the last ten minutes', but all he did was to give a little sketch of a bow and say, "Mrs Barrington, I may have no proof at the moment, but don't be too sure that I won't find any. And I shall keep up the search."

"Search away, but you won't find any."

"Have you concealed it so well?"

She took a quick step towards him and he caught her upraised hand. "No, I should have to arrest you for assaulting a policeman in the course of duty."

"Well?" Rodgers' voice brought him back to the dusty disarray of his office. "You've been gazing out of the window for the last five minutes."

"I'm sorry. I said that I had nothing on Soulis: maybe I do, maybe I don't." He told Rodgers of his visit to Diana earlier, omitting to mention the scene that he had witnessed.

Rodgers grinned as he said, "Sorry to encroach, but I'm wondering if that over-sexed young woman is important in either your case or mine. I'm not horning in on your territory, but I'm here to look for unexplained happenings. An unexplained murder, vanishing face powder and the connecting link with Paris are unusual enough to merit further investigation. I'm probably wasting my time in thinking along these lines, but I've nothing else to go on." He got up and reached for the phone. "I'm going to ring the AC and ask that you be brought into the picture. You can't help or know what to look for unless you know the problem that we're up against."

The Assistant Commissioner demurred at first. "The more people who are told about this, the bigger the chances of a leak." His voice travelled faintly over a hissing line.

"But, sir," Rodgers was at his persuasive best, "if Superintendent West is to assist me to the best advantage and in view of the recent developments – which I agree, may have nothing to do with our problem..."

"All right, Rodgers, with the Minister on my back I can only say do it your way, but God help you if your judgement is wrong."

The line went dead from Kingston. Rodgers looked thoughtful as he replaced the receiver. What exactly did the old man mean by that remark? Surely West was in the clear? He'd stake his life – yet would he? That was a sweeping sentimental asseveration. What did he know of Richard West? Apart from the fact that he had acquired the reputation of reliability in his work over the years? He didn't know the man. During his time in the Force they'd met briefly, mostly socially at the Police Ball or at the Police Officers' Club. They'd never worked together before. There was a facile surface amity between them that had never cemented into friendship. So where, thought Rodgers, do I go from here? Do I take him fully into my confidence or not?

"Well?" West's voice broke his reverie. "What verdict did the old man give?"

"He's fussing. Pressure being brought to bear. I'll fill you in."

West got up. "Can't wait now. I've got to meet a couple of skin divers in ten minutes. We're going to search for one missing spear-head." He paused, then picked up a small notebook from the desk. "I had a look through Soulis' room. Found this. It looks as if it's in code."

Rodgers took it and riffled through the pages. "A few pages missing," he said.

The jagged edges were evident. "Had anyone else been in his room?"

"Not obviously, or legally. I gave orders that no one was to be allowed in until I lifted the order."

"Then whoever killed him either didn't know of this, or didn't think that it had any importance. We'll get John Terrance on to this." He slipped the notebook into his pocket. "I think I'll come with you. I've done a fair amount of diving. OK?"

"OK," West agreed after a fractional pause.

Rodgers felt some relief as he slid behind the wheel of the Mercedes. The necessity for briefing Richard West was postponed for the time being. He wished that he knew what the AC had meant by his remark.

It was nearing five-thirty when the four divers assembled by a fast rakish-looking launch. The sun was dropping in a sky of bleached grey-blue towards a sea of an oily stillness. The bright blue and green patches of colour, so strong earlier in the day, had paled to a uniform greenish grey, with ripples of gold from the sun's rays turning the surface to shot silk taffeta.

"We'll start from the point where Soulis was found, and work our way west. Right?"

"Right."

The two other divers were young police constables. Clad in tight bathing trunks with oxygen tanks strapped to dark gleaming bodies, face masks pushed up on their foreheads, they both had an air of repressed excitement. This was more like the life of adventure of their youthful dreams; this had more savour than the dull routine of apprehending petty criminals or of serving tickets on careless motorists. They stood poised on the rail of the launch as she rocked gently off the coastline.

"Now remember, Parkes, Ogilvie, cover the area carefully. The spearhead may be hidden by weeds. It may have fallen into a crevice, it may not be there at all. But if it is down there – I want it. Right?"

"Right, sir."

They went in together, snapping their masks into position.

West gave instructions to the pilot of the launch, the fresh-faced young constable named Goodbody, who was mentally lamenting that he hadn't yet mastered the art of skin diving.

"Keep her more or less stationary. Don't close up until you see us break the surface. We'll surface every twenty minutes."

"Yes, sir, understood." Goodbody made up in brisk efficiency that which he lacked in underwater proficiency. He watched enviously as Rowan Rodgers' well muscled body slid into the water, followed by Richard West's lean frame. Although he wished that he was with the divers, he felt that prick of excitement once again – on a case with two of the most well-known superintendents in the Force. Goodbody sighed. That Mr Rodgers drive one nice car too, man. He fell into a reverie where he, Constable Emmanuel Goodbody, solved a crime that had baffled Superintendent Rowan Rodgers...

Rodgers swam easily, cleaving through the soft warm water, his powerful headlamp casting a wide area of light in the clear green depths. Fantastic corals, delicately pink or lavender, loomed on either side, their corrugated fingers or fragile fans draped in clinging tendrils of seaweed, waving tenuously in the constant underwater motion. The soft sand on the seabed swirled in a diffuse cloud as some sea creature darted up and away at his approach. He eased down towards the bottom, tacking back and forth. A shoal of brightly coloured fish came towards him. They divided ranks and passed him on either side, apparently unaware or at least unafraid of him.

It was slow, tedious work; he glanced at his watch. Five more minutes before they were due to surface.

A jagged ridge of rising coral loomed to his right; something glinted dully in the light from his headlamp. He knifed expertly down and grasped the protruding piece of metal. He tugged, and as it came reluctantly from its bed of coral he realised that he had, in fact, a spearhead in his hand. There was no joy in the discovery as it was obvious even in the distortion of the underwater refraction that the spearhead had been in the salt water for very much longer than the one that they sought. He tossed it away and glimpsed the long frame of West ahead. He was also delving into a recess in the coral bed but, even as Rodgers approached him, he flipped his flippers and shot to the surface. Rodgers followed him in a diagonal rise.

The launch was still where they had left it, as the four heads broke the surface simultaneously.

"Any luck?" Rodgers called.

West shook his head. "I thought for a moment down there that I'd found something, but no joy. You?"

"Just an old spearhead that had been there for ages."

"You men find anything?" West called.

"No, sir," Parkes and Ogilvie answered in unison.

"Goodbody! What's with the boat?" West's voice boomed across the still water. Goodbody, roughly woken from his daydreams, throttled the engine into a roar.

"All right, man, no need to over-rev her. Just bring her up gently."

The sun was sinking rapidly now, long golden bands cut like satin ribbons across the silver sea. Daylight would soon dissolve into night and the next probe must be now or not at all.

"Right," West called. "One more try then call it a day."

Twenty minutes later, Rodgers swung aboard the launch. He pulled off his mask and scanned the area. No one else was in sight.

"Keep a look out, Goodbody, they should be surfacing at any moment." He dived off the stern and retraced his earlier area of search. Goodbody watched him go, lost in schoolboy admiration. At that moment his allegiance, hitherto firmly attached to Richard West, now switched to adhere with equal firmness to Rowan Rodgers. He drifted happily into another dream: just as he was dragging the unconscious form of Rodgers, rescued at great personal peril from the bottom of the ocean floor, on board the launch: just as the press were clamouring for an interview, as the television cameras whirred:

"Goodbody – *Goodbody* – where the hell's that boat? Hurry, man, on the double." It was Rodgers' voice sounding anything but grateful. Goodbody over-revved the engine again, which brought an irate, "Watch it, man!" from West.

"OK, we'll call it a day."

The men swung abroad, leaving wet patches on the sun-bleached deck. The launch made a wide U-turn and sped back to the shore, leaving a churning, frothy wake, widening in the now darkened sea. The sun dropped suddenly beyond the horizon and for a few moments the sky and sea merged into a deep blaze of red in the west, whilst the rest of the sky turned a pale green. Then the brief glory of a tropical sunset was over. A few stars winked out and a light breeze ruffled the former stillness of the Caribbean Sea.

Rodgers tamped down his pipe as West lit a cigarette. "Not that we had much hope," West said gloomily. "And possibly not much use, if we had found it."

Rodgers narrowed his eyes through the haze of smoke from his pipe. "Maybe not," he agreed. "Look, when we get to shore, I'll put you in the picture about my spot of bother."

ELEVEN

Rachel put down the telephone receiver. That was the second time Rowan had called to say that he would be late. This time something about skin diving. Skin diving? At this hour? She glanced at her watch: quarter to seven. For the second time that day she wondered if she had done the right thing in coming home. Back to Jamaica, yes, that was the right thing. But back to Rowan? She knew that she was being foolish, that he was on a case. He had to work on it. He'd warned her that they would have very little time together and here she was behaving like a teenager. He loved her – hadn't he proved that last night? Oh God, she said aloud, be your age. What did last night prove? That you'd been apart for a year and that I – yes, let's be honest – I was crying out to be made love to: that's all last night proved. Romantic love didn't enter into it. She'd believed for so long in the concept of romantic love. And then overnight, her safe, secure, happy marriage to Bill had been thrown away. They had loved each other, until that love changed as Bill himself changed. She shut her eyes against the memory. If only she could forget how he used to be before...

The telephone shrilled again.

"Hello, Rachel Groome here."

"Rachel – are you alone?"

"Yes, but – who…?"

"You don't sound like it. You sound as if..."

"Who is that?" she cut in sharply.

"You don't recognise my voice? I'm grieved. I'd hoped that my voice was seared into your memory – it's John. John Terrance. Major John Terrance, JDF."

"Oh, John," she laughed. "Don't be such a clown. What do you want?"

"I thought that you might like to join me in the Pirate's Lair for a drink. And then have dinner with me?"

"John, I can't, I'm having dinner with Rowan."

"You mean that you hope you are. I happen to know that he is skittering at the bottom of the sea at this moment. He may be there for hours."

Rachel hesitated. In the mood that she was in, she didn't want to be alone. Yet to be with John...

"Rachel?"

"Yes?"

"Thought you'd gone. Do come and have that drink. Or, better still, ask me to come up and have one with you there."

"No, John, in my present mood and in view of your avowed intentions, much better not."

"Well, I know about my avowed intentions – but your present mood intrigues me. I'll be right along."

"No," Rachel was firm. "I'll be down in about twenty minutes. But I warn you, I shall drop you the moment Rowan appears." She hung up, lit a cigarette and immediately put it out. She *had* to kick the habit. John was sweet, but quite unpredictable. She wondered what he was doing at the Santa Gloria. She'd known this morning that she had been used to enable John to talk to Rowan in as casual a way as possible. Were they working together on the case? If so it must be big. Army intelligence plus the police. Her natural curiosity was roused, acting like a tonic to dispel her former mood. She entered the shower stall with a feeling of well-being that had been absent since the morning.

Anna Morgan closed the door of her room carefully. She carried the white beauty-case that Rodgers had sent back an hour earlier. From the balcony of her room, she had watched Solange and Peter Horton, apparently on good terms again after their morning spat, go down towards the pool. Madame Yvette was lying down with a headache – the pre-showing headache which she always had. And Girot, she didn't know where he was. He had been strangely absent all day – strange, because he usually fussed over last-minute details and hovered, which increased the tension in already taut nerves.

She paused at the top of the stairs and took a deep breath: she would have to risk it. She had changed her mind about investigating Solange's powder box after the showing and had decided that now, while they were all catching their breath before the mad rush began, was the time.

She went lightly down the broad staircase and crossed the lobby. There were many more people there than usual, all drawn to the Santa Gloria by the magic name of the House of Girot. All to the good, she thought, I won't be noticed in the mob. She was unaware of a pair of dark brown eyes that watched her purposeful passage and the sudden wary look of alarm that filled them.

Anna went to the left out of the lobby and into the dark ballroom. It was closely set with chairs and small tables. She shivered suddenly. The sound of the sea came softly through the opened jalousies of the folding doors along the verandah, and only the diffused light of the moon, lightly veiled by a passing cloud, broke the gloom. The tune of the haunted ballroom swam through her mind and she hurried even more quickly towards the dressing room behind the stage. In her haste, she knocked against one of the tables; an ashtray clattered to the floor. Anna froze, her heart thudding. What a fool I am, she thought, I'm behaving as if I were about to commit a crime. She went almost at a run into the dressing room, shut the door and switched on the fluorescent lights over the mirrors. She put her case on the dresser top and looked round. Yes, Solange's case was still there. She cast a hasty look round the room, still imbued with a sense of guilt. Four movable racks were hung with the clothes the models would show later that evening. Shoes, hats, other accessories were in orderly groups on the long dresser top. Two floor-length, shuttered windows were closed at her left, the shutters tipped up. No one could possibly see her. She opened Solange's case. The lock snapped back and the sound deadened the slight creak that the shutters made as they were turned from outside to the horizontal position. She took the top tray out of the case and picked up the box of powder from the bottom. Behind her the handle of the French window turned silently.

Anna lifted the lid of the box and probed through the powder for the bottom. She had no time to cry out; she barely felt the blow on the back of her head before she lost consciousness and she had no knowledge of being picked up and carried out of the dressing room and deposited on the verandah outside the ballroom.

John Terrance made his way to the Pirate's Lair, which was fairly crowded. He was greeted by a babble of foreign languages and an assortment of English accents: English in its widest sense, from a Texan drawl to an Australian flatness and back again to the indigenous lilt. He found a table for two out on the patio and ordered a Red Stripe while he waited for Rachel and thought over the events of the day – or rather the lack of events. Behind the man-about-town exterior he presented to the world and fostered by his actions was a very shrewd brain: analytical and foreseeing, anticipating people's actions and reactions. At present, though, he had no indication of the likely turn of events. He'd kept a watchful eye on the residents and visitors to the Santa Gloria. There was no one who didn't seem perfectly innocent and genuine. The Girot circus? They had been thoroughly checked by security both in Paris and here. Not that that exonerated them completely; the operators that he was after were masters of the art of subterfuge and presenting a front of innocence. They wouldn't have stayed in business for so long otherwise. And so far no news from Paris in answer to his cable.

"This can't be the John of the flippant phone call? Not this serious-faced young introvert?"

John rose to his feet and looked down at Rachel. He was still serious as he said, "You look very lovely, even more so than usual. And you smell – m'mmm, indescribable."

She sat down as he drew out a chair for her. "And it's not essence of woman," she smiled at him. "It's *Illicite*, sent to me by the great man himself." She nodded in the direction of Girot who stood surveying the crowded bar.

John turned his head to see the rotund figure, a speculative look in his eyes. Girot wove his way to the patio. As he passed, he bowed and sketched a smile but did not stop. He signalled a waiter and gave an order, then continued his slow way towards the pool.

"That's funny," Rachel said. "He sends me perfume and a charming note, invites me to be his guest tonight at the showing, then practically ignores me."

"Probably nerves – if that's any indication." John inclined his head at a passing waiter who was taking a tray laden with glasses, ice and a full bottle of Scotch to where Girot now sat at a table on the edge of the pool. "What's the matter, love?"

She was gazing at Girot, a thoughtful frown creasing her forehead. "I don't know," she said slowly. "I don't get the impression of nerves so much as a drugged state."

"Drugged?"

"Yes, John, I've seen that look on the faces of drug takers before. Bill..." she paused. "Bill had a number of drug addicts as patients over the years. They get a very special look, a certain nervous reaction, a way of beading with moisture for no apparent reason. I'm sure that I recognised that look on Girot's face just now."

"Well, beading with moisture in this climate is understandable," John said lightly, but he felt a tightening of anticipation. If Rachel was right, this could be the lead that he was looking for. If Rachel was right – he wondered how much Rachel's feminine intuition and observation could be backed up by medical opinion. Added to which, one drug taker in such a profession didn't by any means indicate a drug racket. His spark of excitement went out, but he couldn't afford to ignore it. He leant across the table. "Stay here for ten minutes, love. If Girot makes to leave, hold him for me till I get back. Ten minutes. Can do?"

She smiled, her grey eyes shining. "Certainly can do."

He looked at her in pleased surprise. "What a woman, not one question."

"Not at the moment. The questions will be asked – later."

He grinned, "In the wee sma' hours? Lady, I'll keep you to that."

He was gone before she could reply. A waiter brought her drink which John had ordered on his way out. She watched Girot covertly, still motionless except for the frequent raising of his glass. He drank in quick nervous movements, giving his glass a quarter turn after each sip, a turn of frenetic energy that had the effect of building tension in the observer.

John Terrance made his way swiftly through the chattering crowd at the bar, his long legs carrying him at a deceptively fast pace. The lobby was not so crowded as it had been earlier as a number of people were having an early dinner so as not to miss the start of the Girot showing, but there were still more people around than usual. He paused at the reception desk. "Mr Girot's room number, please."

The man hesitated. "Mr Girot gave orders that he was not to be disturbed all day."

"Mr Girot is in the bar. He asked me to get something from his room. May I have the key, please?" He waited. He didn't want to draw attention to himself by pulling rank.

"Sorry, sir. Can't give you the key. It's against the rules."

"It's not against the rules to give me his room number. His secretary will let me in." He hoped that the clerk was not too conversant with the Girot entourage.

"Twenty-one, sir, on the second floor," The man lost interest and turned away to answer the telephone.

Terrance went up the shallow stairs and along the corridor. Twenty-one was the last room on the right hand side. At the end of the corridor were open French doors which led to a verandah. He went through them and saw that the small verandah stopped at the corner of the building. Peering round the corner, he could see the balcony of Girot's room jutting out. It was a matter of only five or six feet from the verandah rail to the rail of the balcony. But the angle of the wall caused a difficulty. Overhead, a metal awning curved round the corner and continued above the bedroom balconies.

He took a quick look back up the corridor – no one was in sight. He peered down into the shadowed garden – it seemed deserted. He climbed onto the verandah rail, reached up and grasped the awning. He swung himself along, hand over hand. It was tricky rounding the corner where there was no purchase for his feet. He hung dizzily for a moment, the metal cutting into his hands, then his feet felt the welcome hardness of Girot's balcony railing. He dropped lightly to the balcony floor and peered through the open French doors. The bedroom seemed to be quite empty. It was large and the balcony on which he stood was spacious enough to entertain a dozen people.

He slipped into the room: it was expensively furnished and had a marked air of femininity. Women's dresses, coats and furs were draped across the bamboo chairs. One of the twin beds was heaped with an assortment of shoes, handbags, belts and hats. On the plate-glass top of a long built-in dressing table were dozens of bottles of perfume, all with the distinctive Girot label.

Terrance stood still, taking in the organised chaos of the room. He was wondering now why he had obeyed the sudden impulse to come there. If Girot was in the drug racket, or even only a drug taker, it wasn't likely that he'd leave evidence where anyone might find it. He opened the drawers between the beds – nothing. On top of one of the bedside tables was a large ashtray half filled with stubs and ash. Terrance sniffed then peered at the gold tips – no brand name. He took out of his pocket a small polythene pouch and unzipped it, revealing many small vertical compartments. Carefully selecting a few of the stubs, he put them in one of the compartments then rezipped the pouch and returned it to his jacket pocket. He looked keenly around the room: two large cardboard cartons stood against the wall, striking a mundane note in the prevailing luxury. He crossed the room to examine them: they were marked *Maison de Roger Girot, Paris, France*. Underneath was lettered: *Cosmetiques: Poudre pour la figure. Douze-douzaine boites. En blanche.* The other carton was similar but instead of *blanche* was marked *translucent* and *au naturel.* Powder? Face powder. Both cartons were firmly sealed with adhesive tape.

He looked at his watch. He'd been away from the bar for seven minutes: three minutes to go. He went into the bathroom: there was a lavish assortment of towels, some in a damp heap, some hanging primly folded on the racks. On the ledge of a deep blue hand basin lay a hypodermic syringe. He examined it without touching it: a one-cc capacity. Its presence didn't mean that the man did take drugs – he might be a diabetic – but it didn't preclude it either. The syringe was quite empty. He opened the cabinet above the basin and saw a box with some small phials in it. He took one and added it to the polythene pouch.

With thirty seconds of the allowed ten minutes left, John was back with Rachel. The stocky figure of Girot was still by the pool. He had been joined by Solange who was leaning across the table talking volubly, her long slim hands gesturing dramatically.

Rachel smiled at John. "Any problems?"

"None. And possibly no results either – it was a long shot. But tell me, do ladies wear white face powder, ever?"

"White? No, only clowns in circuses. Why?"

"Because..." he began then stopped. Rachel's eyes were focussed on the entrance where Rowan Rodgers stood, obviously looking for someone. "Ugh! I thought that my luck was holding too well," Terrance murmured, then called, "Over here, man."

Rodgers wove his way through the press of bodies. He, like Terrance, was in formal evening dress, his white shirt front contrasting pleasantly with his dark good looks.

"You look very handsome, both of you, all dressed up," Rachel said. "Are you trying to compete with the models? Silly question. Trying to impress them, no doubt."

Rodgers signalled a waiter. "Thanks for looking after Rachel, John. Perhaps," he didn't look at Rachel, "perhaps you'll have dinner with us?"

Rachel bit her lip. She'd hardly seen him all day; now he was adopting a proprietory tone and inviting a third to dinner. John didn't look at her but there was a glint in his eyes that told her that he realised what she was feeling. He said, "Thanks, Rowan, I'd like that – if Rachel doesn't mind?"

She shook her head.

"Fine," Rowan said. "We'll have a quick drink and then dinner. What time is this fashion show?"

"Nine or nine-thirty. I'll check." John got up and went over to the bar.

Rowan took Rachel's hand but she was quite unresponsive. "Are you annoyed because I asked John to join us?"

"I know it's silly of me but I haven't seen you all day. Well –

hardly."

"I know. Don't think that I'm not regretting it, but I asked John for a purpose. Don't ask any questions yet."

She laughed suddenly. "All right. But if this is a preview of the pattern of our life..." She was saved further commitment by Terrance's return.

"Nine-thirty in the ballroom. There's great excitement rising at the imminence – and eminence – of the occasion."

The dining room was crowded. The whole of the fashionable island society seemed to be present, but Rodgers had reserved a table earlier in anticipation of such an event. As Rachel accepted her second cup of coffee, the waiter arrived with a cablegram, white and blue on the silver tray.

"Major Terrance, sir?"

Terrance took the envelope and with a hasty apology, opened it. He narrowed his nostrils in a characteristic way. He studied the message intently then said, "Rachel, would you excuse us a moment?"

She put down her untasted coffee and rose to her feet. "Of course. I have to powder my nose. It will look better if I leave, anyway."

"That's quite a woman," Terrance murmured as he handed the cablegram to Rodgers. It was from Paris: COMMODITY MAY BE DIFFICULT TO ACQUIRE STOP OVERSEAS BRANCHES POSSIBLY STOCK STOP.

Rodgers asked, "And translated?"

Terrance's lips barely moved as he said softly, "SOULIS AGENT WORKING NARCOTICS TRADE STOP LARGE SHIPMENT LAST WEEK STOP PRESUME JAMAICA."

"You broke that down quickly."

"No credit; I planned the code."

"So, Soulis was an agent and undoubtedly your missing contact. So the two cases become one. Which brings us back to Diana Barrington. What was his interest in her?"

TWELVE

For the second time in nearly twenty-four hours, Carlisle Linton almost stumbled over a body. He'd been sent to check the tables in the ballroom, to see that each was complete with ashtray, book-match folders and fresh hibiscus blossoms floating in balloon glasses.

He was walking jauntily along the verandah, whistling the award-winning reggae tune of the Independence Festival celebrations, when he came upon the still figure of Anna Morgan. She lay on her back, her dark hair loosened. There was a grey tinge about her coffee-coloured skin that he didn't like.

He stopped.

He felt a sudden fear. The memory of last night was too close and the picture of the dead man on the beach filled his mind. His instinct was to run, but then Anna gave a slight movement and her eyelids fluttered.

He ran and knelt beside her. "What 'appen, miss? You fall, nuh?"

She opened her eyes slowly, the effort making her wince. "Get – get Madame Yvette." She had a struggle to get the words out.

The boy looked blank. "Ma'am?"

She was too weak to feel annoyance at the boy's inability to understand. "Get someone – anyone – quickly."

Carlisle nodded. This was more in his range of comprehension. He felt a vast relief that the pattern of the previous evening had not been repeated. He hurried back to the lobby and to his joy saw his cousin Delroy Smith going towards the bar. "Delroy! Help me, nuh, man. One o' the lady, she fall – look so she hurt bad."

They hastened back and Carlisle, forgetting Richard West's warning, recounted his fears in relation to the events of the previous evening.

Anna had recovered somewhat and was now fully conscious. With the help of Carlisle and his cousin, she reached her room.

"You want me to get the doctor, ma'am?" Smith asked.

"No, thank you. I shall be all right. I – I must have slipped. Would you kindly ask the lady in the next room, Miss Susan Taylor, to come to me?"

Susan Taylor was half dressed, a terry robe over her bra and pants, her hair in rollers. "Anna – Anna, darling, what is it? The waiter said that you'd been hurt."

Anna felt the back of her head. "I slipped – on the verandah downstairs and must have hit my head rather badly. Would you look? Is the skin broken?"

Susan examined the area. "No, but you've got quite a bump. Your hair must have saved it from being worse. I'll tell Girot that you can't go on tonight." She picked up the receiver of the telephone on the bedside table, but Anna stopped her. "No – no, please, Aunt Susan. I'll be all right. I've got about an hour and a half before I need go down. I'll just rest. Perhaps I could have a drink?"

"Of course. I'll get room service." She went on speaking as she dialled. "Darling, you ought to have a doctor see that bump. Say you're conscussed or... Room Service? Would you send two...gin?" Anna nodded. "Two gin and tonics to Room Seventeen. And a lot of extra ice. Yes, Miss Anna Morgan." She replaced the receiver. "Do let me get a doctor?"

"No, I feel all right now. I promise you that if I don't feel well I'll have you call one – please?"

Susan sighed. "All right, but I feel so responsible."

"Oh, really, darling, I've been on my own in Paris for the last three..." She turned away. "I know – I'm sorry."

Susan kissed her. "Forget it. All that's over now."

When the drinks arrived, Susan made an ice pack out of a shower cap and held it against Anna's head. "Oh, that's bliss!"

After Susan had left to finish dressing, Anna stayed on the bed and sipped her drink slowly. She knew that she should have told Rodgers earlier about her suspicions regarding the powder box; she knew that it was important but she wanted to find out something more definite before she said anything. Why she had concealed, first from Smith and then from her aunt, the fact she had been hit over the head then carried from the dressing room to the verandah, she didn't quite know. She lay back on the pillows and hoped that the throb in her head would lessen before the start of the showing of the collection.

By nearly nine o'clock, the ballroom was crowded. As Rachel, Rowan and John entered, they were escorted by a waiter to a table on the aisle with a perfect view of the stage. "Mr Girot's compliments," the waiter murmured.

They glanced round. The room was on two levels, shaped like a triangle with rounded points. The stage filled one point, its apron curving into the audience. Full, rich velvet curtains hung convexly at the back and would swing open in an arc to reveal the models. Ceiling lights added brilliance to the setting of ornate gowns and glittering jewellery. The buzz of conversation was at a high level as waiters moved deftly amongst the tables taking final orders. There was a 'welcome to the club' ambience – the club of wealth and position. Rachel felt an air of unreality about the evening which was as unexpected as it was unpleasant. She had been so looking forward to the occasion and now she wished that it was all over.

"Why, hullo there."

The two men rose to their feet as Diana Barrington paused by their table. She was magnificent in a white ankle-length sheath that clung to her figure, revealing the perfect lines which Rowan remembered only too clearly from the morning. The white gown was a foil to the rich coffee patina of her skin. Her red-gold hair gleamed, reflecting the lights from above.

Rachel felt a stirring of jealousy and a frisson of alarm as she saw the way that Diana smiled into Rowan's eyes. "Hullo, Diana. I haven't seen you for years." She tried to instil warmth into her greeting but to her own ears it sounded curt and dismissing.

"Rachel? Why, I'd no idea that you were back. You look – divine." Diana's eyes narrowed as she looked at Rachel then quickly back to Rowan. Her smile was calculated now as she asked softly,

"And how are the – children? Six – did you say? All tucked up and asleep, I hope?"

Rachel felt her face stiffen at the shared intimacy of the mocking query.

Rowan grinned easily, quite relaxed. "As you surmise. Are you alone? Won't you join us?"

Diana lifted her head arrogantly. "I'm sure Rachel loathes the idea – so I will." She flashed a brilliant smile at Rachel and sat down with lithe grace. Large angular earrings of red gold studded with small emeralds swung with her every movement. On her left hand was a big square-cut emerald set in a cube of red gold. Rachel gave an inward sigh. Only Diana could afford jewellery made in the modern fashion with an emerald of such depth of colour and clarity. It must be at least six carats. She looked at Diana and tried to keep her voice light and impersonal.

"Why do you think that I loathe your joining us?"

"Of course you do, darling. Here you are flanked by two of the most fascinating males, and I come along." There was the merest stress on the personal pronoun. She didn't need to elaborate further.

Rachel gave a repressed sigh. She knew that she must keep her sense of humour if she was to help Rowan. She smiled at Diana. "You always did have a magnified opinion of the effect of your charms. Which of my 'fascinating males' would you like to appropriate?"

"I – haven't quite decided."

John looked appraisingly at Diana. "If someone would introduce us I might appreciate even further the idea of being appropriated," he said.

Rachel flushed slightly. She had allowed her personal feelings to override her good manners. "I'm sorry, I thought that you knew each other." She introduced them, feeling gauche and swamped by Diana's looks and personality.

Rowan ordered drinks as the tempo and pitch of sound in the now packed ballroom was topped by a protracted and brilliantly executed roll of drums by the leader of the four-man combo that had been playing softly in the background. Applause broke out as the musicians bowed, brightly checked shirts vying with the flash of white teeth in dark glistening faces.

The lights dimmed to the intimacy of a nightclub except for the stage which was a patch of moving coloured shafts of scintillation against the backdrop of the velvet curtains.

There was a feeling of expectant tension which broke into prolonged applause as Roger Girot walked onstage and bowed his head in acknowledgement of the moment. "Ladies and gentlemen," his accent was very pronounced, "I 'ave the great pleasure in presenting to you my Caribbean Collection. This is the *première* showing of most of the pieces you will see. I 'ave designed with your island in mind – your way of life – your year-long summer – your beaches and the sailing – and of course, your love of parties and of entertaining. My associate, Peter Horton, will act as your guide." He bowed again and walked off the stage to renewed applause.

Peter Horton took the stage with an urbanity and self-assurance that spoke of long practice.

The showing began with the traditional beachwear. The audience was now quiet but had an intense appreciation of the clothes that had a quality of tomorrow without in any way being outrageously extreme.

"The man's a genius – even I can see that," Rowan murmured.

"Some of his things are so wildly simple and yet stand out apart. How does he do it?" Rachel asked. She glanced across to where Susan Taylor was sitting, her eyes filled with a mixture of admiration and envy. But, in addition, there was an aura of tension and unease about her that Rachel found disturbing. As she watched, Susan leant forward, the worried look increasing. Rachel switched her eyes back to the stage as Peter Horton announced, "And here is your own lovely Anna in a shocking pink two-piece that..."

Anna came slowly through the half circle of velvet curtains down to the edge of the stage, right out onto the apron. Her lovely face was paler than usual, her full-lipped mouth unsmiling. Rachel touched Rowan's arm. "Anna doesn't look well – and just see how her aunt is gazing at her."

"Her aunt?"

"Oh I forgot, you didn't meet her, it was John – at lunch. She's my dressmaker, the one who made this." She flicked the skirt of her dress.

"Oh," Rowan said. "*The* dress. And she's Anna's aunt. Interesting." He lowered his voice. "I didn't know you'd been lunching with John."

"I didn't know that you'd been sharing jokes with Diana," she retorted. She would not meet his eyes but kept hers fixedly on Anna's slim form.

Anna turned and with the typical sinuous, lithe movement adopted by members of her profession, walked towards the back of the stage. She turned again. The movement made her dizzy and the throb in her head more intense.. She managed one more flounce and achieved a smile. She went back to the dressing room, applause following her. She wouldn't give up. She could rest for the next ten minutes or so, she wasn't on again until the evening wear.

The dressing room was a bustle of excited, voluble activity. The other three models – Tania, an exqusite brunette from Hungary, Lotus, a fragile Oriental from San Francisco, and Solange herself, blonde and svelte from the slums of Paris – were changing their clothes with precise rapidity. Madame Yvette flittered from one to the other, ceaselessly criticising and issuing instructions. Girot brooded in the background, knowing that he was presenting an exciting collection, yet still artist-like, fearful of failure.

Annette, one of the seamstresses who helped the models to change, was in a state of acute worry. This was her first tour with the House and she found it even more bewildering than at a collection show in Paris. She went to help Anna who was struggling with a zip. "Do you not feel well, Miss Anna?" she asked timidly. She rarely ventured remarks to these exalted, luxurious creatures but waited for them to address her. Anna was different. Annette had soon come to realise that underneath the veneer of sophistication was a warm, lovable person.

"Thank you, Annette, I – have a headache. I'm not on till evening wear so perhaps you would, if you have the time, put all the things that I need together? I'll leave dressing until the last minute." She pulled a terry robe around her shoulders and lay back on a day bed, her eyes closed.

"*Cherie*, what is it? You are sick?"

Anna opened her eyes to see Madame Yvette by her side, her carefully made up face creased with worry.

"It's all right, madame, I have a headache. I only have one more to show."

"You are sure you can do it?"

"Quite sure."

Madame seemed indecisive, then moved quickly to where Tania and Solange were engaged in a heated argument. She settled their difference with difficulty. She gave a sharp sigh and for the second time that day admitted that she was tired, that she would be glad – yes, glad – when the tour was over. She perched on one of the make-up stools and shut her eyes for a moment. She had never felt like this before. It was an indication that she was getting old. Getting? She *was* old – a fact that she must face. She opened her eyes with a feeling that too much time had passed, she must have dozed for a while. It must be time to help Anna to dress. *La pauvre petite*, so unusual for her to be quiet and withdrawn. "When you are through, *cherie*," she whispered as she handed Anna a jewel-encrusted evening bag, "I will 'ave a good stiff aperitif waiting for you – 'ow do you say? A pick-me-up."

"Thanks, madame, you're a sweetheart."

The knowledge that this was her last appearance gave Anna the courage to walk on to the stage with all her usual swinging grace and her brilliant smile. As she made the customary turns, she wondered if she could manage to snatch a glance inside Solange's beauty-case. *If* the powder box that she had seen earlier was still there. Solange hadn't seemed to notice anything amiss. She had been extremely vocal and temperamental over everything else. She was not a person to let anything that affected her adversely pass without notice.

Anna smiled at her aunt who was looking more at ease now. And who, she wondered, was that magnificent woman with Rachel Groome and that disturbingly attractive man. Thankfully she made the last triumphant swirling turn and went off to a storm of applause.

The dressing room was empty except for Solange who was struggling into a ball gown of midnight blue. "Fix this zip, Anna," she commanded. "Oh, where is that Annette – never here when she is needed." She twisted to look over her shoulder in the long mirror. Her sudden movement threw Anna off balance. As she clutched at the dresser top, her left arm knocked over a large bottle of perfume. "Oh!" Solange's voice rose in shrill anger. "You stupid incompetent. Look what you 'ave done." She was drenched in perfume from waist to ankle.

"I'm sorry," Anna said. "But you jerked – I couldn't..."

"Excuses – always the excuses. I am sick of you and your prying ways. And now you try to shame me in front of all these people." She was shaking with rage.

"What is 'appening? Solange, you should be ready to go on stage." Madame Yvette had come in, holding a glass which she handed to Anna.

"I am soaked! Look – 'ow can I go on like this?"

"It doesn't show on that colour. Drape your stole down that side. Hurry, child." Yvette handed Solange a mutation mink stole of pale silver-grey.

Solange paused in the doorway and looked back at Anna. "I will see that you do not do anything like this to me again – ever – you understand?" The words were said with quiet venom, completely at variance with her usual manner.

There was a spontaneous burst of applause as Solange walked on stage. Her silver-blonde loveliness against the midnight blue of the Girot masterpiece was reflected in the silver-blonde mink that she trailed with a studied indifference. She stood smiling serenely while Peter Horton began to describe the gown that she wore.

Rachel touched Rowan's arm. "Isn't that a dream? I'd just love it."

"Why don't you buy it?"

"Are you crazy? Have you any idea... Rowan, what's the matter with her?"

The applause was stilled abruptly as Solange made a few tottering steps to the stage apron. There she stayed, swaying. The stole slipped from her fingers as she started to laugh. It was laughter that had no humour in it but had a shrill hysterical note that rose in intensity like a jet engine. The audience froze to a puzzled silence; Peter Horton stopped in mid-sentence and stared at Solange in horror.

"Is the girl drunk?" someone asked audibly. The warmth and approval changed to hostility that swept through the ballroom with the same speed and spontaneity as had the earlier applause. Solange went on laughing, then, as quickly as it had started, the wild laughter stopped.

"The girl's not drunk – she's *ill.*" Rowan was on his feet and moving towards the stage.

Solange still stood there, silent now as her face and body assumed a pallor that, slowly before their mesmerised eyes, changed to a cyanosis that challenged the blue of her dress. She swayed again then, very slowly and with macabre grace, sank to the carpeted stage.

There was an excited hubbub from the audience as Rowan Rodgers reached the girl's side, closely followed by John Terrance. Rodgers held up his hand. "Ladies and gentlemen, would you kindly keep to your seats until we can get the young lady to the dressing room. Is there a doctor – ah, Doctor Montgomery, thank you."

Dr Montgomery had struggled through the crowded tables. He swung himself with surprising ease and agility onto the stage, then bent and felt the girl's limp hand. He wrinkled his nose at the waft of heavy perfume that emanated from her.

"The girl's dead," he said in a low voice to Rodgers.

The manager of the hotel pushed his way to the group. "Mr Rodgers, what has happened?" His face was creased with worry in apprehension of further trouble.

Rodgers spoke quietly, "Mr Deleon, we don't quite know what has happened. Could you ask your guests to go quietly, explain that the young lady is ill? Ah – Phillips, where did you spring from?"

"I sitting at the back, Mr Rodgers, sir. I bring the wife to see the dress dem."

Phillips was at his stolid best, unaccustomedly resplendent in a well-fitting grey button-down shirt and a tie that caused Rodgers to give a mental blink. "Young Goodbody and Pearson here too, sir."

"Good, man. Go and get them. Let them mix with the audience as they are leaving or lingering in the lobby. Tell them to keep their eyes and ears open for anything – but anything – that's odd. Tell them to be exceptionally discreet. And ask Mrs Groome to come here, please."

Deleon had spoken to the now restless audience and the guests were beginning to drift out of the ballroom.

Rachel and Diana were still at the table, Rachel calm through experience of sudden attacks of illness and Diana calm through an inability to show interest in another beautiful woman's misfortune. Phillips gave Rodgers' message to Rachel.

Diana got up. "I'm going to the bar. I need a drink after all that drama," she announced. "When things are more normal and you can be spared, perhaps you will all join me?"

Rachel looked at her coldly. "Thank you, perhaps we will." She walked away, her carriage expressing the contempt that she had concealed from her voice.

Richard West had joined the group by Solange's body. "Anything I can do?"

"Yes, make a quick note of who was in the audience, anyone that might be connected. Rachel, will you do the same?"

"Of course. Heavens, what a scent!"

"I know, she reeks. Must have poured half a bottle over herself. Let's get into the dressing room."

The dressing room was in a state of utter confusion. Girot was demanding to know why the show had stopped. His high forehead was glistening with sweat as he lashed Peter Horton with a spate of invective that was rapidly becoming completely Gallic.

"But, sir," Horton managed at last. "It was impossible to continue. The audience thought that Solange was drunk and were becoming restive. There was nothing I could do. Then Mr Rodgers asked the manager to dismiss the guests."

"Mr Rodgers? Who gives anyone the right to dismiss guests from my showing? H'm? *Hein*? Tell me that?" The veins were knotting at his temples.

"The right of the police of this country, Mr Girot." Rodgers' voice quietened Girot. He stood quite still for a moment, then turned to face Rodgers.

"Police? You are of the police?"

Rodgers nodded. "I am. As is Mr West here whom you met last night." He didn't mention John Terrance who had propped himself against the dressing table top.

"Always the police, last night and again tonight. What interest do your police 'ave in..." His voice trailed off and for the first time he looked at Solange. He tried to speak and finally, in a voice from which all belligerence had disappeared, asked, "What is the matter with her?"

"She is dead, Mr Girot." Dr Montgomery rose from an examination more extensive than that which he had been able to carry out on the stage.

"Dead? But how? A heart attack?"

"No," Dr Montgomery said slowly. "Not a heart attack. There are a number of factors that I do not like and, until proven otherwise, I think that we must assume that the young lady was – murdered."

THIRTEEN

The dead body of Solange Barnave had been removed to the local hospital for a post mortem examination. The guests in the ballroom had slowly dispersed to a hum of conversation, uneasy and speculative. The evening of festivity had ended in tragedy and to many was an anticlimax. Most people had departed to their homes, some nearby, others as far away as Kingston. Some had taken refuge in the hotel's bars whilst a few were kept uneasily waiting, by police request, in a room near the ballroom.

Richard West had detailed two uniformed constables to stay at the entrances, and Rodgers had detailed Phillips to assist him with the necessary questioning. At West's request, Rodgers had assumed command.

"Where's young Pearson?" Rodgers asked.

"Here, sir." Although in plain clothes Pearson snapped to attention.

"All right, relax, man. Did you see or hear anything that might be of use out there in the lobby?"

"No, sir, sorry, sir. Most people don't rightly know what happen. Most think the young lady drunk, sir."

"Well, they'll soon learn otherwise when the press gets on to it. Goodbody," he turned to the other young constable, "did you gather anything of use?"

Goodbody would have given a year's leave to be able to come up with something. "Sorry, sir."

"Don't be – it was a long shot. Well, you two, just stay in the background while I question these people. Listen and look – and learn."

Rodgers surveyed the gathering: Roger Girot, his round, chubby face somehow thinned since the death of his chief model, was slumped in an armchair, smoking continuously. Peter Horton, his thin, effeminate features strained and haggard, restlessly prowled round the long room. Madame Yvette, her carefully made up face as composed as ever, had a watchful look in her dark, hooded eyes. It was only by the nervous plucking of her small veined fingers that she betrayed any emotion. Tania and Lotus sat close together, their make-up smudged with easy-flowing tears. Anna Morgan, dry-eyed and remote, was apart from the others.

"Ladies and gentlemen." At Rodgers' quiet deep voice, they gave a nervous attentive forward movement in unison, like puppets linked by one thread. He looked round dispassionately. "A death has taken place which occasions some careful enquiries to be made. These will, I hope, clear up the cause of death but, until we have the medical report, I must request that each one of you will guarantee that you will not leave the hotel grounds." He walked to the shuttered French windows that led to the verandah and spoke in a low voice to Goodbody and Pearson. "Pearson, sit down and take notes. Goodbody, stay at the door so that you can observe those inside and those who I question. I'll see them on the verandah." He raised his voice: "Mr Girot, may I see you first?"

Girot nodded. He raised himself laboriously, like an old man. He stubbed out a barely lit cigarette before he followed Rodgers to the verandah.

Rodgers waited until the couturier was seated at a small round table then asked, "Your name, sir?"

Phillips and Pearson sat a little behind him, notebooks at the ready.

"Roger André Furneaux – Girot is my – how do you say? – professional name."

The routine questions dealt with, Rodgers asked, "How long have you known Solange Barnave?"

"Oh four, maybe five years. She came to me after I had just achieved some little notice in the world of *haute couture*."

"She was one of your top models?"

"She was my *première mannequin*, Mr Rodgers, It will be hard to – replace her." He stopped and mopped his perspiring brow with a silk handkerchief. "Forgive me, but it has been – a great shock. I cannot quite grasp the fact that... you say that the cause of death was not natural? How can you be sure?"

"We cannot be certain, sir, but from what I know of the medical profession as a whole and Dr Montgomery in particular, I don't think that it would have been stated so strongly if the facts had not pointed definitely to the conclusions drawn." Rodgers had purposely phrased his reply in a pedantic way.

"I see. You think it was suicide?" Girot looked almost hopeful.

"You feel that Miss Barnave had some reason to commit suicide?" Rodgers countered.

"Oh, no, no, no," Girot sounded shocked. "But if it was not, then – murder? I do not see how."

"Neither do we yet. That's what we've got to find out. Now, sir, what were your feelings towards the young lady?"

"My – feelings?"

"Yes," Rodgers felt irritated at the obtuseness. "How did you get on with her, apart from the professional standpoint?"

Girot, even from a sitting position, seemed to pull himself up. "I do not have any feelings apart from professional feelings towards any of my *mannequins*," he stated coldly.

Rodgers pursed his lips, "Then," he asked patiently, "how did you get on with her professionally?" he stressed the last word lightly. "Did you ever quarrel – ever disagree?"

Girot laughed, a mirthless sound that was at odds with his looks and the situation. "That question proves, Mr Rodgers, how little you know of artistes. Of course we quarrelled, over big things and over little things – it is all part of our life."

This was getting him nowhere, Rodgers thought. The man was hiding, either intentionally or by habit, behind a barrier of professional foibles and artistic eccentricities which could so easily cloud the true picture. He got up in a movement of dismissal. "Thank you, Mr Girot. If there is anything else that we want to know," he tried to keep the irony out of his voice, "we will let you know. One last point." Girot turned at the door. "Do you know if Miss Barnave was in the habit of taking drugs?"

The question caught Girot off balance. His light blue eyes came alive for a moment, then he said evenly, "No, Mr Rodgers, I do not know, nor have I any reason to suspect that she did." He left.

Rodgers looked at Phillips. "Well?"

"Difficult, sir. Being a foreign gentleman it hard to judge."

"What about you two?" Rodgers said to Pearson and Goodbody.

"The gentleman don't like you last question, sir. I right beside him and him screw up him hand and draw in him breath," Goodbody said tentatively.

"Good. Pearson?"

"It seem, sir, that him voice – it not so foreign as him like us to believe."

Phillips looked in pleased surprise at the young constable, and Rodgers said, "Good observation. I agree. His understanding of English is much better than he wants us to believe. I deliberately threw some difficult stuff at him – it didn't faze him one bit."

Next to be questioned were the two models, Tania and Lotus. They were questioned together as it seemed obvious that their mental make-up didn't extend beyond wearing clothes with distinction; certainly not to planning a crime, still less its execution. They could add nothing very much to that which Girot had said, but they were both in agreement that Solange had been more than just a model in the Girot establishment. They wouldn't or couldn't commit themselves that she had been Girot's mistress – Rodgers thought this most unlikely from his observations of Girot – but that she had been in Girot's confidence and wielded a certain amount of power they were certain. That both girls had disliked the *première mannequin* was obvious. They spoke bitterly of her tantrums and petty jealousies, especially apparent if any one of the other models was more favoured by the public.

"These tantrums that you speak of," Rodgers asked Tania. "Has this always been so since you have been with the House or is it a new thing?"

" M'sieur," her eyes opened wide, "it was not always so. Always the temperament – we all 'ave that – but for the last months, maybe for one year, she 'as been – 'ow do you say? Impossible! Always up in the air, or down on the ground, and so unreasonable – about every little thing."

"I see. Well, thank you, Miss – er – Tania." Rodgers stood up in polite dismissal. Tania flashed him a charming smile, then remembered the occasion and switched it off again.

Phillips looked up from his notebook. "The young lady dem," he began, heavily idiomatic. "Seems like dem all come out the same mould – not real, eh, Mr Rodgers, sir? Like puppet, nuh?"

Rodgers stretched to his full height, his arms above his head. He grinned down at Phillips. "For a country bwoy," he drawled, "you pack a solid philosophy. They may be puppets," his tone changed, "what we have to discover is who is the puppeteer and does he pull the strings for good or evil?"

"Sir?" Phillips looked blank then grinned. "Yes, I see what you mean, sir."

"Right, let's see the little Madame Yvette," Rodgers said more cheerfully.

"Your full name, madame?" he asked after she was seated.

"Yvette Louise Blancharde."

"You are married?"

"No. Madame is – 'ow do you say? A title of – *politesse* – courtesy?"

"I see." He regarded her with interest: her hair, metallic grey and moulded to her small head, gleamed in the soft light of the verandah. Her face was a smooth mask. She sat perfectly still and composed without the nervous fussiness that he had noticed previously. She was gowned – no other description was possible – in a dress of a dull black broken by metallic threads. The material clung to her small figure with a dramatic understatement that proclaimed the cut of the master.

She smiled. "You observe with care, m'sieur. It is very many years since a young man has looked upon me with such interest. Of course, I realise that your interest is of your profession, not the interest that so pleases a woman." Her voice was light but her eyes were hard.

He bowed slightly, "Forgive me, madame. What is your position with the House of Girot?" Getting the jargon, he thought.

"I am the *Directrice Technique* – that is to say – er – the manageress? – that does not have the grand sound in your language, no?" She didn't wait for an answer but went on rapidly, "I am in charge, m'sieur, of the day-to-day running of the House. I engage the models, subject to the approval of the *Directeur*, of course. I act as chaperone when there is a showing or when we go on tour. I supervise the fittings and arrange in what order the girls will proceed from the *cabine...*"

"Cabine?"

"Yes. The – dressing room you say, eh? In fact, m'sieur, I am the general plate washer and chef."

He smiled at her Gallic version of the well-worn phrase.

"I see. Now tell me, madame, about Solange Barnave. You have known her long?"

"*La pauvre petite*. Of course, she came to us four, maybe five years ago. Such a tragedy." Her expression of sympathy extended no further than the utterance of the words.

"You got on well with her?"

"She was – difficult at times. All the models are temperamental and 'ighly strung. Solange was no more than most."

This was not the impression he had received so far but he let it pass. "How did the young lady get on with the other girls?"

"Oh – so-so," she hesitated. Rodgers felt that she was keeping something back.

"Yes?" he prodded.

"It – is nothing, I think. Perhaps Solange did not get on so well with Anna. There were the frequent spat, you say? Only today..." she stopped.

"Yes? Today?" His voice was sharper. Her tone had taken on an evasive quality that made him wonder whether she was deliberately hiding something or deliberately trying to make him believe that there was something to hide. A spat with Anna? The one that he knew of or another one? Well, all right, he would get it from Anna. Aloud he said, "Madame, I do not think that you realise that this is a very serious matter. If there is anything that you know that may help us in our investigations, then it is your duty to tell me, even if it involves someone else."

He waited. She regarded him levelly. "Of course, m'sieur, if I knew anything of importance, I would tell you."

Stalemate again. Rodgers held her eyes for a moment then asked, "How long had Miss Barnave been taking drugs?"

There was no pause before she answered calmly, "About a year, I should think." The faintest spark of triumph showed in her eyes, as if she realised that he had not expected her to admit her knowledge.

He took an exasperated breath. "You tell me one moment that you act as the girls' chaperone and in the next that one of them took drugs with your knowledge. Did you do anything to stop her?"

She gave a slight shrug. "I said, m'sieur, that I am their chaperone in the – dressing room – and during our tours. I cannot overlook all their actions."

"Maybe if you had not overlooked this action, she would be alive now," he muttered.

"M'sieur?" She was puzzled.

"Never mind, just one of the vagaries of the English language. You say that you never tried to stop her?"

"I did not say that."

He asked with restrained patience, "Did you try to stop her?"

"Many times. She just laughed and said that I was old-fashioned – not with it, you say, no? She said that she took drugs just for the kicks – oh, she used all the arguments that the young employ when they are set on doing something. I did not approve but there was nothing I could do about it."

"Nothing? Could you not report the matter to Mr Girot?"

She gave him a strange look, "I did that too. It did no good." She seemed as if she was about to say more, but folded her lips and kept silent.

Rodgers leant forward. "So Mr Girot knew – and did nothing?

Yet only half an hour ago he denied that he knew anything about her taking drugs. Does he, in fact, take drugs?"

Her expression was stony as her eyes went blank. "That I do not know."

"But you do suspect that he does? Answer me, madame."

"There is no need to shout at me, m'sieur. I neither know nor suspect. And now, if you have finished, may I go?" She stood up. She was very small even with the high heels that she wore.

Rodgers got up and looked down at her. "Madame Yvette," he said slowly, "where did Solange procure the drugs that she took?"

"That also is something that I do not know. Goodnight, M'sieur Rodgers." She left them, head erect, heels tapping out in high staccato on the terrazzo tiles of the verandah.

Rodgers pulled out his pipe and tobacco pouch. "What do you think, Phillips?"

"Lord, Mr Rodgers, sir, she lie fe sure."

"Maybe – but all the way? Or was there truth as well? The devil is, we can't take any action for deeds committed in their own country. Goodbody – Pearson?"

"Mr Phillips right, sir. The lady lie," Goodbody said.

"She 'fraid too," Pearson added.

"Afraid? What makes you say that?"

"She get up sudden like. She don't like you ask 'bout the drug. She say you shout, an' you don't. She try to tek you mind off the question."

"Very perspicacious." Rodgers looked at his watch: nearly midnight and still Peter Horton and Anna Morgan to see. He hesitated then said, "Right, let's have in the elegant long-haired boy." He puffed thoughtfully at a freshly lit pipe while he waited for Peter Horton. He hadn't discovered anything so far, except that personalities were beginning to emerge, and when that happened much more was likely to follow.

He looked up as Peter Horton came out onto the verandah, followed by the stoical Phillips. He still had a haggard air about him, his frilled dress shirt was less crisp than it had been earlier in the evening. He had assumed an amused pose and asked as he approached the table, "Well, well, Inspector – oh, I do beg your pardon, *Superintendent* – is this to be a first or a second degree? One never hears of them, does one? Surely the lights are a little dim for such macabre activities? No strong light to blind the victim? Or does that switch on later?"

Rodgers tried not to show his feelings and said as mildly as he could, "Mr Horton, sit down, please. Your flippancy under the circumstances is a trifle misplaced. Does the death of a colleague mean so little?"

"But of course, dear man, I'm desolate." Horton spoke lightly with a complete absence of sincerity or any attempt at sounding convincing.

"Come, Mr Horton, I'm not here to play verbal games. A girl died tonight – it may very well be murder."

"But surely. Inspector – Superintendent – you don't suspect me? I was under your eagle eye the entire evening."

"Mr Horton, that is no criterion of innocence. If she was poisoned – as seems very likely – the fact of your not being physically capable of killing her during a given time has no saving grace. You may have planned for just such a happening."

"A happening? My, aren't you dated in these parts! But I grant you it was indeed a Happening." Horton looked steadily at Rodgers, then he dropped much of his preciousness although he still retained a relaxed mien. "Whether I planned it or not is something which you would have to prove – which would be an impossibility – because I did not kill her." The last words were spoken in a completely different tone, one of firm sincerity that carried conviction.

"We shall do all in our power to find the guilty party, Mr Horton. What were your feelings towards the young lady?"

"I loathed her. She was a conceited, vain little bitch. I've often felt like murdering her." He made the statement in a casual conversational tone that made even Phillips jerk his head up. If Rodgers felt any surprise at the words, he concealed it admirably and merely asked, "And did you?"

"Murder her? I've already told you that I didn't."

"Why not, if you felt so strongly about it?"

"Why not?" Horton gazed at Rodgers, his assumed mask wholly down. He laughed, "God, Rodgers, you're a man after my own heart. You've a sense of humour behind the snarling red tape." He laughed again. "Why didn't I kill Solange? For the simple reasons that she wore clothes to perfection and she photographed like a dream."

"Those two points," Rodgers remarked gravely, "do constitute a strong deterrent to murder." He got up. "As you say, you were under my eye during most of the relevant part of the evening. Just remember, please, not to leave the hotel compound until you're given the go-ahead."

He watched Peter Horton lounge elegantly away. That young man, he thought, is by no means what he seems. The outward effeminacy was, he now felt sure, just a pose. At times another personality showed through the facade.

He wondered why. Just for professional reasons? Rodgers remembered with annoyance that there were a number of questions that he had failed to ask owing, no doubt, to the initial flippant remarks made by Peter Horton.

Was that chance – or had that too been calculated? Rodgers had the feeling that he had been manipulated by a very clever operator.

FOURTEEN

Dr Montgomery washed his hands thoughtfully. The strong perfume which had drenched Solange still clung to them. Although her clothes had been removed and the scent had dispersed somewhere in the clinical surroundings of the morgue, there was still enough in the atmosphere to provide a most unclinical climate. I'll never get Joan to believe that I've been on a case, Montgomery thought. "Right, Davis," he told the morgue orderly. "She's all yours."

"Yes, sir. Goodnight, doctor."

The doctor hurried from the chill of the post mortem room to the warm softness of the tropical night. He strode along the wide verandah that ran the length of the hospital. Soft shaded lights glowed at intervals through the jalousied windows. The driveway encircled a smooth green lawn with oleander shrubs in bloom, their delicate blossoms clear in the moonlight. From a spreading poinciana tree that grew in the centre of the lawn, a chorus of tree frogs sent out their nightly entertainment. A dog barked in the distance and was answered by a rising crescendo from the strays that congregated in the nearby settlement each night to scavenge in the refuse heaps. Apart from these sounds, all was calm and peaceful, except for the occasional wail from a sick child and the responding muted voice of a nurse on duty. Dr Montgomery was inured to the fact of death, but even his calm professionalism was shaken by the coincidence of being called out on two successive evenings, each time to a case of murder. He shook his head in a puzzled manner; he didn't envy Rowan Rodgers. Two murders and both victims visitors to the island. He turned into an open doorway.

"Good evening, nurse. May I use your phone?"

"But of course, sir." A sleepy probationer engaged in sorting instruments jumped to her feet. She nervously indicated the telephone then scurried out.

Montgomery dialled, preoccupied as he listened to the ringing tone.

After a long interval, the receiver was lifted. "Santa Gloria Hotel. May I help you?"

"Dr Montgomery here. Would you ask Superintendent Rodgers to come to the phone? It's most important. I'll hold on." He waited, in unhurried thought, going over in his mind the events of the evening. "Rodgers? Montgomery here. I thought that you'd like to know my findings right away. This is, of course, subject to confirmation by the lab, but I am convinced that the young lady died as a result of an overdose of nitrobenzene – probably aniline." He heard Rodgers give an inward breath.

"But how was it administered?"

"In the perfume that her dress was drenched with – it was wet from waist to ankle."

"In the perfume?"

"Yes. I was suspicious of it from the beginning. By the way, if you got any on your hands when you carried her to the dressing room, better wash off thoroughly or you'll be noticing some symptoms yourself."

"Luckily I've already washed. I smelt like a perfume counter – my jacket still stinks to high heaven."

"I'll let you have the complete findings tomorrow. If the lab boys find methaemoglobin, that clinches my diagnosis."

Rodgers walked slowly away from the telephone booth. Nitrobenzene in perfume? This joker, if it was the same one who killed Soulis, certainly came up with a choice selection of murder weapons and methods. He went into the dressing room. As he entered, he felt that he was in suspended time: the harsh bright lights, emblem of the dressing room and show business, blazed down on the rails of dresses, gowns and bright beachwear. The dressing table top was a jumble of cosmetics, used tissues and odd wisps of cotton wool. A fine film of face powder lay over all. Bottles of perfume, nail varnish and hair spray, some with the tops left off, gave off an assortment of scents and odours, but predominant was the thick, cloying scent of the spilt perfume, so strong that it seemed to hang like a pall in the still air; it had an alien undertone that Rodgers could now identify as nitrobenzene. There was the almost empty bottle still lying on its side. It was a big bottle – he bent and looked at the label: *Illicite. Girot. Paris, Rome, New York. 450 grms.* 450 grammes, that was sixteen ounces. At the price of an ounce of perfume these days, it was worth a small fortune. He realised that it was the twin of the one that Girot had sent Rachel. The bottle had a screw cap, so that it must have been deliberately unscrewed; it hadn't come open by being knocked over. From his experience, women were fanatical about putting the stoppers back on perfume bottles, although he admitted in a set-up like this, where perfume could be had for the asking, perhaps carelessness crept in. He took out his handkerchief and, handling the bottle with extreme caution, he wrapped it up, after screwing on the cap. Then he returned to the verandah.

"Goodbody, take this at the double – but with great care, mind you – to the hospital and give it to Dr Montgomery. Tell him it's the container. He'll want it for analysis. And after that, knock off duty. You've done enough for one day – and done it very well, lad."

"Yes, sir. Thank you, sir." Goodbody beamed. How he had wanted to impress the great man from Kingston, to show him that he wasn't just a 'little country bwoy'. And now he'd been commended. He saluted smartly and went off in a flurry of self-importance. Rodgers grinned as he watched him go. Such zeal was commendable, he thought, and augured well for the lad, if only his dreams of glory didn't get in the way of the dull and dreary day-to-day routine. He remembered that he hadn't locked the door of the dressing room and went back to do so.

"Mr Rodgers –" a worried voice made him turn. The manager of the hotel was by his side. "I know that you're very busy, but can you give me any idea as to the position? You were good enough to conceal for a time last night's shocking event, but tonight – in full view of five hundred people…" He mopped his brow, which even in the comparative cool of the night was dripping with moisture.

Rodgers looked down at the rotund little man with sympathy. "I know that you must be worried, Mr Deleon, but as you say – in view of five hundred people. It'll be splashed across the headlines in the morning." He thought bitterly of the possible comments by the Assistant Commissioner for 'allowing' a murder to take place under his very nose... Not only would he be on the carpet but also West and Terrance. Whew! The press would have a field day.

"What am I going to do?" Deleon was almost wringing his hands.

"There's nothing that you can do." Rodgers gave a short laugh. "If it's any consolation, it doesn't seem to be a case of 'the natives rising'," he added ironically.

"But, Mr Rodgers, surely that's what the other guests will think? Imagine what this will do to our image abroad."

"Mr Deleon, all that I can say is, don't worry. If this drives a few people away, they'll come back – or others will take their place. There are always people who enjoy a murder, you know."

Rodgers gave the man a brief goodnight and went back to the verandah, thinking that the manager seemed much more concerned with his existing guests than with the fate of his two recently departed ones. He gave a grin at the thought which took him back to his schooldays and the recurrent theatrical offering of *The Dear Departed*. On the verandah, Anna Morgan was waiting to be questioned.

He sat down opposite her. She was pale and tired. The memory of her appearance earlier in the evening when Rachel had said that she looked ill gave him a sense of guilt at having left her until last to be questioned.

"I'm sorry to have kept you so long. These things take time."

"Of course I realise that." She leant forward. "Mr Rodgers – is it true that Solange was murdered?"

He nodded. "Everything points in that direction."

"But how?"

He hesitated. There were a few answers that he wanted before he revealed the information that Dr Montgomery had just given him.

"That is something that has to be determined," he said evasively. "Now, Miss Morgan, I understand from Madame Yvette that you had a difference of opinion earlier with Miss Barnave. Is that the same incident you told me about?"

"Yes – and thank you for getting my case back to me." She still didn't say anything about the attack made on her. She wasn't quite sure, even now, why she was reluctant to mention the incident.

A shadow loomed out of the garden and up the steps. "Do you mind if I join you?" Terrance's slim figure stepped into the circle of light.

"Not at all, John. I hadn't realised that you had left."

"Went to make a phone call when you were called to the phone."

"Sit down, we'll soon be through." Rodgers turned his attention back to Anna. "So, these flashes of temper were not uncommon with Solange?"

"It was uncommon these days if she was not in a rage. She would fly into a tantrum over the slightest inconvenience." She paused, conscious that she was speaking of one so recently dead. Rodgers sensed her thoughts.

"Don't feel guilty about saying what you really felt about her, Miss Morgan. That rather outdated 'not speaking ill of the dead' approach should not apply in an investigation of murder."

"I'm sorry. It's just – when you've known someone for a number of years, worked with them under often trying circumstances, laughed and fought with them, it's very difficult to accept that – suddenly – they're... they're gone. Why should anyone want to kill her?"

"You've just said that she was difficult to get on with."

"Yes, but one accepted that. She was Solange: the highest paid model in Paris. One accepted – and mostly forgave her idiosyncrasies."

"Well," said Rodgers dryly, "someone was driven beyond acceptance and forgiveness. So this afternoon you had a fight. What about tonight? Were you on good terms in the dressing room?"

For the first time she would not meet his eyes. Moments passed as she stared out at the garden.

"I asked you a question, Miss Morgan," he said eventually.

"Yes, I'm sorry. Tonight? I wasn't feeling very well. I had a bad headache so I was rather late in getting to the *cabine* – the dressing room. I didn't have anything to do with Solange until – until just before she went on – for the last time." Her eyes flared wide as she realised the significance of her words. Rodgers waited and Phillips looked up expectantly from his notebook. Constable Pearson drew in an audible breath and Terrance, elegant and suave in evening dress, was silently watchful.

There was an atmosphere of tense anticipation that was heightened by the surroundings: the shadowed gardens beyond the verandah railing, the soft sight of the warm night breeze through the feathered palm fronds, mingled with the surge of the surf on the coral reef that curved the smooth unruffled waters of the bay.

"Yes, Miss Morgan?" Rodgers' voice broke the silence. "What happened before Solange went on for the last time?"

"It was unfortunate – it couldn't be helped. The dresser had left the dressing room, I don't know why. Solange asked me to zip up her dress. She was turning and twisting and the bottle of perfume on the dresser top was knocked over. She was drenched from the waist down. It didn't show, the wetness on the dark dress, and she held her stole to cover it. You must have noticed that she was reeking when – you carried her back." She wet her lips at the expression on Rodgers' face. "Why, Mr Rodgers, it was an accident. I don't know who actually knocked over the bottle, but Solange was almost hysterically furious. She said that I would never again do anything like that to her. She sounded threatening." She looked helplessly from Rodgers to Phillips, stolidly silent over his notes.

"You may or may not be aware, Miss Morgan, but that action was probably the cause of Miss Barnave's death."

Phillips jerked his head and Terrance gave a slight intake of breath. Anna gazed at Rodgers in complete bewilderment. He went on, "That perfume – subject to laboratory tests – was heavily loaded with one of the nitrobenzenes. She was subjected to absorption over a large area of skin and, of course, through inhalation as a result of the fumes given off from her dress and body."

Anna rose quickly to her feet; her face paled and she swayed. "Surely you don't think that I..." She was unable to finish.

Rodgers got up and took her arm. "Sit down, please. I am not drawing any conclusions yet. I just want to present to you the known facts. It is the unknown facts that I want to uncover. The point is, was it intended to drench Solange with her perfume, as indeed did happen, or was it intended to be over a period of time, a slow absorption, which would eventually prove fatal?"

Anna swallowed and spoke with difficulty. "Mr Rodgers, I don't think that either of those assumptions can be correct – because, you see – that was not Solange's perfume. It was mine. I think that I was the intended victim."

FIFTEEN

"Do you realise just what you are saying?"

"Yes," Anna was calmer now. "That bottle of perfume was mine. I'm the only one in the group who wears *Illicite* and I noticed at the moment that the bottle fell that it was mine – I had spilt nail varnish on the label. The strange thing is, though, I didn't take it down to the *cabine*."

"Are you sure of that?"

"Quite sure."

"Do you remember when you last saw it?"

"It was on my vanity dresser this afternoon. I don't remember seeing it after..." She stopped.

"After?" Rodgers prompted.

"As I told you, I wasn't feeling well and I suppose that now I'll have to tell you why." She sounded incoherent but Rodgers felt a quick surge of satisfaction. He'd experienced this before on a case. Everybody lying or concealing facts which they knew to be important but the revelation of which would be embarrassing. Getting nowhere, time being wasted, then suddenly a witness or a suspect would decide to talk. That was always his cue for a surge of optimism as to the final outcome of the case, although weeks could pass before the final resolution.

He pulled out his pipe, gave Phillips a quick nod and asked, "Right, Miss Morgan, what have you got to tell us?"

She leant back in her chair, quite composed now. "I know that I should have told you long before – whether my silence had any bearing on what happened tonight..." She stopped and gave a little shrug. Then she recounted in detail the glimpse that she had had in the dressing room of a box of face powder before Solange snatched it away from her.

Terrance raised his eyebrows. "A box of face powder, Miss Morgan? Why should that be remarkable in a make-up box?"

She gave a start; she had forgotten his presence. "Because, Major Terrance, there was only a thin layer of powder on the top, covering a polythene partition."

"Whose make of powder was it?" Terrance's voice was controlled, almost bored.

"Why, Girot's, of course. We all use it."

"Why did you think that this particular box had a false bottom – and why did you think that it was important?"

"I don't know. I saw it by accident and thought it odd. Importance was added by the way Solange acted – out of all proportion of what was a natural mistake. When a box of powder was stolen from my own beauty-case, I became very curious."

"Why didn't you tell us about this before?" Rodgers asked.

"I don't know. It seemed so trivial."

"Why have you changed your mind?"

"Why?" She thought a moment then went on quickly, "I decided to do a little investigating of my own." She told them of her endeavour to examine the box again earlier in the evening and of how she had been attacked.

"You little fool." Rodgers exploded. "What do you think that we're here for?"

"I know," she was contrite. "But you were so busy over everything. I didn't think that it was important enough."

"Not even after you'd been knocked on the head? What more do you want?"

She was suddenly near to tears. "I'm sorry – but I felt so ill – and by then it was nearly showtime."

"How did you get back to your room? Have you any idea how long you were out?"

"Only a few minutes," she answered the last question first. "It was the little boy, the bellhop Carlisle, who found me. I'd been taken from the dressing room and dumped on the verandah. The poor boy thought that I was dead at first."

"That infant seems to have a singular talent for finding inert bodies. Then what?" he went on quickly before she could ask what he meant.

"Well, he fetched his uncle – no, his cousin – the barman, and they helped me upstairs. I told them that I'd slipped on the tiles and hurt my head."

"When you went back to the dressing room for the show, did you look for the powder box again?"

"Yes. I looked – while Solange was on stage – just when..." she gulped. "It had been changed. There was a perfectly ordinary box in its place." She looked near to exhaustion as she asked, "Mr Rodgers, I heard that Simon Soulis had died. Was his a natural death?"

Rodgers shook his head. "No, it was not. But I don't think that you are in any shape to worry about that now." He stood up. "There are still a number of questions that I should like to ask you but I can see that you've just about had it. I want you to go to your room and lock the door and the windows. Put on the air-conditioning. Could you possibly get one of the other girls to stay with you?"

"I could get Aunt Susan. You mean, you don't want me to be alone because someone might...?" Her eyes widened in sudden fear.

"Phillips, would you escort Miss Morgan to her room? Pearson, stay outside Miss Morgan's door until two AM Phillips – arrange for young Goodbody to relieve Pearson at two until he himself is relieved."

"Yes, sir."

Rodgers smiled at Anna. "It's for your protection, no other reason."

She nodded her thanks and said goodnight in a voice made small by tiredness. She seemed very slight beside the burly Phillips and the tall young constable.

"What do you think, John?" Rodgers asked after they had gone.

"I'm interested in those boxes of face powder. It would be as easy as hell to bring in powdered drugs in boxes with false bottoms. Whoever examines the powder in a lady's beauty-case?" John got up and stretched. "And for your information, my friend, Girot has two cartons of face powder in his room."

Rodgers got up. "Let's go and have a look. But stop – how do you know?"

Terrance grinned. "I paid an unofficial visit earlier this evening. But how do we make this official? We've nothing on Girot – yet?"

"If he's in his room, I'll think up something. If not, we take your former route."

Rachel Groome glanced again at her watch: nearly midnight. She'd been waiting in the hotel lobby for hours – or so it seemed. She decided that she would go up to her room, see how Bamboo was, then down to the bar and wait for Rowan. She thought again with unreasonable irritation that ever since she had arrived back in Jamaica, she had spent nearly all the time waiting for Rowan.

As she opened the bedroom door, a fretful whicker greeted her and a small cream bundle of fur hurled itself at her ankles. Rachel scooped the little cat to her shoulder where immediately the irate swearing turned to a deep contented purr.

"Poor darling." Rachel stroked the soft fur. "You do get left alone – you and me both. Never mind, we'll soon be home and you'll have lots of space, lizards to chase and all the love in the world."

She sat on the edge of the bed and waited while the kitten snuggled down again in the middle of the bed, then she got up and went to the door: Bamboo didn't stir. She closed the door quietly and went down the dimly lit corridor. It was very still and deserted. Abruptly she was possessed of a deep fear. She knew none of the details that surrounded Solange's collapse but the look on Rowan's face and the convergence of Richard West and Phillips, their grave expressions and subsequent actions, convinced her that the collapse was not due to natural causes. She looked quickly over her shoulder as a door closed softly – there was no one in sight. The fear grew – fear of what, she had no idea. It swamped her reason, made her legs numb so that she felt as if she were in a nightmare, running, running and getting nowhere. Her high heels clicked on the tiles with an unnatural clarity, the only sound in all the world. She tried to run, but her long dress impeded her so that she stumbled. Her breath came in sobbing gasps and the fear threatened to become panic. Thankfully she reached the wide welcome of the shallow staircase. She entered the crowded Pirate's Lair bar, still breathing quickly and with her heart pounding, yet with a feeling of shame at her exhibition of childish fear.

"Why, darling, you look as if you could use a drink," Diana called. She was seated on a high bar-stool and, as she spoke, she swept her evening bag off the stool beside her. "I was saving this seat for that gorgeous policeman – or should I say *your* gorgeous policeman?"

Rachel ignored the question and sat down in silence. Her shame at her recent panic was more pronounced in the warm intimacy of the bar. "A double whisky on the rocks," she ordered to Smith's query of "What'll it be, Mrs Groome?"

"Why, darling, you are knocking it back." Diana's tone was still mocking.

Rachel swivelled round and looked at her. She wasn't tight but she'd obviously been drinking steadily. "I'm sorry, Diana. I was a bit – upset – I'm all right now."

"Have cigarette. Have one of mine. I always believe in supporting my own."

Diana held out a packet, dark blue with silver embossment. "Barrington Specials – a legacy from my late husband. My late but not lamented husband."

"Oh," Rachel showed her surprise. "No, thank you – I'm trying to kick the habit. I'd no idea that Barrington Specials were you."

"But of course, the bastard left me a whole factory. I can smoke all day if I want to. These babies bring in a lot of bawbees – oh yes, a great many..." She stopped suddenly then asked in a completely different tone, "What's going on? Or hasn't your policeman told you yet?"

"For heaven's sake, Diana, don't keep calling him 'my' policeman. I don't know any more than you do."

"Well, the grapevine has it that the girl's dead – and not by natural causes."

It was no surprise to Rachel. She had suspected as much at the start – but how? And more important, who and why? She pushed the unanswerable questions to one side as Diana went on. "Two deaths by violence in twenty-four hours – we haven't had so much excitement on the island since 1980 and the Cuban scare."

Rachel sipped her drink and glanced round the bar which had a heavy smoky atmosphere despite the fact that one side was open to the dispelling breeze that came from the north. Although it was so late the bar was still crowded. Girot sat at a table for four with Madame Yvette and Peter Horton. They were talking volubly, half in French and half in English, in that high-pitched state of excitement that so often follows a tragedy. Anna Morgan was nowhere to be seen. In possession of the patio bar was a group of prominent businessmen accompanied by their wives – presumably, Rachel thought, but she had been out of touch with island gossip and scandal for so long that it was difficult to keep up with the rapid change and interchange of marital partners – and there was a constant trek from them to Girot's table to dispense both condoling and congratulatory remarks. Rachel felt sorry for the little man but realised that even an event like this and the abrupt termination of the showing could do nothing to shake his world-famous prestige.

The door from the foyer opened and Susan Taylor entered. She glanced round casually, then her eyes rivetted on Girot. For a moment she seemed undecided, then moved to the bar and spoke to the barman. Rachel looked across at Girot's table. Yvette had her hand on his arm and was murmuring in low rapid tones. He swung round and looked at Susan Taylor, frowned and slowly nodded his head. He rose deliberately and crossed to the bar. Rachel heard him ask, "Excuse me, madame, but surely we 'ave met before?"

Susan turned, an unfathomable expression in her eyes, but she said easily, "I'm flattered that you should remember me, Mr Girot. I'm Susan Taylor – Anna Morgan's aunt. We met in Paris, briefly, about two years ago."

"Of course," he bowed. "You visited your niece before the

Spring Showing. But I understood that you were going to the States?" He waited but she made no reply. There was a quiet menace in his bearing as he asked, "You – still follow your profession, madame?"

Rachel waited for Susan's reply. Since Girot's accusation the previous evening, she had had a growing conviction that the arm of coincidence was being stretched too far. She was surprised and relieved when Susan answered calmly, "I went to the States for a few months but I'm happier at home. And yes, I am still a dressmaker."

Girot gave his usual involuntary wince at the description. His voice hardened as he asked, "Do you, just by chance, madame, happen to be – dressmaker – to Madame Groome?"

Susan regarded him levelly, turned her gaze on Rachel for a long moment, then said evenly, "Why, yes, Mr Girot – and just by chance – Mrs Groome is wearing one of my most successful creations."

Rachel dropped her eyes to her empty glass as Girot turned and looked at her. There was a long pause before she heard him say. "Certainly one of your most successful creations. I remarked on it only last night to Madame Groome. Perhaps, *mademoiselle*, we could have a little talk about clothes in general – and one dress in particular?"

Susan's voice was still calm and unruffled as she replied, "I'd be delighted at some other time. If you will excuse me now, I have to get back to Anna. She is not very well."

Girot stiffened. "Not well? What is the matter with her?"

Susan took the two glasses that the barman handed her and asked, "You do not know? Then may I suggest that you ask the police?" She walked away, leaving Girot motionless, a look on his pudgy face that Rachel was unable to define.

"And what," Diana Barrington's voice held only a cursory interest, "was that all about?"

"I'm – not quite sure." Rachel tried to catch the barman's eye but he was carrying on a graphic discussion with one of the waiters. In one of those utter silences that sometimes fall on a crowded room, she heard Smith pronounce clearly, "I tell you, man, the young lady done murder. Not the first. What 'bout the other gentleman las' night?" There was a ripple through the room, then silence settled again.

"Me hear nothin' 'bout that. Who tell you, man?"

"Young Carlisle. Him not only fin' the body, but him see who do it."

Rachel sat up straight. Surely this was hearsay and imagination? Rowan would never – she leant across the bar as Smith continued, "An' not only that man, what 'bout the other young lady? She say she fall but Carlisle say that him did see..."

"Bartender. Mr Smith." Rachel's clear, incisive voice cut through the barman's gossip and simultaneously the babble of conversation welled up again. Smith broke off sharply at Rachel's imperative call. He looked aggrieved. He'd thought that this lady was different from the usual autocratic jet-set. "Yes, ma'am?" He sounded sullen, but his expression changed as Rachel admonished him gently. "Smith, I'm sure that Superintendent Rodgers or Superintendent West cautioned you not to speak about recent events. It could do damage, you know."

Smith's dark round face took on an aspect of guilty aggression. "I don' see how, ma'am. Everyone know now..."

"Everyone knows now, yes, Smith, thanks to you," Richard West said curtly. He stood behind Rachel and smiled down at her. "You did quite right, Mrs Groome."

"You heard? I didn't see you."

"I come in from the other bar. Let's hope that no one else babbles." He looked at Diana. She gave him her wide, embracing smile. Her voice was huskier that usual as she said, "Why don't you join us, Mr West?"

"Thank you, I will." He slid onto the stool on the other side of her. "What are you drinking? Whisky on the rocks?"

"Please. How clever of you to remember."

"Mrs Groome?"

Rachel hesitated. "I don't think that I'll have anything else. I was waiting..." She broke off as Rodgers, closely followed by Terrance, entered the bar. They both had an air of quiet frustration. Rodgers crossed directly to Rachel.

"Sorry to keep you, but things are a little hectic and complex right now." He seemed about to say more but stopped as he saw that Diana was one of the group. His eyes narrowed as he saw her bright head beyond Rachel's dark sleek one. She raised her glass to him then drained it.

"Aren't you flattered, Mr Rodgers, two ladies waiting for you? I'm sure that you would like to repay our devotion by joining us in a drink?"

He held her gaze for a moment then said, "There is – almost – nothing I would like more, Mrs Barrington, but there are one or two points that I have to clarify." He turned to Rachel. "Shall we go outside where it's quieter?"

He took Rachel's arm as Diana said huskily, "What a pity, Mr Rodgers. I was hoping that afterwards you could have conveyed me home and we could have had that swim."

Rowan swung back to her. Rachel felt his fingers dig into her arm. "A tempting invitation – but not tonight. Perhaps," he went on with advised insult, "Major Terrance or Mr West would kindly volunteer, if you are nervous about driving alone late at night."

Diana's smile didn't falter but there was a flash in her eyes that made Terrance give a mental whistle. As Rowan and Rachel moved away, Richard West spoke quickly, "Let me follow you home, Mrs Barrington. Or you can leave your car here and have it collected in the morning."

The smile left her face and her eyes lost any vestige of softness as she snapped, "You have just witnessed the grand brush-off. Thank you, Mr West. As your colleague saw so clearly, it takes more than the violence that we've had in the last day or so to make me scared of driving home alone. I'd love one last drink and then you must get to your bed."

West opened his mouth to protest but said nothing as he watched her take out a cigarette with a slightly shaking hand. "Have one of these, Richard. My special home-grown variety."

He took one from the dark blue and silver box. "I didn't know that you could buy these on the local market?"

He didn't look at her but examined the crest on the cigarette with intent scrutiny. As he raised his eyes, she exhaled a cloud of smoke and flipped her lighter for him.

"You can't buy them on the local market – I export only, but I have a constant personal supply." He took her hand to steady the light that she held for him and felt again the emanation of her erotic personality. He knew that he was a fool to be taken in by her blatant charm but he was powerless to resist. He ordered drinks and barely noted that John Terrance had drifted away and that at last the bar was beginning to empty.

SIXTEEN

Rowan and Rachel settled down at a small table on the edge of the patio. Rachel noted that Rowan positioned himself so that he could observe the inner bar.

"You were very rude to Diana. Whatever came over you?"

"I don't like women who fling themselves at me. I suppose I wasn't very gallant, but can't you see that she's trying to make trouble between us?"

Rachel wanted to say that, as far as she could make out, he must have encouraged Diana by his earlier actions – which she could only guess at. She touched his arm and said without much conviction, "Rowan, if you want to take Diana home it's all right."

He put his hand over hers. "Sweetheart – I know and you know that it's not all right. I have no intention of taking her home." He smiled at her and murmured softly, "At this moment I would like to kiss you until you faint. Instead I'll have to settle for this." He gave a quick look round then leant across and kissed her. Brief though it was, it left them both shaken. "Woman, what you do to me," he murmured. He took out his pipe and pouch of tobacco, and said more briskly, "Don't look at me like that. It's much too distracting and I want to tell you what I've learnt tonight and have your reactions. If I remember rightly, you've come up with some useful deductions and ideas in the past."

He beckoned a waiter and ordered drinks, then over his smouldering pipe, the blue haze wafting between them, he recounted the information that he had gathered during the course of the evening.

As Rachel listened, she gazed out at the moonlit garden. It was very quiet now with only the insistent chorus of tree frogs and crickets, and occasional harsh, discordant note from a croaking lizard, and the accompaniment of the sea surging against the rocks on the shore.

"Rowan," she said at last, "it all seems so inconsistent. Two people have died, connected professionally, I know. But are their deaths connected? A murderer usually sticks to one method of killing."

"Usually they do, I admit. But you sometimes have your versatile types who will use the best method to fit the circumstances. Whether the two deaths are connected remains to be seen; my hunch is that they are. We ask whether Anna's experience with the vanishing powder box in Solange's beauty-case and the disappearance of a similar powder box from her own case has any significance or whether by some extraordinary quirk the two events are also coincidence. Well, that remains to be seen."

"The fact that Solange was killed in mistake for Anna doesn't really alter anything, does it?" Rachel asked.

"Not really. And yet it might." He narrowed his eyes and thought for a moment, then he reminded her about John Terrance's unofficial visit to Girot's room and the presence of the two cartons of face powder. "And yet," he ended, "when we both went back half an hour ago, there was only one carton."

Her eyes widened. "I wonder if that has any significance. These big fashion houses have their own range of cosmetics and perfumes. The missing carton could have been brought for sale – or even a special order for one person. Was that why John was asking about white face powder?"

He nodded. "And that's the one that's missing."

"I shouldn't have thought that either a sale or a delivery would have been made between the time that John saw the carton there and when you both saw that it wasn't."

"No," he agreed. "Especially under the circumstances. We'll have to follow it up tomorrow. The whole set-up has a tenuous quality that I don't like."

"Well, really, if you call two unexplained deaths in twenty-four hours 'tenuous', what do you call concrete?" Rachel leant forward. "If that attack on Anna earlier was an attempt to kill her and the poisoned perfume was really meant for her, surely she's in danger?

Should she be left alone?"

"Sweetheart, I'm not as obtuse as that. She's not alone. Her aunt is with her and outside her door is an eager-beaver young constable standing guard."

"I see. This poison – you say that it was one of the nitrobenzenes?" Rachel asked.

"Subject to lab confirmation, yes."

"You realise, of course, that nitrobenzene is used in cleaning clothes?"

He smiled at her teasingly. "That, too, hadn't escaped my notice, or the equally deducible fact that nitrobenzene is available to every member of the hotel staff – they have a dry cleaning department – as well as being available to every member of the Girot circus. Which means," he went on wearily, "an awful lot more questioning. The estimable Phillips and his cohort, young Pearson, can take on that little chore."

Rachel was very tired. She'd drunk too much too quickly and she was not as alert as she was normally. There was an insistence at the back of her mind that something had happened – or that something had been said – that Rowan ought to know about. Was it something she'd seen? Or something she'd heard? Surely she could remember. She had a strong conviction that it was vitally important. "Rowan," she began, then realised that his attention was elsewhere. She turned in her chair and saw that the Pirate's Lair was now practically deserted. Diana Barrington had slid off her stool and was saying in a voice that carried clearly, "No, Richard. No, I shall be quite all right. Goodnight and thank you." Her walk as she left the bar had a seductive quality, one that Rachel could appreciate and resent. Rachel turned back to Rowan. He was watching Diana with a calculating expression that was alien and disturbing. She got to her feet. "I think that I'll go to bed, I'm very tired."

He nodded and got up without a word. He piloted her, his hand lightly under her elbow, quickly through the bar and across the now empty foyer to the stairs that led to her room. John Terrance joined them, appearing apparently from nowhere.

"Calling it a day?"

Rodgers said with relief, "John, be a good chap and see Rachel to her room. Goodnight, Rachel. I'll call you."

Before she could reply, he had gone with long loping strides out of the main entrance. She heard a deep-throated roar as the pale yellow Quattro with Diana at the wheel, her red-gold hair shining in the moonlight, flashed past the colonnaded porte-cochere.

Rachel stood where Rowan had left her, a bitter unbelief welling up. Then she heard the answering roar of Rowan's dark grey Mercedes as it too passed the entrance. As the silence of the night returned, Rachel looked at John. "Well," she said in a light choked voice, "what do you make of that?"

"Probably not what you make of it," his voice was almost caressing. "Don't look so tragic. I'm sure Rowan has a good explanation. I've been commissioned to escort you to your room. Are you going to ask me in for that drink that you refused to offer me before?"

Her bitterness turned to reckless anger. "I might do just that," she said.

Rodgers drove at a careful distance behind the Quattro. Diana drove with a dash and brilliance – a careless brilliance – that complemented her looks and personality. Rodgers kept his mind firmly on the matter in hand. He didn't want to anticipate the hurt in Rachel's eyes that he knew he would see when next they met. He understood what she must be imagining – probably believing – at this moment. He couldn't blame her but it was better this way. She was a good actress, that he knew only too well, but it would be more convincing in this case to experience real emotions and to react accordingly. He only hoped that the reaction wouldn't be something that he couldn't handle.

He switched off his lights as he closed the gap between the two cars, then drove past the entrance to the Ripple driveway as Diana swung the Quattro in a squeal of protesting tires off the highway and up the long steep curves to the house. He drove on for half a mile.

The road wasn't wide enough to make a full U-turn and he reversed in whisper quietness, then completed the turn and drove back a short distance before pulling onto the soft shoulder and into the shadow of a clump of bamboos.

The soft tropic night was alive with sound, the whirr of assorted insects, the occasional crow of a clock-happy cockerel and a cacophony of yapping dogs from a nearby village. Far below him, the sea beat rhythmically on the white sands of the cove.

He hoped that Diana had been unaware that she had been followed. He didn't think that she could have heard him turn the Mercedes, as the sound of her own engine revving in low gear up the steep driveway would have drowned any other sound. He lit a cigarette and waited. The moon was almost full, low in the sky to the west. Its brilliance cast a radiance across the sea and sharp black shadows of the bamboos across the white dusty road. He peered at his watch: nearly one-thirty. He would give Diana until two AM before he made his move. He glanced up at the rocky hillside with its tangle of vegetation. He could see the lights at the top of the hill: someone was still awake at Ripple.

Fifteen minutes went by.

He filled and lit his pipe and settled deeper into the bucket seat.

The sharp splutter of an inboard motor brought him upright and out of the car in one swift movement. The sound of the engine was far below him and going eastwards. He moved silently through the shadows until he came to the white steps that led down to the beach. He swore at the decision that he had made to park so far up the road for as he reached the steps the sound of the rapidly moving launch receded into the distance. He raced down the steps, automatically noting that the gate hung open, onto the smooth sand of the cove. The launch had gone. There were no lights to be seen out at sea and the sound of the engine was now barely audible.

Had Diana taken the launch?

If so, why?

There was only one way to find out. Like a black shadow, Rodgers climbed back up the steps, crossed the road and began to make his way with caution and the utmost speed up the driveway.

The great house, with its lower floor of Spanish wall, its elegant, curving double stairway that began at the stone carriage blocks and ended at the entrance to the upper floor, was a featureless black mass as the moon sank towards the sea.

He stood quietly in the shade of an overhanging creeper that spilled fragrant clusters of pale flowers from the verandah above. There were dogs – that much he knew. He would have to get upstairs without alerting them. He kept to the grass strip that bordered the driveway then stole softly to the foot of the stairway. The treads were of stone so there was no fear of giveaway creaks. He reached the landing at the top, conscious that he was in silhouette to any watcher from the side. His fingers explored the high heavy double doors and he gave a sigh of relief as they swung open soundlessly to his touch. So Diana Barrington, with all her sophistication, still kept to the old trusting country ways. She was asking for trouble in these days of mounting crime when most people grilled and barred their houses – even in the country parts.

He slipped into the square entrance hall. The high tray ceiling was a white blur above him, the rest was in shadowed gloom. He wondered if he dare risk a light and if the servants slept in or did they, as in all old houses, have their quarters separate from the main house? He'd have to chance it.

Which way?

West had said that he went through a door by the stairs; that must be the inner stairway leading to the lower floor. He could just make out a deeper darkness in the centre of the hall – that must be the stairway. He moved silently through the hall and followed a passage to a side verandah. This must be it: he threaded an unaccustomed way through the cane furniture to a pair of open French doors. He inched round them and peered into the room. It was in darkness. There was no sound at all. He entered cautiously and as his eyes grew used to the gloom he made out a huge four-poster, with pineapple carvings and soft white hangings. He went over to the bed. It was quite empty, not even rumpled, white sheet turned sedately down awaiting its occupant.

So – it could have been Diana in the launch.

Why?

Why return home by road only to leave immediately, retracing by sea the route travelled by land?

He was about to turn from the bed when something hard and cold was pressed into his back. He stiffened and slowly raised his hands.

"I'd like to shoot you right now, you damned to hell sneak thief."

It was Diana's voice, low and cutting yet with an underlying fear. Without turning he said, "Well, here's a nice way to treat an invited guest."

"Rowan!" She dropped her arm and the gun clattered to the floor. He spun round, she was very close. "I was, believe it or not, frightened."

He took her by the shoulders and realised that she was clad only in a wrap of white lace. Her hair was damp and she smelled deliciously of bath essence.

"Where have you been?" As he asked the question he knew the answer.

"Having a shower. I didn't really – expect you. Not after the way you humiliated me in front of everybody."

"I'm sorry about that but you brought it upon yourself with your sly intimations. You must learn to shut and lock your house. Do you realise that anybody, friend or foe, can just walk in? That front door was unlatched, the French doors wide open. Don't you read the papers about the rise in crime or hear of the atrocities that have become a commonplace?"

She shrugged. "I don't like to be caged." She was still very close. His hands slid from her shoulders to her waist.

"Did you know that someone took your launch – about half an hour ago?"

She put her arms round his neck and involuntarily his hold tightened round her. He could feel the warm, firm flesh through the lace.

"Do we have to worry about that?" she murmured.

"Unfortunately – yes." He released her reluctantly.

Surprisingly, she laughed. "Either my charms are rapidly fading or you have built-in resistance. Or is it –" the mocking note was back – " a stern devotion to duty at all hours? Or perhaps – Rachel?"

"Your charms are as potent as ever – and we'll leave Rachel out of it." He pulled her close and kissed her. "Now go and get some clothes on and we'll see if we can discover who has taken your boat."

She went into the adjoining dressing room.

Rodgers padded to the big mahogany vanity: it was a beautifully preserved piece of furniture, its polished surface almost black with age. A battery of bottles, boxes and jars greeted his gaze. He picked up a square box with the distinctive Girot logo: he opened it and saw it was half full of powder. He poked a finger in and felt the bottom of the box, replaced the lid and wiped his finger on a tissue.

"Interested in cosmetics, Superintendent?" Diana asked behind him. He turned and surveyed her appreciatively. She wore close-fitting black pants and a black shirt.

"Isn't this appropriate for sleuthing at night? Much more than that." She flipped a finger at his white shirt front, then said sharply, "You didn't answer my question?"

"I'm interested in most things that concern you," he said easily. "Do you always use Girot's cosmetics?"

She glanced indifferently at the littered vanity top. "Mostly. I like some of his things."

"Are they on sale in the island?"

"Are you serious? With the foreign exchange bind as it is? I bring a supply back when I travel. Girot was supposed to have brought some – I hope that he has."

Rodgers studied her in the half light that spilled out from the dressing room. Her brown eyes were warm with a candid innocence that convinced him that she was concealing something more than smuggling a personal supply of cosmetics duty-free through customs.

"Right, let's go."

He followed her through the open French doors. Instead of turning to the left and retracing the steps that he had taken, she went to the right and down a wrought-iron flight of steps to the verandah below. She crossed the verandah and opened a gate in the railings. A flight of cut-stone steps, similar to the flight that led down to the cove from the main road, went straight down through the lush, studied informality of the hillside garden. Rodgers' eyes narrowed: another route to the house other than that by the driveway. He glanced at the luminous dial of his watch and again when they reached the road and saw that the steps cut the time needed to reach the house by nearly ten minutes, which, even allowing for the difference in time for going uphill, was a formidable saving.

The gate at the top of the beach steps was closed but not padlocked. Who had closed it after he had used it, he wondered. They went soft-footed down to the cove...

He was not surprised to find the launch safely moored in the softly lapping shallows.

SEVENTEEN

At about the same time that Rowan and Rachel were discussing the latest developments over a drink on the patio, a phone call was being made from a public call booth in a secluded corner of the Santa Gloria.

The insistent ringing was loud in the close, night-stuffy atmosphere of a little shop that served the needs of a settlement further east along the coast. The proprietor, grumbling audibly, his dark face creased with sleep, answered reluctantly.

"Yes? Jim Chin Yu speakin'. Wha' you wan?" He listened, annoyance increasing. "You no know, man, is de middle of de night? Who I goin' sen' fe it? All right, man, you don' ha' fe shout eena me ear." He slammed the receiver back in its cradle. "Cho, who 'im t'ink 'im is? H' ignorant."

Chin Yu shuffled back through the dark shop with its mixture of pungent smells: saltfish; pimento; coffee; garlic; the sickly sweetness of soft brown sugar in crocus bags: and the overpowering kerosene oil and strong white rum, intermingled with the acridity of wood smoke. Startling predatory cockroaches, he disappeared into one of the recesses behind the jumbled counters where he slept with his common-law wife, ancient mother and an assortment of offspring. He pulled on a pair of stained trousers and thrust his feet into broken, once-white sneakers. Then he made his way, not too silently and muttering audibly, out of the shop and into the moonlit night. He shuffled along the highway for a few yards, passed the postal agency and one or two tawdry, brightly-painted houses, then he turned off and began to climb a well-worn track up the rocky hillside – well-worn but still rough to the feet with sharp stones breaking through the red, bauxite-laden earth. The track led sharply uphill by devious ways through a tangled underbrush of trees, ferns and tall waving grasses. He passed one or two shack-like dwellings which clung precariously to the hillside: dwellings of a type becoming obsolete, except in remote country parts, of wattle and daub with palm-thatched roofs. He finally stopped, short of breath and even shorter of temper, at the door of a shack that had even less pretentions to modernity than the others. The door hung drunkenly in an opening that was too large for it, the wood rotted with age and termites. Chin Yu knocked loudly with knuckles grown thick with long years of manual labour. It was not until his prolonged third summons that the door was opened.

A blowsy, half-drunken woman peered out. Her hair was a mass of little sticking-up braids. Her dark skin was blotchy, the features blurred and coarse. She tried to focus her eyes – small, dark and red-veined – on her caller, with very little success. When after many attempts she became articulate, her voice was slurred and reached him on breath that was foul and heavy with the fumes of cheap rum. "Wha' you wan', man? Wakin' decent folk from they bed?"

He looked at her in disgust as she leant against the rotting lintel, her sagging breasts obscenely visible from a tattered, ill-fitting cotton dress. A powerful gust of sweat, both fresh and stale, wafted to his nostrils.

"Carlisle 'ere?" He spoke abruptly, even in his own indelicacy resenting her further degradation.

"Sure. Wha' you wan' wit' 'im, man?"

"I get a message, from one Superintendent Rodgers; me 'ear tell of him, 'im one big man from Kingston, an' 'im say he wan' Carlisle back at the 'otel, right now."

"Lord, man, me poor pickney, 'im tired fe true. It cyaan' wait till mornin'?"

"No, missi, 'im say to meet up wit' im same place on de beach. 'Im say Carlisle know de place, by de rock dem. 'Im say it h'urgent."

"What a way it go. Car-lis-le!" She raised her voice, stressing the second and third syllables on a rising note.

Jim Chin Yu nodded and shuffled off again into the night, thankful to be out of the woman's way. He'd heard of the steady drinking that she did – in fact he supplied her excessive wants from his shop – of how she took all young Carlisle's wages and tips for rum, but this was the closest that he'd come to her. Poor little bwoy, he thought with a sudden surprising compassion. Him work hard an' deserve somet'ing better.

Inside the one-room shack, Medorah Wells called again to her sleeping son. "Carlisle, wake up nuh, bwoy."

Carlisle stirred uneasily on his hard bed, returning unwillingly to wakefulness. He opened his eyes and sleepily focused on his mother's face. "Is time, Mumma?"

"Still night, me chile, sun nuh come up, but Mas' Jim bring message from one police – wha' 'im name? Is Rodgers, me t'ink."

"Superintendent Rodgers? 'Im one big man, mumma." Carlisle sat up, wide awake now. "What the message, Mumma?"

She thought, searching the recesses of her drink-fuddled brain. " 'Im say fe go a de same place on de beach – by the rock dem." She bent and gripped his shoulder so that he winced in sudden pain. "Wh' appen, bwoy? Why you mus' meet up wit' de police? Y'in trouble me tek stick to yuh, sure as yuh barn."

He wriggled free and swung his legs to the floor and began to dress quickly.

"Cho, Mumma, is nothing like that. Is help I help de police."

His mother eyed him suspiciously but her mind, not over-intelligent at its best, was now incapable of any reasoned thought, so she let her unkempt body sink slowly onto Carlisle's vacated bed. "Min' nuh, bwoy," she managed a feeble admonishment as Carlisle prepared to leave. "If is trouble fe yuh, me tek stick." She was back in sodden slumber as Carlisle called, "I gone, Mumma, soon come."

He ran lightly down the rough track, so lately laboriously climbed by Jim Chin Yu, glad to be out of the oppressive atmosphere of the one place that he could call home.

Though still warm after the heat of the day, the night was yet cool enough for comfort. He reached the main road without breaking out into the state of perspiring disarray that normally accompanied hasty physical exertion. He looked up at the dark blue sky with stars that glittered and winked like living points of light. Like, he thought, the diamonds that some of the guests at the hotel wore. As he trotted along the deserted highway he thought about his new life at the Santa Gloria and the contrast with his sordid home life. It was a new world, one that he hadn't realised existed. He'd been a bright, intelligent boy at his primary school, he had passed the Common Entrance Examination with ease and was placed in one of the well-known secondary schools, but his mother had said 'no', he had to work, she had no one else to support her. Carlisle felt no resentment against his mother for her decision and he was determined to make good at his job and go up in the world. His ambition had now crystallised and he had decided to be a policeman. He'd developed a hero worship for Rowan Rodgers and Richard West in the last two days and had taken them as his exemplars. He knew that he was too young at fourteen to start police training but he could watch Rodgers and West at work, couldn't he? He could watch Constable Goodbody at the helm of the launch returning with the divers. He could even watch Goodbody on traffic duty in the small main street of the little nearby country town on market day.

He switched his thoughts to the pretty young lady who had fallen and hit her head. He wondered about that as he hurried along the winding highway that bounded the coastline, high honeycomb rocks rising sheer to his left and dropping steeply to the shore on his right. Had she really slipped on the terrazzo tiles – or had she in fact been attacked? His fertile imagination, starved for so long of romance and adventure, heightened now by the artificial sophisticated glamour in which he spent his working hours, took hold and elaborated the possibilities.

He was nearing the hotel now and he decided to take a short cut down the hillside then cross to the meeting place by the white sands which shone in the light of the low-hung moon.

He hadn't stopped to consider or query why Rodgers had summoned him in the middle of the night. His hero had called – that was enough. He wondered once if his disobedience of West's injunctions in recounting to his cousin his gruesome find on the beach was going to bring a rebuke, but decided that that couldn't be termed urgent. Then he remembered that it was Rodgers and not West who had summoned him. That was odd, he thought, he'd never even spoken to Rodgers; but he still went on trustingly. He scrambled the last few feet down the hill and landed silently on the beach. He was conscious of the sound of a motor boat moving at a fair pace towards the shore. Apart from that there was no other sound but the soft susurration of the gently breaking wavelets.

Suddenly he felt very small and alone in the night. He glanced up and back at the dark pile that was the Santa Gloria. There were few lights showing and it presented a brooding sinister aspect quite alien to the cheerfulness of its face in the bright light of day. He shivered despite the enveloping warmth and hurried on to the meeting place. He hoped that the superintendent was ahead of him. He didn't want to wait alone at that place that held such recent memories of death by violence.

He reached the outjut of rock. It cast a frightening pool of black shadow on the bright moonlit sands. There was no one there – just the unknown pilot of the approaching boat, the engine of which took on a new low note as it neared the shallows.

Carlisle ran down the beach to meet the boat then stopped with the awful certainty of what was about to happen. He didn't have time to cry out. He stood frozen into immobility – waiting – as the steel whistled through the air. There was a moment of fierce spreading unimaginable pain – then nothing. His thin little body was dragged a few yards along the soft sand, dabbling its whiteness with quickly gushing blood, then a knife cut the nylon thread that linked the clawed spearhead to the spear-gun.

The beach took back the silence after the boat had made a tight U-turn and the throb of the motor had receded into the night.

Rachel woke suddenly from a deep sleep with the remembrance of what she had wanted to tell Rowan. The knowledge that she had kept the information to herself was like a physical weight. She peered at her watch then sprang out of bed. Five-fifteen AM . Surely, even if her vague fears had any foundation, there could be no danger at this early hour.

As she stood irresolute as to whether to ring Rowan's room – always providing, she thought with an upsurge of jealousy, that he was in his room – she noticed that Bamboo was missing. She glanced at the French doors that stood half open. Oh, what a fool not to have shut them. She searched the room, calling urgently, "Bam – Bamboo – come, sweetheart."

She went onto the balcony. The Siamese kitten could easily have jumped down into the garden. She went back into her room, hastily pulled on slacks and a shirt, and went out again to the corridor: there was a flight of steps at one end that led down to the gardens that ran down to the beach. The feathered palms were black silhouettes against a purple pre-dawn sky as she went slowly, calling softly and hoping for a glimpse of cream fur against the green of clustering ferns. There was no answer to her calls and she scrambled down the steeper pathway that led through overhanging bougainvillea to the beach below. The sky was lightening rapidly now. She was right down on the beach and she let her voice ring out clearly. "Bam – Ba'am – Bambooo. Come, sweetie."

An answering wail came from her right. On the dark grey of a large outjut of honeycomb rock, Rachel saw with relief a small shivering bundle, ears laid back, blue eyes blazing anger, swearing in gutter Siamese. Rachel ran lightly up the uneven rock face and scooped up the quivering little body.

"You little feline nerd. That'll teach you to make unauthorised sorties. Poor baby. It's all right, you can stop swearing now." Bamboo wrapped her darkening paws round Rachel's wrist, her claws needling, then sank her baby teeth into the flesh. "Ouch, little beast. Stop that."

Rachel remembered how Li Po used to do exactly the same thing and she hugged the little cat in renewed thankfulness at having found her. As she turned back she glanced down at the beach.

"Oh, no, NO!"

Her eyes widened in involuntary horror. She was completely immobile for a moment, then she was stumbling, tripping over the depressions and uneven surface of the pitted rock face, down to the white sands that shone so purely in the light of the new-risen sun. The sun shone too, on a prone, still figure on the churned up, darkened track of sand that almost touched the lapping sea.

Rachel knelt down beside the still body of Carlisle Linton. The sight sickened her and her eyes filled with tears. "Poor little boy," she said aloud, with more tenderness and compassion than he had ever heard expressed in life. She looked in revulsion at the wicked looking spearhead that protruded from his chest and the wide open eyes that had glazed but still retained their last expression of fear.

She didn't touch him but got unsteadily to her feet. A shadow passed over her and she looked up – two john crows were circling, their great wings stationary as they drifted on the air currents. The sight spurred her to action. Half running, half stumbling she got back to the hotel. She was sobbing with a mixture of fear, pity for the dead child and remorse. Remorse at not telling Rowan what she had heard and what she had feared. She ran along the corridor to Rowan's room, still clasping the protesting and wriggling body of Bamboo.

Oh God, she thought, let him be there. If he's not – oh God, let him be there!

She didn't knock but flung open the door.

The bed was empty – the room deserted. She leant against the door lintel and shut her eyes, fighting for control.

"Good God, Rachel! Darling, what is it?"

She opened her eyes and there was Rowan coming out of the bathroom, a towel round his waist. His black hair clung wetly to his head, his wide shoulders, deeply muscled, gleamed like dark brown satin in the early morning light.

"Oh, Rowan!" She put her head against his chest, he held her tightly, Bamboo as well. She sobbed the story out, unable to be fully coherent, ending with, "You must hurry – there's john crows..."

She felt him stiffen into immobility, and at last she looked up into his face. It held an expression that frightened her. His black eyes that could be so tender were hard and implacable. His mouth was in a set, cruel line. "The swine," he said in a low voice. "The unutterable swine. To do that to a little boy." He looked down into her wide grey eyes and his softened. He bent and kissed her gently. "My poor love. Now listen to me. You are to go to your room, take a couple of tranquillisers and rest. There's a lot that I have to do but I must know that you are safely in your room. I'll order you some coffee and then leave word that you are not to be disturbed under any circumstances. You stay there until I get back. Right?"

"But, Rowan – I..."

"No 'buts' – you'll do just as I say. It'll get you used to the idea." He kissed her again, not quite so gently. "I'm serious, sweetheart. I'll be back as soon as I can."

He led her to the door and saw her safely back to her room, then dressed with concentrated speed. He left a message with the desk clerk to contact Phillips right away as well as messages to West and Terrance. Then he made his way down the rocky path to the beach and its silent, sprawled occupant.

EIGHTEEN

The familiar detailed, routine investigations were over. Dr Montgomery had made his examination and remarked dryly, "We have no vaccine for an epidemic of this nature."

The camera crew had photographed the area from every possible angle until at last the body of Carlisle Linton, so recently an aspirant to the constabulary force, was borne away to a waiting ambulance.

"No speculation about the cause of death in this case. The spear-head was still in the body," Rodgers said gloomily to Phillips.

Phillips' normally cheerful face looked grim – he had a boy just about that age.

"Who goin' to tell the mother, Mr Rodgers?"

"I will, right now. Phillips, I want you to question the Girot circus again, find out about the nitrobenzene, if they have it on tap and who has access. You have Pearson, put him back in uniform. Put the fear of God in them all until someone breaks. Wait, though... I need somebody with me now. What about young Goodbody? Oh, Lord, he's been standing guard outside Anna Morgan's room."

"I'll check, sir." Phillips went swiftly up the hillside, light and sure-footed, despite his outward appearance of stolidity.

Rodgers checked the time. Six-thirty AM. He thought longingly of a cup of coffee but knew that it would be an hour or two before he could have one. He wanted to see the boy's mother before the grapevine could get the news to her. He looked up; two disappointed john crows were still circling – he wouldn't mention them to Rachel.

He climbed the hillside with long, lithe movements. He was about to get into the Mercedes when Goodbody presented himself. He was smart and trim in his blue and white regulation shirt, dark blue trousers with their distinctive red stripe down the side seams. His cummerbunded waist with its gleaming leather belt was stretched taut as he said crisply, "Constable Goodbody, sir, reporting for duty." His salute was military in its precision.

"Morning, Goodbody. You've had some sleep, I hope?" The boy hesitated and Rodgers went on, "Were you on guard from two AM? You should have been relieved at five."

"Yes, sir. But I'd like to go with you, sir. Mr. Phillips say to get someone else. But I'd like to go with you, sir." The military facade cracked a little, showing the boy underneath.

Rodgers smiled. Who was he to crush such enthusiastic zeal? "Right, Goodbody, I need your help. We'll be an hour or so. Then you're to go off for the rest of the day. I'll square it with Mr West. Right?"

"Right, sir. And, sir, the lady – one Mistress Groome – she send this for you."

He held out a plastic bag containing a thermos, a paper napkin which was wrapped round two Danish, and a hand of bananas.

"Ah, coffee, just what I needed. Bless the girl. Pour me some and have some yourself. I should think that you could do with it too."

The hot coffee tasted good and the young constable sat beside Rodgers in the big powerful Mercedes in a glow of well-being. Who'd have thought that he, Emmanuel Goodbody, just a few weeks out of the Police Academy, would be helping the great Rowan Rodgers on a murder case. He came out of his roseate thoughts as Rodgers said, "Let me put you in the picture, Goodbody."

He gave Goodbody as many of the facts as he thought he needed to know as they drove eastwards along the coast road while the early morning sun cast long shadows across the dusty roadway and the coolness of the first hour after dawn started to give way to the increasing heat of the day.

Rodgers parked the Mercedes close to the soft shoulder of the road. "We'll ask our way here." He nodded at the little general shop that graced the other side. A white painted notice nailed to the rough wooden door stated: JAMES CHIN YU (Prop.) LICENSED TO SELL TOBACCO SPIRITS & WINE.

At Rodgers' imperative knock, Chin Yu shuffled once again from the dark recesses at the back of the store. He had been just about to open up in the hope of catching early shoppers before they went off to their daily work but nevertheless he was not pleased at the summons. He pushed wide the wooden door and revealed the usual clutter of a general shop of a district or settlement. A strong gust of pent-up stale air greeted Rodgers. He wrinkled his nose at the sharp acridity.

Chin Yu regarded his visitor from slit, sleep-filled eyes. "Mornin'," he offered tentatively.

"Morning" Rodgers returned briskly. "Could you tell me where I can find Mrs Linton?"

Chin Yu shook his head. "No one me know call so."

"The mother of young Carlisle Linton – he works as a bellhop at the Santa Gloria."

A slight gleam of intelligence entered the opaque black eyes and Chin Yu nodded his head. "Is Medorah Wells you wan'. She de mother." He regarded Rodgers' well-dressed figure with distrust then glanced down slyly at the still form of PC Goodbody standing by the expensive car. A wary look came into his red-rimmed eyes. "You the police? Wha' the boy do?"

"Why do you think that he has done anything?"

Chun Yu hawked and spat with accuracy into a patch of grass. "One Superintendent Rodgers phone in the night. Say I mus' carry message to de bwoy."

"Superintendent Rodgers?" Rodgers asked slowly. "You spoke to him yourself?"

"Same time."

"Did the voice sound like mine?"

The man hesitated. "Me nuh know. Why you ask?"

"Because I am Superintendent Rodgers and I did not phone you." He called across the road. "Goodbody, come here with your notebook." He turned back to Chin Yu who, now uneasily wide awake and watchful, began to whine, "Me nuh know who phone. 'Ow me know? Why yuh 'ave fe ask me question? Is nothin' me do..."

"All right, man. I just want you to give a statement to the constable here. Just tell him all you remember about the phone call. That clear?"

"Yes, sir." The man was alarmed at the close proximity of the law.

"May I use your phone?"

"Yes, sir. It back o' the counter."

Rodgers went to the back of the cluttered shop and took up the receiver. He dialled the local exchange and asked if any trunk calls had been put through to – he gave a quick look to check the number.

"I don't know, sir."

"Check anyway, this is an urgent police matter."

He got through to the Santa Gloria and put the same question. Any calls through to the switchboard at... "What time was the call, Chin Yu?"

"Sir?"

"What time you hear the phone ring?"

"Me nuh know fe sure; 'bout one-two inna de marnin'."

Rodgers sighed. The island propensity for ignoring time always presented difficulties. He spoke again into the mouthpiece. "Check all calls out of the hotel between midnight and three – no, better make it between midnight and four AM..."

The murderer – it must have been the murderer – might have used a call box. He thought a moment. There wouldn't be all that number of call boxes around this part of the country. He dialled again, waiting impatiently as he listened to the ringing at the other end of the line and in the background, the monotonous painstaking questions from Goodbody to Chin Yu.

The receiver at the other end was lifted. "West here."

"Richard, good – Rowan Rodgers, Listen, man I want you to have every call box in the area printed. The same at the pay phones at the Santa Gloria. Right away, before the guests get active." He thought a moment then said, "Check with the Telephone Company about any calls put through the exchange in the area between midnight and four AM."

"Right – will do," West answered crisply; he didn't waste time in questions.

Rodgers felt that it would yield nothing but he had to cover every possible lead. Together with Goodbody he returned to the Mercedes armed with the knowledge that Medorah Wells' dwelling was but 'a chain or two' along the road going east, then another 'half chain' up the hillside. Knowing that the country man's conception of distance complemented his conception of time, he drove slowly.

"Here, sir." Goodbody spotted the narrow pathway winding up the hill. They left the car parked close to the low dry-stone wall at the side of the narrow highway. The sea, far below, glittered in the early morning sun and the brilliant patchwork rippled in merging shapes and colours from light aquamarine through azure to deep turquoise.

Rodgers and Goodbody trudged up the pathway that was little more than a track. They pushed aside the tangled bushes and overhanging branches of close-packed trees. Clouds of insects rose from the disturbed vegetation and darting lizards fled in agitation at their approach, a dry rustling accompanying their retreat.

They came at last to the mean little shack. The door hung open and from the dark interior the slack and unlovely figure of Medorah Wells lounged into view. She watched their approach with the belligerent apprehension that the uneducated experience when confronted by the police. She was even more unprepossessing in the clear light. Her hair, partly braided in a myriad of little tails, partly frizzed as she made an ineffectual effort at grooming with a filthy metal comb that had more gaps than teeth, had the brittleness of neglect. Her dark skin had the dull, leathery, bloated texture of an alcoholic, her eyes were dark brown discs rimmed in yellow whites, streaked with red veins. Her voice when she spoke held a sullen whine which reached them on a gust of stale, rum-laden breath.

"Wha' yuh wan' wit' me? Is Carlisle yuh wan'? I tell 'im I tek stick iffen..."

"Good morning," Rodgers cut in. "You are Carlisle Linton's

mother?"

He viewed her with a distaste he dared not reveal and silently commended the young bellhop on his independence and strength of character at escaping from such an environment. Not that it had done him any good in the end, he amended.

"That right, an' if is trouble 'im..."

"Mrs Wells," Rodgers addressed the woman with what he was sure was a courtesy title, "unfortunately, I have to tell you some bad news. Is there somewhere where you can sit down? This is going to be a shock..."

She didn't tell let finish but darted forward, bringing the sickly stench of her unwashed body too close for his fastidious nose. "Shock? Wha' yuh mean? Somet'ing 'appen to the bwoy?"

"Yes, I'm afraid so." He tried to keep in mind that whatever her appearance she was still a bereaved mother. His voice was gentle as he said, "I'm afraid that your son is dead."

She let out a loud keening wail, startling in its suddenness but holding more of a dramatic quality than convincing grief. She held her head in her hands and crouched forward, racking sideways. Then the wailing stopped as suddenly as it began, and she turned on Rodgers and spat at him, "How 'im dead? Heh? Is the police kill 'im? Wh' appen?"

"The police had nothing to do with his death," Rodgers' voice was stern.

"How it is they sen' fe the bwoy long 'fore sun up? One Super Rodgers sen ' fe 'im."

"So I hear. That message was sent by someone we have yet to find. I am Superintendent Rodgers and I know that message was not sent by me or by any other member of the police force. The boy was helping us in a case. He was a fine little chap, you should be very proud of him."

This was news to Medorah Wells. She began to wail again and to demand, "Wha' goin' happen to me now? No one fe care fe me. Lard – wha fe do?"

Against his better judgement, in the knowledge that it would be squandered immediately on rum, he gave the woman a hundred dollars. "Don't worry about the funeral," he said. "I'll see that all arrangements are made."

She took the note with a flash of cupidity and gave him a sly look that spoke of hope for another if she displayed yet more grief. With a jerk of his head to the silent Goodbody and a brief good morning to the woman, Rodgers turned his back and went hastily down the hill track.

On the way back to the Santa Gloria Rodgers asked Goodbody to read out his notes on his interview with James Chin Yu. The young constable read diffidently at first but gained confidence as he progressed. Chin couldn't swear if the caller was a man or a woman. He said it was a light voice but that was all. He was definite that the caller had stated he was Superintendent Rodgers and equally definite that the meeting was to take place on the beach by the big outjut of honeycomb rock. There was nothing of real value in the statement yet Rodgers felt that the boy had shown intelligence and patience in eliciting what little information he had.

"Good work, Goodbody. Efficient note-taking well presented."

Goodbody glowed with delighted embarrassment.

At the hotel entrance, Rodgers swung the Mercedes in a wide arc and parked neatly beside Richard West's new Rover 220 Turbo Coupé. He noted that it was the latest model, completely automatic, fitted with stereo, two-way radio – the lot. He twitched a mental eyebrow; old Richard was spreading himself a bit. The fact that he drove a Mercedes 230 SL was no comparison, ancient as it was. Everyone knew his background and the fact that he didn't need to work for a living but he hadn't realised that West was seemingly in the same happy position. He dismissed the matter from his mind and went quickly through the hotel lobby, along the corridor and up the stairs to Rachel's room. He knocked gently, then entered. Rachel was asleep, her normally sleek dark hair ruffled. Her long eyelashes curved in a crescent against the smooth coffee-coloured skin of her cheek. Her pointed face held an expression of peace and a child-like innocence that gave the lie to the age he knew her to be. She stirred then opened her wide grey eyes. She smiled at him and stretched out her arms. "What a lovely way to wake up."

He kissed her, mentally comparing her fresh loveliness with the malodorous slattern he had just left. "It could be the customary way," he said.

Her smile went, whether at his words or because she had suddenly remembered the events of the early morning, he wasn't sure.

"Have you found out anything?"

He shook his head, "Not really, except that the message that got the boy to the beach purported to originate from me."

"Oh no, how awful."

She got up from the bed. She had changed from the shirt and slacks to a frothy lace wrap, in a deep shocking pink. "I feel so terribly responsible for that poor child's death," she said painfully.

He looked at her in amazement. "You? How can you be in any way responsible?"

She told him how she had heard the barman announce that Carlisle had seen someone on the beach the night Soulis was killed.

"But that's not true – the boy swore to West that he had seen no one. Go on."

"I told Smith to stop gossiping. He blustered a bit but Richard West backed me up."

"West was there and didn't stop the man talking?"

"He came in in the middle of it – at least I didn't actually see him come in. He was just suddenly there."

"Who else was there who could have heard?"

"Oh, masses of people. Diana Barrington was next to me. Girot, Madame Yvette and that King's Road young man – what's his name? Peter Horton. Susan Taylor had been at the bar, but I think she'd left by then." She then told him of the scene that she had witnessed between Girot and Susan Taylor. "There's something strange between them. Her manner was pleasantly defiant and he – well I don't know, but he had a sort of menacing uneasiness. Oh Rowan, I'm sorry, I should have told you about Smith talking like that. I knew last night that there was something I had to tell you and – I forgot. I feel terrible..."

"Don't worry, my sweet. It wouldn't have made any difference. If the boy talked to his cousin he may have talked to others."

"I know, but the barman wasn't telling the truth. Why did he lie?"

"Probably because it made a better story. On the other hand, Carlisle may have told West that he hadn't seen anyone, when in fact he had. We'll never know now." He kissed her. "Don't worry about it any more. What about having some coffee sent up?"

She picked up the phone. "I'll order some breakfast."

He grinned at her, his black eyes gleaming wickedly. "That'll be a nice snippet for the gossip columns. No one will believe that I haven't been here all night."

She looked at him unsmiling. She wanted to ask where he *had* been all night. Instead she dialled room service and gave an order in a cool, impersonal voice.

"Talking of gossip columns, ask them to send up the *Gleaner*." Rowan sounded as if he sensed her thoughts but had no intention of enlightening her.

They breakfasted on the balcony. The golden wedges of pawpaw were cool and refreshing, their smooth sweetness cut with the tang of lime, but Rachel ate only a little then drank cup after cup of coffee whilst Rowan worked his way heartily through fruit, eggs and bacon with fried plantain followed by toast and marmalade. Then he lit his pipe and scanned the headlines.

"Oh, God, the press is having a field day. Listen to this: 'POLICE WATCH WHILE MODEL DIES.' Then they go on: 'With two top-ranking police officers present at a well-known north coast hotel, why have the tragic deaths of two visitors to the island been accomplished under their very noses? Is our police force held in such contempt that crimes may be committed while they look on and do nothing?' "

There was much more in the same vein, accusing the police of idleness, of luxurious living at the taxpayer's expense, of encouraging the escalation of corruption, while pointing out the damaging effect on the tourist industry of such crimes as those recently committed and so on.

The telephone by Rachel's bed rang. She went in and answered then called, "It's for you – Kingston."

He took the receiver from her and sat on the edge of the bed. "Rodgers here... Petrie?... You have?... What was that again?.... Yes, yes indeed. Very enlightening. Thanks a lot, you've helped tremendously. 'Bye." He replaced the receiver and looked up at Rachel with a smile. "I see the faintest glimmer – but the very faintest glimmer."

He pulled her down beside him and kissed her. Her mouth remained closed under the demanding pressure.

"As soon as this is over we'll really take a holiday. Where would you like to go? Cayman? Tobago? Up north?"

She pushed him away and sat up. "Aren't you rather taking it for granted that I'll accompany you?"

His face became set and serious. "I rather understood that you would. Why the change of plans? Or is it a change of heart?"

She jumped up and faced him. "You ask me that? When you've spent as much time as possible with that – that whore."

He got up abruptly. "So it's a case of simple jealousy. I suppose that I should be flattered. I'm not. I'm disappointed that you trust me so little – and that you are so..." he was about to say 'blind' but caution stopped him. "Never mind. Let's leave it at that."

He walked to the door and without a backward glance left her standing by the bed. As he hurried to his own room, his thoughts were not on the recent scene but on Petrie's report. He wondered if he had enough information to force the issue or if he should wait for further confirmation. He hastily showered and was just finishing dressing when his phone rang.

"Rodgers here."

"Rodgers – John Terrance. I've got a bit of information that might interest you. May I come up?"

"Sure – right away." He paused then said, "I've had a bit of a break too."

He had barely hung up when Terrance arrived. "That was quick."

Terrance took a notebook from his pocket and said, "We had this notebook of Soulis gone over by the cypher boys. They've broken the code. Interesting: a list of names, addresses, dates and place names. Here – take a look." He handed Rodgers a sheet of closely typed foolscap.

London, Paris, Kingston, Montego Bay, St Ann's Bay were mentioned frequently against a name and a date. One name that caught Rodgers' eye had occurred many times over the previous six months. This was under the heading: OUTGOING.

"Good God!" he breathed softly.

"Surprised?"

"Not really – it ties up strongly with some information that I received earlier." He recounted the conversation that he'd had with Petrie and explained why he had requested the information in the first place.

Terrance listened intently. "It's beginning to add up. There were some pages torn out of that notebook – that gives one cause to wonder."

Rodgers looked back at the notes that he held. Under another column headed: INCOMING was a name against Montego Bay that caused him to whistle in surprise. That same name appeared at an earlier date against Trinidad and Caracas.

"Well, well – somebody on the other side slipped up in failing to collect Soulis' little book."

"So it seems that his death was definitely part of the drug set-up," Terrance stated. "As the same method of killing was used for the boy, we can assume that there's a tie-in there. And with *this* to go on," he flipped the notes, "the girl's death must be connected." He rose and stretched his elegant frame. "We've had a break with these killings; they've revealed info on the drug racket that we'd never have had otherwise. All that remains now is to find out how it's got out – and how it's brought in. And, of course, whose is the organising brain behind it all. Simple, eh? Then we just corral the lot. No problem."

Oh, yes," Rodgers agreed wryly. No problem."

NINETEEN

Detective Sergeant Phillips spent the morning making exhaustive enquires at the hotel, ably assisted by Police Constable Goliath Pearson. The news of Carlisle Linton's death had not circulated yet but there was an air of gloom and muted tones among the guests as they speculated about and discussed the events of the previous evening. To the manager's relief there had been surprisingly few cancellations, although he was still in a state of nervous alarm and foresaw empty rooms in the weeks ahead.

Phillips decided to tackle the Girot group first. In view of Anna Morgan's belief that the poisoned perfume was meant for her, he needed to pursue a new line of enquiry.

Yes, they all admitted to being able to obtain nitrobenzene. No, there was no special care taken with it, they were all fully aware of the danger it presented but it was one of the essentials of the profession. To his probing as to their feelings regarding Anna, they all agreed that she was a charming girl, not tempestuous or temperamental. As Peter Horton phrased it, "No one was surprised when Solange was the presumed target – one was only surprised that she hadn't been murdered before. But Anna – no, Sergeant, you'll have to come up with something better than that."

Phillips remembered his chief's comments on Peter Horton's overt racial feelings towards Anna and wondered at his championing of her now, but decided to let it pass, at the same time keeping it in mind.

To his cautious enquiries regarding the bellhop, no one remembered seeing him after nightfall. Phillips left that line for the moment. "We'll question the hotel staff before we tackle Anna Morgan – and her aunt," he said to Pearson.

Pearson said nothing but he was all eyes and ears. He was thrilled to be working again with the redoubtable Sergeant Phillips and was determined to learn all that he could.

They went into the deserted Pirate's Lair Bar. Delroy Smith was at his usual place behind the curved bar counter polishing glasses and checking levels in the battery of bottles. The grey tinge to his dark face proclaimed that he had only recently become aware of the fate of his young cousin.

"Lard, Mr Phillips, why anyone wan' do a t'ing like that? Him jus' a little bwoy!"

"Someone must have thought that he knew too much. When did you see him last?"

" 'Bout half-past seven. The young lady, one Miss Morgan, she trip an' fall. Carlisle fin' she an' ask me fe help him wit' her. She trip on de tile – or so she say..." he added with a sceptical look.

Phillips looked thoughtful. "You don't think she trip, then?"

"Me don't know nothing, sir."

"But you think, eh? And you talk?"

Smith became uneasy. "Mrs Groome say so, sir?"

This was news to Phillips. His question had been rhetorical but he nodded. "Is what you say *exactly*?"

"Me don't rightly remember – jus' that Carlisle fin' Mr Soulis an'..." He paused, his small brown eyes suddenly wary.

"Yes?" Phillips prompted sharply.

"Me jus' say – that Carlisle see de person – who kill Mr Soulis."

Phillips' expression was one of disgust. "You know that not true? Carlisle don't say that?"

"No, sir." Smith was frightened now as he realised the enormity of the effect of his statement made only to create an impression.

"You see now – you signed the boy's death warrant. He might still be alive."

"Lard, Mr Phillips, sir – I sorry – honest to God – me never did t'ink."

"Then think now and try and remember who was here who might have heard you."

Smith gave a list of names, most of which were unconnected with the matter but among which were members of the Girot circus, with the exception of the three remaining models.

Phillips left a shaken, contrite Smith and went to the reception desk. "You on duty last night?" he asked the desk clerk.

"Until nine." News of Carlisle's death had reached him and he was nervous and ill at ease.

"Did you see young Linton last night?"

"Yes, sir. I see him when he go towards the bar, about half-past seven."

"Why do you remember that?"

"The bellhops not allowed in the bar, sir. But him say him going for his cousin, Delroy Smith – but him never reach as Smith meet up with him – one of the young ladies fall an' hit she head."

That tied in with Smith's testimony.

"You see Carlisle after that?"

"Yes, sir, just before he went off duty – about half-past eight. I get a call from the French gentleman for Carlisle to fetch a package." He paused and licked his lips. He disliked and feared this close contact with the police.

"The French gentleman? Mr Girot?"

"Yes, sir."

"You see the package?" Phillips sounded bored but he was wondering why Girot had denied seeing the boy at all that evening.

"Is a cardboard carton, sir, about so big." He sketched the size with spatulate fingers.

"And where Carlisle take it?"

"Me don't know, sir. Him say is a car him have to put it in."

"He say whose car?"

"No, sir, him jus' say it one pretty pretty car."

"Did he speak to you earlier about Mr Soulis?"

"Mr Soulis? No, sir."

"Sure?"

"Yes, sir."

Phillips regarded him for a long moment. Probably the man's unease was due to some past brush with authority and nothing to do with the present case. "Okay, man. If you think of anything which may be useful, let me know. Right?"

"Right, sir." The desk clerk breathed his relief as he watched Phillips' stocky figure and Pearson's tall slim one go towards the main entrance.

"What do you think, lad?" Phillips asked.

"I think he speakin' the truth, but he scared of something, sir."

"Of us – or something else?"

"Of us, I think, sir. Is a shame, eeh, sir?"

"It is indeed. Let's press on."

The next on the list were the car park attendant, the porters on duty at the main entrance and the two surviving bellhops. They all denied that Carlisle had talked of the gruesome find that he had made even when pressed to do so by the youngest bellhop, Gladstone Ogilvie, a diminutive, cheeky round-faced youngster whose black eyes sparkled wickedly in his cherubic features.

"Is ask me ask why the police talk to him. Him say he can't say as 'im mek a promise an' 'im wan' to be a police when 'im reach age fe join."

"I see." Phillips felt that they had lost a good recruit. "Thanks, son."

No one other than the desk clerk remembered seeing Carlisle after seven-thirty and certainly at no time carrying a large carton. The car park attendant was vague to a moronic point about the owners of the cars that had been parked the evening before.

"Is like this, sir," he explained to the patient Phillips. "Me tired, y'see, sir. Me been on duty all day an' me know we goin' get plenty plenty car at night. So 'bout seven me jus' tek a likkle break like..."

"How long?" Phillips cut in to stem the flow. "How long did this little break last?"

The man rolled his eyes to the sky. "Jus' – likkle time. Jus' till 'bout eight – mebbe likkle more."

"Maybe nine, or maybe nine-thirty?"

"No, sir!" The man was aggrieved. "No so it go. Is jus' nine o'clock, me did see on Mrs Barrington's car clock when me open the door for her."

"Mrs Barrington was here at nine?" Phillips thought back to the night before. It had been well after nine when she had entered the ballroom. He made a mental note to check on her whereabouts between nine and nine-thirty.

"Yes, sir. Mrs Barrington come back at nine. She here earlier. I park the car for her jus' before me go off at seven. She mus' have driven off while me tek a likkle break."

Phillips thanked the man and tucked that further bit of information away. He had gathered that any snippet of information concerning the attractive Mrs Barrington was of equal interest to both Rowan Rodgers and Richard West. He felt disappointed in Rodgers; he had firmly believed that at last his roving chief was about to settle down with Rachel Groome. He returned to the lobby in a rather depressed state of mind and inquired through the desk clerk if Miss Anna Morgan could spare him a few minutes.

She would be down directly.

Phillips waited stolidly as he watched the passing parade of the hotel guests. They milled around window shopping in the innumerable gift shops with their display of locally made articles: inlaid mahoe or mahogany cigar boxes, jewellery of hand-carved tortoiseshell or coconut shell, exquisite embroidery and cutwork linen. All very expensive and often quite useless back in a different environment. There were frequent loud greetings to each other, an easy camaraderie occasioned by wealth and position. It made Phillips wonder, in his unsophisticated way, if all that he saw was but on the surface, a facade of friendliness which belied the true and deeper feelings. He gave an inward shrug,out of his depth in a new world of wealth and a different social standing.

"Me did never know a place like this," the usually silent Pearson voiced Phillips' thoughts. "Cost plenty plenty too, you hear, sir. All these people, mus' all be millionaire."

"Some, no doubt, but most have saved long and hard to come to a place like this."

"Me rather be at your cottage or up in the hills."

Phillips grinned. "You're all right, bwoy. Ah, here comes the lady."

"You wanted to see me, Mr Phillips?" A soft voice, still

retaining a slight Jamaican inflexion, brought them both back to the business in hand. Phillips turned and looked appreciatively at Anna Morgan. He remembered how some years back she had been the favourite for the Miss Jamaica title and how disappointed he had been when she was awarded the second place. She was even more beautiful close to. Her large, slanting brown eyes were fringed in the sweeping curl of thick lashes that most Jamaican girls accept as a right. Her skin was like coffee-cream velvet and her high, wide cheekbones had a beauty of structure that was ageless. Her long dark hair was impeccably styled as usual but she had an air of tension and unease that showed itself in the quick movement of her hands and the slight termor of her full lower lip. Like a child about to cry, thought Phillips with an unusual rush of sentimentality.

"How you feel this morning, Miss Morgan? You sleep well?"

"Not very, I'm afraid – even with this nice young policeman on guard. Thank you so much, Constable. You must be tired; I'm so sorry."

Pearson blushed and stammered, "Is all right, miss – a pleasure."

Anna smiled at him and he became even more embarrassed. She put him out of his exquisite misery by devoting her full attention to Phillips. "It's so hard to believe that Solange is – dead. And more difficult to believe after all that someone should want to kill *me*." She gave a quick glance round the lobby and Phillips had the impression that she didn't find it quite as difficult to believe as she was suggesting.

He took her elbow. "Perhaps we could sit down in a more quiet spot?"

She smiled. "Would it be against all the rules to ask you to have a cup of coffee? The coffee shop is just over there."

"A very good idea, Miss Morgan. As I recall I had no breakfast, so coffee will be very welcome."

The coffee shop, called The Galley, was very nautical in appearance but with the modern coffee shop slickness of service. It was nearly empty at that hour, but the sounds of swimmers and enthusiastic surf riders reached then clearly from the beach where waiters armed with the traditional machete expertly prepared coconuts for drinking the cool water, with five clean, cutting motions. The sweet coconut water, naturally insulated by the hairy outer covering, was more than welcome to the sun-parched guests.

Phillips guided the girl to a corner, where the 'ship's rail' bounded two sides. While Pearson went to collect coffee and Danish from the serve-yourself counter, he pulled out a chair for her.

"Thank you," she smiled at him as she sat down, at ease again. "Are all policemen as nice as you and Mr Rodgers? Not to mention the shy young constable – what's his name?"

"Pearson – Goliath Pearson."

She gave an unexpected giggle. "Oh dear, I shouldn't laugh – how unkind."

"No, I had the same reaction myself. As to all policemen being nice – no, I'm afraid not – but that's neither here nor there at the moment. Ah, Pearson, that looks good."

After they had sipped the strong, hot coffee and finished their Danish, Phillips smiled at the girl, showing very white teeth in his dark, rather heavy face.

Pearson took out his notebook as unobtrusively as possible as Phillips said, "You say that you can't understand why anyone would want to kill you. That's not really true, is it? You do have some idea?"

The switch from the friendly social atmosphere to a professional tone threw her off guard. She choked over her coffee then asked evasively, "Why do you think that, Mr Phillips?"

"Because," he took a chance, "it's obvious that you think so. You protested just a little too much."

She gave a mirthless laugh. "They always say that sooner or later you pay for what you've done, don't they?"

He nodded. "And have you done something that you now have to pay for?"

"Yes, I have to pay by the embarrassment and pain of confession. I thought it was all over."

She paused, her eyes looking back into the past.

Phillips waited, then whispered to Pearson to get more coffee. She thanked him without a smile. "You're very kind. Do you treat all criminals like this?"

"It hasn't been suggested that you are a criminal."

She took a deep breath. "I was. I was a drug addict."

Phillips' outward stolidity was unchanged but inwardly he felt a surge of hope and the belief that he was about to hear something of importance. He wondered if he should stop her now and have her make a formal statement, but thought that if she stopped she might not be so willing to talk later. Pearson's notes would give the required formality.

"You don't seem surprised?"

He shook his head. "You learn not to be surprised at anything in my job, ma'am. Please go on."

"I said that I was an addict. I'm not now. About three years ago, just after I started to work for Girot, I discovered that a number of people in the world of high fashion took drugs. More for kicks than for anything else, a try-anything-once attitude. But they did help to relieve tension and anxiety before a showing. And I started too. It's like a roller coaster, once you've started you can't stop. I started on ganja but moved quickly to the hard stuff. My aunt, Susan Taylor – she's with me now – she found out and was appalled. She made me go into a nursing home for a cure. It worked. She didn't want me to go back to Girot's but I insisted. I knew that I was cured – for good. I'd learnt a bitter degrading lesson. I had to go back to prove to myself and to her that I was cured." She paused, her lovely face haggard at the memories she'd conjured up.

"And were you?" Phillips' voice was sharper than he intended and she paled at the question.

"Oh yes, I haven't touched it since."

He leant forward. "Why are you telling me this now? What bearing does it have on an attempt on your life?"

"Because I'm convinced that some drugs have been brought into Jamaica. I saw one of the boxes. The face powder box in Solange's beauty-case – it had a false bottom. And once, when I took the stuff,

I was given some from a similar box."

"You mean that Girot is trading and smuggling drugs?"

"I don't know – I doubt it very much. But it must be someone in the House. It may have been Solange herself; she certainly acted suspiciously over my touching her case."

"Or," said Phillips deliberately, "it could be you, and Solange found the box in your case and you tried to switch the box to her case. The rest that followed would explain everything."

Anna looked at him wordlessly, her face paled to an ashen grey. At last she said, "You can't believe that? If that were so, would I have told you that I had been an addict? Would I have humiliated myself by such a confession?"

"You might; in fact, you very probably would have done. But I didn't say that you had switched the boxes. I merely said that it was possible." He got up; his voice was grave as he said, "Miss Morgan, what you have said may be very important information. I want you to come with me and when Pearson has typed the notes which he has taken, I must ask you to read them carefully and then sign them."

"Anna!" Susan Taylor swept into the coffee shop, her normally meek manner replaced by anger. "What are you doing here? What have you been saying to this man?"

Anna stood up to face her aunt. She was still shaken by Phillips' accusation. "Why, Aunt Susan – you startled me."

"What have you been saying?" Susan gripped Anna's arm.

"Please – you're hurting me. It's just something that I discovered and felt that Mr Phillips should know."

"Know? About what?"

"I think that Solange was smuggling drugs – I know that she took them..."

"And you told him? You little fool, do you realise..." Susan was about to add more but the comprehension on Phillips' face made her appreciate the implication of her words and the construction that might be put upon them.

Phillips looked down at her sternly. "Miss Taylor, I had hoped to interview you later this morning but what you have implied in your outburst leads me to believe that you are in possession of certain facts that may help us in our investigations. Miss Morgan is about to sign a statement in the presence of witnesses. I must ask you to accompany me and make a formal statement."

TWENTY

Rowan Rodgers left John Terrance in the hotel lobby. There was a lot to be done. He must check with Phillips – he hoped that he was having success in his enquiries – but he had to see Rachel before he went out. He could understand her feelings although he was hurt and angry at her attitude and wished that he could give her a convincing explanation for his conduct. She was usually so rational. He knocked softly at her door.

"Why, hello. I didn't expect you back so soon." Her greeting held a cool aloofness that made him pause. He pushed the door open and followed her into the room. "Rachel, sweetheart. I'm sorry. That's what I came to say."

She crossed to the French window and said distantly, "Being sorry now doesn't mean that you won't behave in exactly the same way again. As soon..." She broke off as the telephone rang. "Rachel Groome speaking...Yes, he is... It's for you, John Terrance."

There was a note in her voice as she said the name that made Rowan give her a sharp look, a subtle change in contrast to her previous cutting tone, but she kept her eyes lowered as she handed him the receiver.

"Rodgers here." He listened intently, then said, "You have, have you? Good work, man, it could be the break that we're looking for." He listened for a few moments more then put down the receiver with a pleased sigh.

"What is it?" Rachel was interested in spite of her mood. "Good news at last?"

"Could be. They've been watching the airports for anything suspicious or unusual. It's been noted that a certain man has been boarding an aircraft at Sangster regularly, twice a week. He always carries a package then leaves the plane at Kingston – minus the package."

"Well?"

"He was followed onto the plane. He placed the package on the hand luggage rack. Later a flight attendant removed the package."

"Well – what then?" Her eyes were wide and questioning.

"On the next trip, the package was intercepted. It was six cartons of cigarettes."

"Taking cartons of cigarettes *onto* a plane?"

"Exactly. But they weren't ordinary cigarettes." He paused. "They were very special – all ganja. Also, although the packets weren't branded, the cartons had a Barrington Special wrapper. Which bears investigation."

"Of course." She was distant again. "I'm sure that you're only too anxious to start."

Rodgers left Rachel in a state of frustration. Why did he have to have these complications in the middle of a difficult case, he asked himself as he reversed the Mercedes skilfully from between two closely parked seven-passenger tourist limos. The fact that the complications arose *because* of the case he was too disturbed to appreciate. He took the circular driveway of the Santa Gloria too fast with a high squeal of protesting tires and turned left along the coast road.

The sun beat down hotly on the shining black highway, a constantly moving heat haze shimmered above the surface just ahead of him. Then the barber green smoothness ended and he was riding through a cloud of white dust, his shock absorbers registering the change. To his right, the Caribbean Sea sparkled in the morning light, its bright patchwork of blues and greens broken by sundry small sailing boats of the Sun Fish class, racing each other, tacking to and fro to catch the fresh mid-morning breeze.

He kept at a steady sixty-five to seventy miles an hour along the winding road, knowing that his power brakes were his insurance if necessary. He overshot the sharp left turn that led to Ripple and reversed with a high-pitched whine. He took the many hairpinned bends of the steep driveway too fast and went into a tight, quickly controlled skid. His front wheels stopped only inches from the edge and he shuddered involuntarily as he looked down at the highway that he had so recently left, lying below. He drove the last few yards at a more sedate pace and parked smoothly beside Diana's Quattro. He spent a moment admiring its sleek lines and thought that even that driveway would offer no problems to its road-hugging four-wheel drive.

He viewed the house appreciatively. Such perfection of reproduction must have cost a fortune, he thought, as he climbed the elegance of the exterior stairway. The wide, panelled mahogany doors stood open and he stepped into the square entrance hall. The dark patina of the floor was a contrast to the white scatter rugs that echoed the white paint of the tray ceiling. The walls were panelled in different coloured woods, blonde satinwood balanced against the deeper yacca and green mahoe. The windows, set in deep embrasures, had jalousied shutters. The whole ambience spoke of a time long since passed. This was echoed in the old-world courtesy of Peters who spoke from behind Rodgers.

"Good morning, sir. May I be of help?"

Rodgers turned from his admiring appraisal and looked at the wide-coated manservant, whose crinkled, greying hair was a caracul above his wrinkled dark face.

"Good morning – Peters, isn't it? Is Mrs Barrington at home? I'd like a word with her."

"She's just come up from her morning swim. I've ordered coffee. Perhaps you would care to join her, sir?"

"Thank you."

Rodgers followed Peters along the corridor to Diana's suite. He contrasted the hovel that housed Medorah Wells with the insolent opulence of Diana's establishment. It had an old colonial aura, a sort of Scarlett O'Hara magnificence which, in the light of knowledge, left him with a strong feeling of distaste.

Peters offered him a seat in one of the deep bamboo chairs on the wide verandah. Through the white curtains of Diana's bedroom that fluttered against the open shutters, Rodgers glimpsed a veiled movement. He remembered again the perfection of that room, the huge four-poster with its graceful half tester draped with soft white hangings. The folded-down counterpane, he remembered too, was white, fine, intricate crochet work.

He sighed – sometimes he disliked his job.

"Well, how nice to see you again so soon." Diana sat down opposite him, a round cane glass-topped table between them. He looked at her without a word. Her dark red-gold hair was still slightly damp, clinging closely to her head. Her brown eyes were soft, with none of the arrogance that so often filled them. She wore white designer jeans and a white top, cut full like a poncho, edge with bobbled fringe that barely covered her ribs, leaving exposed a seductive expanse of warm brown flesh. Her expression hardened as he said nothing. She lit a cigarette as Peters returned, wheeling a laden trolley on which was a large coffee percolator, bananas and slices of pawpaw and pineapple.

There was an exotic mixture of smells: the fruit, the hissing percolating coffee, cigarette smoke which mingled with Diana's heavy perfume. Rodgers got up abruptly and went to the verandah rail: he knew that he would never smell that particular mixture again without evoking this moment. He gazed unseeingly at the curve of the bay – he knew that he was prevaricating and the nearness of Diana with her unabashed sexuality wasn't helping him to pursue the course that he had to follow.

He turned and faced her.

"I want to ask you a few questions – and I want straightforward answers."

She put down her coffee cup slowly. "Well, don't stand there glowering. You can at least sit down and have a cup of coffee."

"This is not a social call. There are a number of points to be elucidated and you can be of help in the matter."

"Oh God, you've gone all Scotland Yard again! Points such as?" Her voice and eyes were hard now.

"First of all, your finances are in a bad way. Your factory – Barrington Specials – has been running at a steady loss over the last four years. Why keep up a business that is losing money and has to be heavily subsidised from your own pocket?"

"Who gave you the right to pry into my affairs? What business is it of yours if my factory is losing money? It's *my* money."

"You like money too well to throw it away on something that's not paying its way. Either the books are faked for tax purposes, or the factory is a front for other activities."

"What do you mean?" She was on her feet now and went towards him. "You goddamned policeman – I should have known. You come here pretending to be interested in me and all the time it was just to conduct your filthy spying... Get the hell out of my house."

"I'll go when I'm ready. You say that I was interested in you. On the contrary, *you* were interested in *me* – no, don't do that..." He caught her wrist as she raised her hand to strike him.

She glared at him for a moment then pulled her wrist free. "How did you get your so-called correct information about my financial situation?"

"From your attitude I adduce that it is correct. Your lawyer told me. He is also, I believe, your business adviser?"

"He told you that? Who in hell's name do you think you are? To get – by what means I don't know – to get private information about a law-abiding citizen. What are we living in – a police state?"

Rodgers kept his voice at a conversational level. "Your lawyer was acting under instruction, yes, but the methods used were not police state methods, only those which come into being under a special code."

"I don't understand," she said. She had grown still, all anger gone and in its place an icy wariness.

"I think that you understand very well. Under the international code concerning the trafficking of drugs, local police have special powers."

She watched him, immobile. "How does that concern me?" she asked at last.

"Inasmuch as your cigarette factory, whilst losing money on its regular sale of Barrington Specials, is netting you a nice little fortune in Barrington *Extra* Specials – the cigarettes with ganja substituted for tobacco." He regarded her with hard eyes. "How much do they fetch per carton? Between two and three thousand US dollars on the Canadian and United States markets? Probably more on the British market? After all, one stick on the local market is a dollar – yours are four times the length and all prettied up."

He had to admire her calmness and wondered briefly if he had made a mistake in assuming her guilt. She lit a cigarette with steady fingers. "You talk a lot, Mr Rodgers, but you have no proof."

"No? Your courier on the airline talked. We've been watching him for weeks. He was picked up today after he had passed six cartons to the flight attendant. You must have made it worth his while – he took a long time to crack."

She flung her cigarette savagely over the railing. "Damn him – I knew that he wasn't to be trusted. I told..." She stopped, her nostrils flaring in alarm.

"Go on."

"I've nothing more to say. Apart from what you've told me, you have no proof that I have anything to do with it."

He took a deep breath. He'd got to get her to reveal whether she was the brain behind the export of ganja. From the slip that she had made, it seemed that she had a partner – a senior or junior partner? The organising brain? Her complicity now was apparent but he needed confirmation to complete the case against her and throw it wide open.

"I have more proof than Simon Soulis had – and you killed him for what he knew. We know that your boat was used that night. Was he still alive when you put him in it?"

She went grey under the golden-brown skin. "I didn't – I didn't do that – he was dead when I..." Her hand flew to her mouth. She stood looking at him with wide, fear-filled eyes. All the arrogance and anger evaporated as she slowly sat down at the table.

Rodgers lit a cigarette and said, "So Soulis was dead when you found him? Where was that?"

"On the beach. I... oh God, it was horrible." She seemed about to break down. He went across to the liquor trolley and poured a triple whisky. He added ice and handed her the glass. "Drink this, then tell me slowly and in detail."

She drank the whisky in gulps as if it were water.

Soulis had approached her one evening in the bar at the Pirate's Lair. He was attractive and amused her. They had dinner together and then went back to Ripple to swim. She told him that he could borrow the Quattro whenever he liked. He told her that he was a professional photographer and was in Jamaica to cover the Girot showing. She'd had no reason to doubt his story as she had seen many signed photographs stamped with the touch of the master. On the evening of his death he had arrived at Ripple at about seven PM He told her that he was a member of Interpol and that he had evidence that she was engaged in the drug traffic. Here Diana paused, took a deep breath, then continued, "He said that he had fallen in love with me and if I would marry him and take him in as a partner – he would destroy the evidence."

"And how," Rodgers asked sarcastically, "did he propose to do that? He would have had the police forces of the whole world after him."

"He said that he would stage a mock death."

Rodgers leant forward. "Either you are a fool to expect me to believe this fairy story or you were a fool to believe him – and you are no fool! NOW – I want the truth."

"I'm telling you – that is what he said. Perhaps it was a trap, to get my confidence so that..." She stopped, then went on, knowing that she had committed herself so deeply that a few more words couldn't matter. "I don't know how he was going to do it. He said that he would take my launch back towards the hotel. I was to go down to the beach half an hour later and then report that my launch had gone. I waited. I knew that Peters would be bringing up dinner, so I left the shower running and went down to the beach. The launch was still there. And so was Simon – dead." She stopped again and held out her glass.

Rodgers poured her another drink and waited. Either this was the truth or she was a superb actress.

He waited.

"Yes, he was dead, with that fiendish hook in his throat. I – got him into the – water and – towed him back to the Santa Gloria beach."

"*Towed* him?" Rodgers felt nauseated at the callousness of the woman: she sensed his mood.

"I had to. If I got him into the boat there would be blood – and a body is not so heavy in the sea. I got him onto the Santa Gloria beach – then..." She shut her eyes against the memory, "I reversed quickly – in the hope that the spearhead would come out. It did – so I cut the line."

"Why didn't you just drop him in the sea?"

She looked her contempt at his obtuseness. "There would have been more questions when the body was eventually found – someone night have seen him arrive at my house. This way there was nothing to connect him with Ripple – or me – on the Santa Gloria beach."

Rodgers had to admire her cold-blooded reasoning even under the shock of the gruesome discovery. But was it, he asked himself, was it a shock *or* a discovery?

"You sound convincing – but then you're the type of woman who sounds sincere when uttering a lie. If you didn't kill him, someone did. Someone who used your beach, your spear gun – and presumably your boat. Someone who wants to get rid of you by saddling you with an unexplained body. Perhaps you would like to tell me who that someone could be?"

She was beginning to recover her composure. She finished her drink, lit a cigarette and viewed him through a blue haze. "Why should I even try to help you? You come here with preposterous notions and accusations."

"Don't bother to try and bluff now. You've as good as admitted your complicity in the outgoing traffic in ganja. What about the incoming traffic in pethidine?"

She sat up straighter. "Incoming traffic in pethidine?"

Rodgers was convinced that this was news to her. She was

becoming possessed of a growing inward anger that she could not conceal or control.

He watched her expression with satisfaction – at last he'd got through to her. She was angry and it was not too difficult to guess why.

"So your partner held out on you, did he? He had a nice little sideline and kept all the profits?"

"Damn you – yes – and damn..." She just stopped short of saying the name. Not even anger could make her lose all caution.

"So Soulis was killed. And the girl, Solange? Why?"

"I don't know. Surely there's no connection? I'd never seen her before the night of the fashion show."

"What about the girl Anna Morgan? What connection does she have?"

"Anna Morgan? The Jamaican model? What has she to do with all this?"

If it was true that Diana knew nothing of the pethidine angle then it was probably true that she had no knowledge of the attack on Anna or Solange's death. But what about Carlisle Linton? His death was surely connected with Soulis – same method, same place…

Same place?

If Diana was telling the truth then Soulis had died on *her* beach and not where he was found.

"And what about the little bellhop? Why did he have to die?"

She got up slowly, her eyes widened and her face paled so that he thought she would faint. "What little bellhop?" Her voice was hoarse, unrecognisable.

"Young Carlisle Linton. You must have known him. He was found at the same spot where Soulis' body was found. This time, though, you hadn't been able to get the spearhead out of his chest. He was dragged along the beach – and the head had to be left in."

"No, NO! Stop it! Oh, God – that little boy." She put her hands to her face and began to shudder.

Unless she was a superb actress, this had to be authentic. He took her by the shoulders and gave her a little shake. "Pull yourself together. That lad was a good, hard-working boy. He had ambition and the will to get where he wanted to go – now he's dead because of you and this filthy soul-destroying traffic that you live by. Now tell me who this man is?"

"No, I can't. I – can't. What are you going to do with me?"

He was silent for a long moment – thinking. She could still be lying. This was a very cunning woman.

He had the germ of an idea. It might work. God – it had better. He said at last, "I'm going back to get a warrant for your arrest. Don't imagine that you can get away. This is a small island, remember, and every policeman would be on the hunt for you. Just occupy your time by getting a few clothes together."

She watched him go with cold eyes. She stood motionless until the roar of the Mercedes had become a receding purr, then she went through the French doors into her bedroom. She swung aside an old painting in the panelling by her bed and inserted a key into a skilfully disguised keyhole. A door opened smoothly. She slipped through and closed the door behind her. She was in a tiny, closet-like room which was occupied by a small but powerful transistorised two-way radio.

She manipulated the control panel.

"DB calling the *Arawak Maid.* Come in, *Arawak Maid.*" She waited then repeated the call. "Come in, *Arawak Maid.* DB calling. Over."

The receiver crackled. "*Arawak Maid* receiving you, DB. Over."

"Stand by to pick up launch *Katinka.* Keep out of sight over the horizon, due north from Flat Point. Will join you within an hour. Emergency. Repeat, emergency. Be ready to get under way at top speed as soon as I join you. Over."

"Message received and understood. Over and out."

Diana reset the controls and spoke again. "DB calling. Come in, BS. Urgent. Come in, BS."

The response was immediate. "BS receiving you, DB. Over."

"This is an emergency. Plan A. Have all merchandise at main gate in half an hour. All merchandise in whatever condition. Over."

There was a delay before the answer came through. "Impossible to do that. Contrary orders have been received. Over."

"Damn you to hell. I'm still the owner, you do as I say. Understand? All merchandise at the main gate – or you'll be in jail by tonight. Over."

The response was immediate, "Right, DB. In half an hour. Over and out."

Diana returned to her room. She took a suitcase from the big, old-fashioned press and began to pack with an ordered feverishness. She took a thick wad of US dollars from a wall safe and stuffed it into her handbag. Her jewels she tumbled carelessly on top of her clothes.

Without a backward glance at the place which she had called home for so many years and with no word to the faithful Peters, she swung the Quattro in a tight circle and went down the driveway at a pace impossible for any other car.

TWENTY-ONE

As Rowan Rodgers got out of the Mercedes in the Santa Gloria car park, it began to rain. The sky had clouded over quickly and the rain was sweeping in from the north-east, accompanied by the familiar rumble of its approach. The horizon was misted out and the sea had turned a sullen grey. He sprinted across the roadway with the smell of rain on hot concrete rising and enveloping him. The sound followed him as he entered the foyer as the downpour increased in volume to become a wall of falling water.

"Do you know where Sergeant Phillips is?" Rodgers asked the desk clerk.

"Yes, sir. He left a message that he'd gone to the police station with Miss Morgan and Miss Taylor and could you join them there."

"Right." This would take up time, and time was too valuable to waste at this juncture. He went into a phone booth.

"Sergeant Phillips, please. This is Superintendent Rodgers."

There was a short pause, then, "Phillips speaking."

"What's the position, Phillips?"

Phillips told of Anna Morgan's revelations and her aunt's reactions. "So I thought we'd better get signed statements, sir," he concluded. He then gave a brief resumé of his other enquiries and findings. Rodgers cut in, "You were quite right but there's been a new development. I need you here, so get back at the double. Bring West with you. We can get those statements later."

"Right, sir."

One of the many good things about Phillips, Rodgers thought as he hung up, one of an abundance of good things, is that he doesn't waste time in idle questions or objections.

He spoke rapidly to the desk clerk.

"Yes, sir, I understand. In the main lounge, right away."

The rain was pounding on the steeply shingled roof as a group of people assembled in the main lounge twenty minutes later. There were Superintendent Richard West and Major John Terrance talking to Rachel Groome. Roger Girot, looking mutinous, with Madame Yvette. Peter Horton, hiding any anxious feelings that might be his behind his usual facade of bored amusement. The two models, Tania and Lotus, sitting close together like frightened birds, uneasily aware that something unpleasant was about to take place. And finally, Anna Morgan and Susan Taylor, ushered in rather breathlessly by Phillips. Girot was smoking one of his long exotic cigarettes, looking annoyed but quite calm, although his high, domed forehead was beaded with sweat and his cold blue eyes were watchful.

Rodgers crossed the room to Rachel's side. He ignored the circumstances of their recent parting and said in a low voice, "Watch everyone carefully, and note the reactions."

She nodded.

Rodgers turned and faced them all. "Please sit down, ladies and gentlemen. I've called you together to let you know the latest developments. As you are all aware by now, three deaths by violence have taken place in the hotel and its environs in the last thirty-six hours. Those deaths were all connected with an investigation which has been taking place on a wide scale with reference to drug trafficking. We have reason to believe that one of you – maybe more than one – has been using the overseas tours of the House of Girot as a cover for the distribution of the drug pethidine."

There was a rustle of movement throughout the room and Girot erupted to his feet.

"You make a ridiculous statement, Superintendent. If that were so then I would be aware of the fact."

"Exactly. It has not yet been proven that you are not."

Girot's complexion became suffused; a vein beat strongly at his temple. "Do you not realise that I am a world-famous figure in the world of fashion? Would I jeopardise my reputation by such practices?"

"You might – it's probably much more lucrative than your

profession. It is a well-known fact that the world of high fashion does not command so much allegiance as it did a few years ago. With the swing to mass production, there is not the call for clothes as you make them."

Girot glared at him. "What proof have you for such an allegation?"

"You refer to the drug-running, I believe, and not to my remarks about the world of fashion?"

Girot didn't answer. He sat down again, suddenly drained of belligerence.

Rodgers went on. "We have reason to believe that the drug was brought in in face powder boxes with a thin layer of polythene. The incidence of pethidine addiction has risen alarmingly following your tours of Caracas and Trinidad. You brought with you on this trip, two cartons of face powder, one of which was as it appeared, innocuous face powder. The other, which we believe is by no means innocuous, was taken by the late Carlisle Linton to a certain person's car. You, Mr Girot, directed the boy to take the carton from your room last night, yet you denied in your statement that you had seen the boy."

"That is still true. I did not see the boy, nor did I direct him to do any such thing. I noticed when I returned to my room last night that one carton was missing but I was too upset about Solange to make any enquiries. I thought that perhaps Mr Horton had taken the carton – he is in charge of the cosmetics department."

All eyes turned to Peter Horton; his effeminate elegance was unruffled. "My dear Superintendent, you're quite wrong. We always travel with cosmetics and they are all – innocuous was the word you used."

"Where is the missing carton?"

"I've no idea," Horton gave a delicate shrug. "I've not seen it since we arrived."

"Very well. But if you think that we have no proof – it is you who are wrong. At this moment the Paris police are investigating your cosmetics factory. Their findings will be interesting."

Madame Yvette made a quick movement but Girot checked her. "They will find nothing – nothing."

"Perhaps not. I only hope that your staff can be trusted not to reveal what they must know. It is difficult not to talk under pressure. Perhaps you've trusted too many people."

Girot was on his feet again. He was breathing heavily, the veins at his temples standing out more prominently than ever. He glared at Susan Taylor. "It is you who has done this – you – you..." He took a step towards her but Rodgers caught him by the arm. "No violence, please. We have had quite enough already."

Girot dropped his hand and shrugged off Rodgers' hold. "You have no proof – no proof," he muttered.

"All the same, you will all stay here until we do have proof – one way or the other. You may not leave the island – in fact, you may not leave the hotel and its environs. Simon Soulis died because he had proof, proof of the importation of pethidine and of the export of ganja."

They were all silent now, watching him uneasily. He went on, "It has been established that Mrs Diana Barrington has been actively involved in the export of ganja, and it is very probable that the two activities are connected by one controlling brain. I believe that brain is among you here."

Again there was a rustle of uneasiness and they viewed each other with covert suspicion.

Rachel looked at Rowan in bewilderment. What on earth was he up to? Surely he didn't have sufficient evidence to back up these sweeping accusations? She studied each member of the company in turn. What did he want her to look for? One thing that she had noticed, which the astute Pearson had remarked on, was that Girot's Gallic accent became less and less the more infuriated he became. So it was a studied idiosyncrasy. If it were natural he would become *more* Gallic under pressure, not less. What else? Nothing really. If the guilty party was amongst them, it would most likely be the one who evinced no reaction.

Rodgers glanced at his watch.

"Superintendent West, would you go to the station and get a warrant for Mrs Diana Barrington's arrest and then go and execute it? She should be ready by now. I told her that I was going to arrest her on suspicion of murder and of trafficking drugs. I hope that she will give us a statement that will clear up a lot of obscure points."

West stood up, his lanky frame towering over them. He seemed uncertain. "Do you think that she'll still be there?" he asked.

"Where could she go? The airports have been alerted; every policeman in the island would be on the lookout within minutes."

West looked at him. He seemed to be in doubt of Rodgers' reasoning but all he said was, "Right, I'll get her." He left the room in long, hurried strides.

Rodgers glanced at his watch again. He seemed to be making some mental calculations, then said, "That is all for the moment, ladies and gentlemen. May I warn you again that it is useless to try and leave the island. In this weather," he added ironically as the rain beat more thunderously on the roof, "it is even inadvisable to leave the hotel. Mrs Groome, would you come with me? Major Terrance, would you get on to Paris and check their findings?"

He gave a half bow to the group who were still sitting in an uneasy silence. He held the door open for Rachel. "That'll give them something to think about," he murmured.

She caught his arm as they hurried towards the reception desk. "Rowan – I don't get it. What are you trying to do? Flush out the murderer? Wasn't all that mostly bluff? Surely Diana, even as she is, couldn't have...?"

"My love – haven't you yet discovered that anyone is capable of anything?"

"Anyone?"

"Anyone," he said firmly. "Now we've got to work fast if my supposition is correct." He picked up the phone and dialled. "Constable Forbes? Superintendent Rodgers. Is young Constable Goodbody there?... Right, let me speak with him. Goodbody? Superintendent Rodgers here. Now listen, take Pearson and..." He spoke rapidly for a few moments then hung up. "Rachel – I have to go. You stay here and keep an eye on the Girot circus. John will be here."

She touched his arm. "Can't I go with you?"

"No, not this trip. It may be messy."

"Rowan," her grey eyes filled with tears. "Be careful. You're – you're very precious to me."

He smiled down at her. "I'll take you up on that later. I was beginning to think that I was anything but precious."

She shut her eyes in sudden pain. "I know – I've been such a fool. I see that now."

He bent and kissed her, a hard and demanding kiss, watched appreciatively by the desk clerk and disapprovingly by an elderly female guest. "Take care," he whispered and then was gone into the pounding rain.

ઉ₰ᘐ

Diana Barrington drove the Quattro out through the gates of the Barrington cigarette factory. Beside her on the seat was a large package wrapped in polythene. She had paid the foreman lavishly and warned him to burn every scrap of evidence relating to ganja and told him that the police would be there shortly. She had to trust that fear for his own skin would protect hers.

The road led downwards in sharp curves. The surface was bad and the potholes filled with water. The rain drummed on the roof like bullets bouncing, the windscreen wipers were useless as water poured in a steady sheet over the windscreen. She entered the main highway in a slipping slide, testing even the Quattro's holding power on the foaming, slippery surface. In a way, she felt, the rain was an advantage: no other car could overtake her in this weather. If she could only get to Ripple beach, she would be all right.

It became darker as the rain increased in intensity. She could hardly see where she was going. The road was like a river with deeper streams cutting across as cascades poured down from the hillside. She knew every inch of the road, every corner, every dip, every cross drain – even so, she nearly missed the white gate that led down to the beach and had to reverse through water that was now above the hubcaps. She braked. Nothing happened, then the car began to slide backwards. In a sudden panic, she slid the gear stick into park and hauled on the hand brake. The Quattro came to a stop. She flung open the door and with difficulty got hold of the package in one hand – it was heavy and she nearly dropped it. She put the strap of her handbag over her shoulder and grasped the package in both hands. Thank God she had had the forethought to leave the gate open. She accepted the fact that she would have to abandon her suitcase with her clothes and – she felt a momentary pang – her jewels. But it was her freedom, perhaps her life, that she was saving now and a sense of panic and urgency seized her. She was wet to the skin in an instant. Her shoes filled and squelched with water, impeding her progress, so she kicked them off and scrambled down the white steps that gushed now like a waterfall.

She ran across the wet heavily clinging sand to the launch which bobbed crazily in the choppy sea. She tossed the mooring rope over onto the deck, then threw the package after it. She followed clumsily, her dripping clothes restricting her movements.

Her fingers were wet as she fumbled for the starter. Suddenly she sensed that she was being watched and turned to see the man as he came down the white steps. She froze into frightened immobility as she recognised him, even through the curtain of rain.

"No, don't," she screamed as she saw him raise his arm. The wind whipped her cry back to her.

She was scrabbling again at the controls.

As the engine roared into life she tried to fling herself to the deck but the bullet caught her below the left shoulder and she sagged across the control panel. The launch shot forward in an uncoordinated swerve as the man raised his hand to fire again. There was a report, distorted and muffled through the rain, and Richard West looked down in disbelief at his useless right hand.

Rowan Rodgers, closely followed by Phillips, ran out of the beach hut.

"What the hell, Rodgers," West gasped in pain. "She'll get away. I was trying to stop her."

"Trying to kill her, you mean, so that she couldn't testify against you. Take him in, Phillips."

Rodgers peered anxiously seawards where the launch was pursuing its erratic course, then saw with relief a police launch, Goodbody at the helm, round the point and close rapidly with the pilotless runaway.

TWENTY-TWO

Constable Emmanuel Goodbody studied the morning paper with a mixture of feelings. He'd made the headlines, that much was certain. 'YOUNG CONSTABLE RECOVERS BODY OF WANTED WOMAN,' said one. Underneath, in smaller type, was: 'Dramatic sea ordeal in blinding rain.' Another proclaimed: 'COMPRESSED GANJA WORTH TWO MILLION TAKEN FROM SLAIN WOMAN'S LAUNCH.' There was even a picture of him, his uniform plastered to his body by spume and rain, giving a sheepish smile at the camera.

But somehow the reality of publicity did not correlate with the dream. He felt a faint contempt for his childish visions as he remembered too vividly the body of Diana Barrington as he carried her from the rescued launch. It was his first close contact with a woman like that and his first close contact with death. The combination was overwhelming – maybe the daily routine held more satisfaction than he had realised. He went slowly into the guard room to receive his detail for the day.

It was not until dusk that Rodgers, Rachel and John Terrance met for a drink in the Pirate's Lair. "Now," Rachel said as she sipped an ice-cold Red Stripe beer, "tell me all that's been going on. Rumours have been floating round all day – each one contradicting the preceding one."

Rodgers slowly filled his pipe. He looked tired and there was pain in his eyes as he said, "I don't know what you've heard but the facts don't make for pleasant hearing. Richard West of all people, a man who has been in the Force all these years, with as fine a record as you could wish for."

Rachel leant forward. "But why? How long has he been involved?"

"In answer to the first question – money. To the second – about three years. He was in Paris about three to four years ago, studying their methods of procedure and deduction, and he got entangled with the pethidine angle through that same girl – Solange. It was about the same time that Anna Morgan was going through a bad patch.

"He didn't know how much Anna knew of his involvement in the drug racket and he couldn't be certain now that she wouldn't remember him. That's why he tried to kill her, or at best incapacitate her, while he was in the hotel. He was afraid that she might recognise him and start asking awkward questions. It was just unfortunate that his colleague, Solange, was the victim. I had his record checked and discovered that he had been in Caracas and Trinidad at the same time as the Girot showings there. The coincidence was too much to ignore."

"But why didn't he worry about Anna recognising him then?"

"Because he wasn't there in his official capacity; presumably he kept a low profile."

"But Solange gave no indication of having known him."

"Well, she wouldn't, would she?"

"Was only Solange involved in the Girot set-up?"

"No. Peter Horton is the man in charge there. Apparently Girot himself was an unwilling participant, but he was in too deep before he realised it – then he had to go along with it or lose everything."

"What about Soulis?"

"He was a member of Interpol. He'd been on to them for a long time but could get no proof. That's why he'd attached himself firmly to the Girot circus. He was an excellent photographer and could have passed anywhere but Peter Horton distrusted him and was always quarrelling with Solange about her friendship with him. He'd also got a lot on Diana Barrington and cultivated her socially – and sexually – to get conclusive proof. Richard West realised this, and also that he might be spotted by Soulis. They had both been in Caracas and Trinidad. It was West who killed Soulis in that fiendish way. How he got him down to the Ripple beach we'll never know."

"And now Diana's dead," Rachel said thoughtfully. "Perhaps it's as well, though. Imagine someone like Diana in prison."

"I wish that she had lived to pay the penalty in personal misery."

Rodgers' voice was hard. "Do you realise that for years she's lived in luxury through the degradation of thousands of human beings, most of them teenagers? Have you any idea of the increase in addiction in Britain alone in the past few years? It's more than doubled. The increase here in Jamaica is phenomenal. People like Diana Barrington and Richard West could never pay too high a price in punishment."

"I'm sorry." Rachel put her hand over his. "I've never seen you so bitter – you ought to be jubilant that you've cracked the case. After all, the London and Paris police, not to mention Interpol, have been working on it for years, and you and John have cracked the whole thing wide open in just a few days."

Rodgers drained his glass and signalled a waiter for refills.

"Rachel, my love, I hate to disillusion you and shatter your image of me as a great detective, but I didn't crack it – I just happened to be lucky in that I was in the right place at the right time. It was ready to crack because of the personalities involved. If anyone can claim credit for cracking it, it was Soulis and his little notebook. There's enough information in there to be very damning at West's trial."

"But why did Soulis try to run you down? The day that you went to Sangster airport to meet me?"

"That puzzled me at first, but I believe that it was to draw my attention to Solange. He recognised me through the description given him by Interpol. He couldn't contact me openly but he made sure that I noticed him and who he was with. If he'd lived I suppose he would have made direct contact sooner or later. Poor chap."

"What beats me is how West got away with it all these years," John said.

"I don't think that he was entirely above suspicion. The AC practically warned me not to take him into my confidence. I thought then and I still think that if I hadn't taken him partially into my confidence he might have become wary and clammed up. But I'll still have it on my conscience. If I'd listened to the AC that boy might be alive today."

"That's ridiculous. You weren't telling West anything that he didn't know. One thing I can't understand is why did he hand over the damning evidence of Soulis' notebook?"

"I don't think he intended to, but it was on his desk and when he showed it to me I rather whipped it from under his nose. He'd managed to tear out a number of pages but, as the whole thing was in code, it was hit or miss. That notebook first aroused my suspicions that he might be involved, for whoever killed Soulis would surely have suspected the existence of written evidence and would have made some pretext to get into his room. The only person who did this was West, under the guise of authority. From the time Soulis was killed, his room had been placed under observation. Another point which clinched my suspicions was when we went diving for the spearhead I saw him with his arm in a cleft in some coral. I went back to the same spot later on – that's why I was late, Rachel – and found the spearhead tucked into that same cleft. I lelt it there. The next morning, I went down again and it had gone. I'd just got back when you came in from finding Carlisle's body." He bit savagely on his pipe.

"But how was it that *you* didn't see the child?"

"I surfaced higher up the beach. When I think – half an hour earlier, I might have saved that boy." He tamped down his pipe thoughtfully. "There's still a lot we don't know, a lot of ends to tie off, but I suppose that will all come out in the trial."

Rachel sipped her drink. "So when you got us all together then sent West off to bring Diana, you were more or less certain that he was the murderer?"

"Petty certain, but I had to make absolutely sure. He presented us with a nice piece of evidence in the shape of the missing carton of face powder cum pethidine. It was in the boot of his car. That's the real reason why he killed Carlisle – the boy could have said to whose car he had taken the carton. Furthermore, when I asked him about prints on Anna Morgan's beauty-case, he said that it had been wiped clean. That was impossible – Carlisle held it in both hands and I saw Anna open and close it. I deduced that West's prints were on it – so he wiped it clean. Another point, I asked him to check all calls in the area – call boxes that is – for any calls between the hours of midnight and four AM He reported that there was none to Chin Yu's number – but I'd had young Goodbody do a double check – there had been a call put through from a pay phone in the hotel at two-fifteen."

Rachel shivered. "It's hard to believe that someone whom you've known and liked can turn out to be – oh..." She stopped, remembering Bill.

Rodgers took her hands in his; John Terrance might have been on the moon. "Darling – forget. It's not the same. Bill was ill but West is just a cheap, crooked swine, trafficking in one of the filthiest trades known and never hesitating to kill anyone who threatened his safety."

"How did he team up with Diana?"

"Again, we've still got only scanty evidence to go on. This ganja export racket is always with us. They've tried everything, stuffing toys with it, mixing it in with straw for packing china – the lot. All that apart from the blatancy of the illegal airstrips. But to have a ready-made legitimate factory to hand, privately owned by a money-loving tramp, was a gift not easy to pass up. It was not till the night that Soulis was killed that they actually met. He knew who she was, but whether Diana realised who West was before he killed her, we'll never know. Their business had always been done through the foreman at the factory."

"The whole affair has been a nightmare, beginning with the odd accusation about my dress," Rachel said. "That is something which has never been explained."

"It has, in a way. Susan Taylor made a statement when Anna made hers. Apparently Susan was so concerned at her niece's involvement in the drug racket that she went to Girot and threatened to expose him. He was in so deep himself by then that he had to do something to prevent her exposing him, so to keep her quiet he gave her a number of his sketches – a unique form of blackmail on Susan's part – which she has been using over the years to build up a nice little business. When he saw you in one of his designs, it shook him considerably. He hadn't realised what an excellent seamstress she was, who could interpret his sketches so that they really appeared to be a Girot original. He hadn't known that Susan was working in Jamaica. When she left Paris she had gone to the States. He feared that she might make trouble – hence his outburst yesterday morning. By the way," Rodgers turned to the silent Terrance, "did you find out if Girot is an addict himself?"

"He isn't – not now anyway. But he is a diabetic – hence the syringe. Analysis of his exotic cigarettes revealed the mildest tobacco known."

"What will happen to them all?"

"Oh, they'll be extradited and the French police can take it from there. Except Anna – she's staying. She's the only one of the bunch to have come out of this with any claim of self-respect. Even the little Madame Yvette knew quite a lot." Terrance rose to his feet. "Well. I'll leave you two love birds," he said, not looking at Rachel, then slipped quickly off to the bar.

Rodgers gazed gloomily down into his empty glass. He hadn't even noticed Terrance's departure.

"Rowan," Rachel called softly across the small table. "Don't be bitter – it's not like you."

He looked up, his eyes were very black in the shaded light of the room. "No, it's not like me – I'll get over it." He smiled suddenly. "You told me, it seems a very long time ago, that I was very precious to you. I hope that wasn't said because of the imminence of danger?"

She met his gaze steadily. "No, it wasn't. I've been an utter fool. I thought you'd fallen in love with Diana – or at least were having an affair with her. It didn't all seem to be in the cause and course of duty."

"Look, my love, if you agree to forget about Diana, I'll agree to forget John Terrance."

She opened her eyes wide. "But Rowan – nothing…"

He stopped her by leaning across and kissing her. "No more. No explanations. No recriminations. OK?"

"OK." She laughed. "You're going to be fun to be married to."

"I am indeed, sweetheart, and we'll drink to that in champagne." He signalled a waiter.

Rachel got up. "Rowan, not now, I must go. Bamboo will be screaming to get out."

He got up and faced her. "I see that I'm only second to that feline tyrant. We'll both take her for a walk, and then have the champagne sent up – to your room."

She looked up at him for a long moment in silence, then smiled. Her eyes held an expression of utmost tenderness. "All right, my love," she said. "We'll do just that."

ABOUT THE AUTHOR

Jeanne Wilson was born in England in 1920, but has lived in Jamaica since 1944 and became a Jamaican citizen immediately after Independence in 1962.

Mrs Wilson was a novelist, playwright, book reviewer and columnist for the *Gleaner.* Her publications include *No Justice in October* and *A Legacy for Isabel* (one-act plays – Evans Bros. [London], 1969); *Weep in the Sun, Troubled Heritage, Mulatto,* and *The Golden Harlot* (historical novels – Macmillan [London], 1976-80, with editions published by Evans [New York], Arrow [London], Pocket Books [New York], and St Martin's Press [New York]); and *The House That Liked To Travel, Holiday with Guns* and *Flight from the Islands* (children's books – Macmillan, 1977-78). *No Medicine for Murder* and *Model for Murder*, the first two of a series of six whodunits, were originally published by Ward Lock [London] in 1967-68; and *No Medicine for Murder* was republished by Kingston Publishers in 1983.

Mrs Wilson was a member of the Society of Authors of the UK, a Life Fellow of the American Biographical Institute, and a Deputy Director General of the International Biographical Institute, Cambridge. For eight years she was asked by the Swedish Royal Academy to nominate candidates for the Nobel Prize for Literature.

She acted on the local stage and radio for about twenty years, was in over one hundred radio plays and was involved in the School's Drama Festival, as sole adjudicator or committee member, for many years.

She was awarded the Institute of Jamaica Centenary Medal in 1980 and the Prime Minister's Medal of Appreciation in 1983.

She was married to the former Chief Medical Officer of Jamaica, Dr Jeffrey Wilson.

CPSIA information can be obtained
at www.ICGtesting.com
Printed in the USA
LVHW012115291122
734192LV00014B/541

9 789766 570828